The
Stranger
in the
Mirror

ALSO BY LIV CONSTANTINE

The Last Mrs. Parrish

The Last Time I Saw You

The Wife Stalker

The Stranger in the Mirror

A Novel

Liv Constantine

HARPER LARGE PRINT

An Imprint of HarperCollinsPublishers

THE STRANGER IN THE MIRROR. Copyright © 2021 by Lynne Constantine and Valerie Constantine. All rights reserved. Printed in the United States of America. No part of this book may be used or reproduced in any manner whatsoever without written permission except in the case of brief quotations embodied in critical articles and reviews. For information, address HarperCollins Publishers, 195 Broadway, New York, NY 10007.

HarperCollins books may be purchased for educational, business, or sales promotional use. For information, please e-mail the Special Markets Department at SPsales@harpercollins.com.

FIRST HARPER LARGE PRINT EDITION

ISBN: 978-0-06-309044-6

Library of Congress Cataloging-in-Publication Data is available upon request.

21 22 23 24 25   LSC   10 9 8 7 6 5 4 3 2 1

To Honey and Lynn, so much more than sisters-in-law.
You are the best decisions our brothers ever made.

The past is never dead. It's not even past.

—WILLIAM FAULKNER, *REQUIEM FOR A NUN*

PART I

1
Addison

I'd like to think I'm a good person, but I have no way of knowing for sure. I don't remember my real name, where I'm from, or if I have any family. I must have friends somewhere, but the only ones I recognize are the ones I've made in the two years since the new me was born—every memory before that has been wiped away. I don't remember how I got the crescent-shaped scar on my knee or why the smell of roses turns my stomach. The only thing I have is here and now, and even that feels tenuous. There are some things I do know. I like chocolate ice cream better than vanilla, and I love to watch the sunset paint the sky in vibrant orange and pink at dusk. And I love taking pictures. I think it's because I feel more comfortable behind the camera and looking out. Looking inward is too painful when there's nothing much to see.

We're celebrating my engagement on this beautiful September day, and I'm surrounded by people who say they love me, but who is it really that they love? How can you truly know someone when their entire past is a mystery? Gabriel, my fiancé, is sitting next to me, looking at me in an adoring way that makes me feel warm all over. He's one of those people whose eyes smile, and you can't help but feel good when he's around. He is the one who is helping me discover the parts of myself that feel authentic. I take pictures. Gabriel tells me that I'm an amazing talent. I don't know if I'd go that far, but I love doing it. When I'm behind the camera, I'm me again. I know instinctively that this is something I've done and loved doing for a long time. It's the thing that has saved me, given me a living, and led me to Gabriel. He's actually giving me my first break—a show at his family's gallery—in October. Soon, they'll be my family too.

The clinking of a glass gets my attention. It's Patrick, Gabriel's best man.

"As you all know, this clown and I have been friends since we were six. I could stand here all day and tell you stories. But since both our sets of parents are present, I'll spare you the gory details and just say that we've had our share of good times and laughs, and our share of trouble. I never thought he'd settle down, but the minute I saw him with Addison, I knew he was a goner." Patrick lifts his glass toward us both. "To Addy and Gabriel. Long life!"

My eyes scan the restaurant and land on Darcy. Her glass is lifted, but her smile seems forced, and her eyes are sad.

We all raise our glasses and sip. Gabriel's sister, Hailey, is my maid of honor, but she cannot regale the crowd with stories of our shared past because, like Gabriel, she's only known me for six months. Despite the festive mood around me, darkness descends again, and I feel hollow. Gabriel seems to sense my mood shift and squeezes my hand under the table, then leans over and whispers, "You all right?"

I squeeze back and force a smile, nodding, willing the tears not to fall.

Then Gigi gets up and takes the microphone from Patrick.

"I may have only known Addison for a couple of years, but I couldn't love her any more. When she came into our lives, it was the biggest blessing we could have asked for." She looks at me. "You're like a daughter to us, and Ed and I are so happy for you. To new beginnings."

I know she's trying to make it right for me, but it's hard to toast to new beginnings when they're all I have. I do it anyway, because I love her too, and because she and Ed try to be the parents that I don't have. Ed will give me away at the wedding, and while I'm grateful to have him, I can't help but worry that I have a father somewhere wondering what happened to me. That's what makes it so impossible for me to fully embrace anyone with my whole heart. What if my parents are out there somewhere mourning for me, agonizing over what's happened to me or thinking I'm dead? Or even worse, what if there is no one looking?

The doctors have told me that I have to be patient. That memory is a tricky thing. The more I try to force it, the more elusive it becomes. I have no real clues to my identity, no identification, no cell phone containing pictures or contacts. My body, on the other hand, shares some clues—the jagged scars that tell their own story—just not to me.

2
Julian

Julian Hunter had been melancholy all day. Another wedding anniversary coming up in a few months and only memories of happier times to comfort him now.

"Tell me again about the day you and Mommy got married, Daddy." Valentina snuggled closer to Julian and rested her head against his chest. She smiled broadly at him, her green eyes fringed by thick lashes that were as raven black as her hair.

He leaned down to kiss the top of his seven-year-old daughter's head. The familiar feeling of loss swept over him again, but he swallowed and began. "It started out as a beautiful November day filled with sunshine. We got married right here in the house—in the grand living room. Mommy wouldn't let me see her or her wedding dress before the ceremony. She said it was bad luck."

Julian smiled as he remembered how adamant Cassandra had been, insisting upon staying apart the morning before the ceremony. "You don't really believe in bad luck, do you?" he'd asked her, and she'd looked at him, her eyes wide, and said she was just being cautious. Julian considered himself a rational man of science, and his career in medicine had shown him that luck had nothing to do with the course of people's lives. But he'd decided to humor her.

"Daddy, keep going." Valentina pushed against him.

"Right. So . . . it was a very small wedding, with just a few of our friends and your grandfather. A young music student from the university played her cello as Mommy came into the room and walked toward me."

"Did she look beautiful?"

"Yes, Valentina. She looked very beautiful." An image from that day filled his head. Cassandra standing for a moment at the arched entrance to the room, in a high-necked, long-sleeved sheath that skimmed her slender figure and then fell straight to the floor. She smiled, her eyes meeting his as she walked down the aisle. When he noticed a white gardenia in her long black hair, he was touched by her loving acknowledgment of the flowers he'd given her the night he proposed.

"More, Daddy," Valentina urged.

"That's enough for tonight, sweet girl. It's time for

bed." He gently rose from the sofa, but his daughter remained seated.

"No, please. Can't I stay up a little longer?"

He reached down and wrapped her small hand in his, pulling her to her feet. "Afraid not, little one. What would Mommy say if she knew I was keeping you up past your bedtime?"

Valentina's expression darkened. "Mommy wouldn't care. If she cared, she would come home."

Julian had no answer for his little girl. He'd tried to explain it to her so many times, but the problem was that there *was* no explanation.

He thought back to the last time he'd seen Cassandra, and the familiar ache of loss and regret filled him. They'd had their problems like any couple, of course. She could be mercurial and moody. He didn't like to think about the night they'd had their worst fight, both of them spewing angry words neither could take back. Afterward he'd thought all was lost, that he'd have to raise Valentina alone. But then, miraculously, everything turned out okay. For a while, anyhow. Now, two years later, and not a trace of her. It was unbelievable, really, as if she'd vanished into thin air. But he believed with every fiber of his being that she would be found. It was the only thing that kept him going. Well, that and Valentina, of course. She was the image of her mother, with Cassandra's face and hair, but her lips were Julian's, full and generous.

Now he steered his little girl to the stairs, and together they climbed to the second floor. "Teeth brushing and then a very short bedtime story," he said to her.

"Two stories?" she asked as she walked over to the white bookcases that filled one wall of her pink bedroom.

"Don't push your luck, little one. It's late."

After the bedtime ritual was over and he'd kissed his daughter good night, Julian headed reluctantly to his own bedroom. As he entered, his eyes went right to the antique dressing table, where all of Cassandra's lotions and perfumes sat just as she had left them, next to the jeweled hairbrush he'd given her on their first anniversary. He walked over and picked it up, raising it to his nose. He imagined he could discern her scent, but he knew he was kidding himself. Placing the brush back on the table, he moved to one of the large closets—*her* closet—and opened the doors. All of her beautiful clothes hung neatly, untouched since she'd disappeared. He couldn't bear to get rid of her things. That would mean she was gone for good.

3
Addison

"More tea, sweetheart?" Gigi asks me as she closes her fingers around the ceramic pot.

"Yes, thank you." I slide my mug closer and look at the strong fingers as Gigi pours, the nails short, professional and unpolished, the way a nurse's hand should look—proficient and assured. But the rest of her is all warmth and comfort, from the womanly curves and red hair swept up in a soft and loose bun to the blue eyes that always have a sparkle in them.

Sitting at the wood farm table in her and Ed's cozy kitchen always makes me feel cared for and protected.

"Last night was wonderful, Addy. You and Gabriel are so perfect together. Ed and I are thrilled for you."

She looks so pleased, but all at once I'm feeling the same thing in my stomach that I felt last night—

a fluttering anxiety, as if my insides are twisting around each other. I hold my breath, trying to subdue the pulsating, and smile back at Gigi. "I'm very lucky," I say.

"You need to remember that Gabriel's the lucky one too. Right?" Gigi's eyes tell me she knows what I'm thinking. That as someone with no past and no family and barely a career, I have little to offer Gabriel. He is a smart and successful man, popular, well-liked, and from an amazing family. Blythe and Ted Oliver, his parents, opened their gallery in Philadelphia's Old City soon after they married thirty-two years ago. Blythe is an artist and Ted is in charge of acquisitions. The gallery's specialty is contemporary art, and often the two of them travel, searching for new and promising artists, while they leave the day-to-day management to Gabriel and his sister Hailey. They're a close family who make it obvious that they love spending time together. Their dinner conversations are animated and lively, with the topics ranging from art to social issues to world events. For me it's like watching a tutorial on what it is to have parents and siblings, and I always wonder what my own family might be like. Do I have any sisters or brothers? Did we enjoy each other the way Gabriel's family does?

And then I put myself in Blythe's place. How would

I feel if my son were marrying a woman with no past? No health or genetic information. No clue about her own background. I would wonder if there were any mental health problems in her family, or addiction, or . . . or . . . I would have myriad questions that couldn't be answered. Blythe and Ted must surely have the same questions. How could they not?

"Addison." Gigi's stern voice startles me, and I raise my eyes to hers. "You're brooding, and you've got to stop this. It's clear to us that Gabriel and his family love you. You're a lovely woman—kind and caring. Not to mention that you're also smart and beautiful." She smiles at this. "But seriously, you can't keep thinking of yourself as this poor little stray that doesn't deserve happiness."

"I can tell myself that all day, Gigi, but it doesn't make me believe it." I shake my head. "You don't understand. You *can't* understand what it's like to have no past, no memory of who you are."

"You're right, honey. I *don't* know how it feels. But you've got to stop beating yourself up about it. You didn't deliberately choose to forget everything."

"But what if I did? Maybe I did something so awful I wanted to black it out."

"You didn't do something awful. And people don't choose amnesia. It happens as a result of *something*."

Gigi throws her hands out, palms up. "A head injury or some type of trauma. Something."

I sigh and rub my forehead. "I know I've asked you this a hundred times, but can you remember anything from the night Ed brought me here? Something I said or did that seemed unusual?" I knew it was a useless question. I don't even know why I asked.

How many times had I relived every detail of that night two years ago? I was drained, dragging my feet, limping, and feeling as if I would pass out if I had to go any farther. My throat was closing like it was filled with dust and grit, making it hard to breathe. I needed water desperately, and I knew I had to do whatever I could to make someone stop.

I made my way to the road and stumbled along the shoulder until I was unable to walk farther and put my thumb out for the next vehicle that passed. I'm not sure how long it was until I saw the headlights of a big rig coming toward me. It went right past me, and all the air whooshed from my lungs like a balloon deflating, and I felt tears run down my cheeks. And then, miracle of miracles, he stopped, backed up, and reached over and opened the passenger door.

"You need a ride, missy?" His deep voice washed over me like a balm.

"Yes, please," I said, shivering.

"Hop in," he said, reaching his hand out to help me up the steps on the passenger side.

I shut the door and wrapped my arms around myself, and he continued to study me. "You okay?"

I looked down at my ripped pants and the dried blood on my hands. My head was pounding, and when I reached up to touch my forehead, my body jolted in pain. "I'm fine. Could I . . . do you have any water?"

He reached into a compartment next to him and grabbed a cold bottle, handing it to me, before he started driving. He kept his eyes on the road and didn't say anything right away. Then, "Where you headed?"

I thought a minute. I had no idea. "Wherever you're going," I said.

He gave me an odd look. "I'm heading home to Pennsylvania. I've been on the road ten days."

"Pennsylvania. That sounds good." I looked out my window at the tall pine trees we were passing and then turned to him. "Where are we now?"

"New Jersey." He frowned and looked at me strangely, then back at the road. "You have people in Pennsylvania?"

"I'm not sure," was all I could get out.

"I know it's none of my business, but hitchhiking is very dangerous. Do you realize the things that can happen? Especially to a young woman?"

I felt a nervous flutter in my stomach. Was he about to tell me that I'd made a mistake getting in his truck? I said nothing.

He must have realized he'd scared me because he put a hand up. "Don't worry. You're safe with me. I belong to an organization that tries to stop people from being hurt." He glanced over at me again and looked concerned. "You don't look too good. Kinda pale. I can swing off the highway and get you to a hospital. No problem."

My stomach tightened as panic welled up inside of me. I was terrified but had no idea why. "No, please. I'm okay. Really. Please. Don't stop."

He rubbed his chin for a moment. "Okay. But when we get to Philadelphia, you get medical attention." Ed told me later that he'd continued to drive against his better judgment, but there was something in my voice that made him keep going.

I sighed, relieved, and leaned my head against the window, closing my eyes. I felt myself drifting off to sleep when Ed's deep voice startled me.

"What's your name? You from around here?"

My name? I had no idea. I scrunched my eyes shut and tried to concentrate, but my brain felt muddled and hazy. Taking a deep breath, I decided to tell him the truth. It was going to come out sooner or later anyway.

"I don't know. The thing is . . ." I stopped and inhaled deeply again. "The thing is, I don't remember anything that happened before I was walking along the road, holding my head."

"You mean you can't remember how you got hurt?"

"I mean I don't know who I am. I have no memory of anything except walking and getting into your truck."

Ed let out a low whistle. "You have amnesia?"

"I guess so." I didn't have enough energy to talk anymore. "I'm really tired," I said. "Do you mind if I just rest for a little?"

"Sure. Why don't you jump back into the sleeper? You'll be more comfortable there."

Maybe if I had been in a more coherent state of mind I would have hesitated, worried again that he might be a threat, but I was exhausted. Bone-tired. I craned my neck and looked around behind my seat to see a big bed inviting me to stretch out. When he pulled off the road, I crawled onto it and wiggled under a soft green blanket that smelled like fresh evergreens. It felt comforting and warm against my body, and for the rest of the ride I slept like the dead.

When we got to the house, Ed woke me. "Hey," he said, as he gave me a gentle poke. "Wake up. We're here."

I lifted my head, squinting at the bright sunlight

that streamed through the windows and ran my tongue across my teeth, which felt gritty. Ed helped me down from the high truck bed, and I noticed that the trailer was missing from the back of the truck. I looked at him in confusion.

"Had to drop off my load. You slept right through the stop," he told me, taking my hand. "Let's go inside and get that head looked at."

We went up the walk to the house, a white one-story Cape with navy blue shutters and flower boxes at every window, separated from the large garage by a big yard with lots of trees. Pink and cornflower-blue blossoms spilled from the containers, and there was something about the house that said welcome. Before we reached the small porch, the front door opened and a petite woman with a shock of red hair held her hand out to mine and said, "I've been waiting for you two. I'm Gigi. Come on in."

"Hi, honey," Ed said, giving her a quick hug as we entered. "This is the young lady who needs our help." I realized that while I was asleep, Ed must have called his wife to warn her he was bringing home a disoriented hitchhiker.

Gigi wasted no time, taking me into their spotless kitchen and sitting me on a chair. She began examining my head and then turned to Ed and said something I couldn't hear. "We need to get you to a hospital, just to be on the safe side," she said, this time to me. "This doesn't look too terribly awful, but I can't see what might be going on inside. They can run some tests to get the full picture."

It hit me then how hungry I was, and I realized I had no idea when I'd last eaten. As if reading my mind, Gigi put a cup of tea and a buttered English muffin in front of me. "You need to eat something first," she said, patting my back gently. I knew right then that this was a woman I wanted to have in my life, whatever that meant.

4

Addison

I wish Gabriel were coming with me to his mother's tonight, but he thinks it'll be good for me and Blythe to be alone and get to know each other better as we discuss wedding plans. I know she tries to make me feel comfortable, but I still find her intimidating, and the half-hour drive to Chestnut Hill from Gigi and Ed's only serves to heighten my anxiety. I falter for a moment as I pull into the driveway. The strange thing about amnesia is that you forget facts but not skills, so I may not know who I am or if I've ever owned a car, but I remember how to drive. I put the Kia in park, turn off the engine, and grab from the passenger seat the folders that Blythe requested I bring. They're filled with photographs from bridal magazines that she's given me, instructing me to clip out any images I like.

I envisioned a small, intimate wedding with only Ed and Gigi, and Gabriel's immediate family, perhaps a few of their closest friends, but things seemed to go in another direction as soon as we told his parents last month that we planned to get married. We had just finished dinner at their house and were all sitting at the dining room table drinking coffee, and when Gabriel made the announcement, I saw the color drain from Blythe's face. Ted smiled, though, and said, "Well, well, I thought this might be getting serious. Congratulations, son." And then he looked over at me. "Welcome to the family, Addison. I'm happy for both of you."

Blythe recovered quickly and smiled. "Have you chosen a date?"

"We want a simple wedding. The sooner the better." Gabriel looked across the table at me. "Right, Addy?"

"Right."

"Well," Blythe said. "I can understand your wanting to be together as soon as you can, and I think small weddings are lovely. But maybe Addison and I could talk a little more about it before you make a final decision? Would that be agreeable to you?" she'd asked, looking directly at me.

And so here I am tonight with the folders, a little apprehensive as I walk from my car to the house but hoping that we can agree on a small, low-key affair.

She's waiting in the open doorway as I reach the covered porch, wearing a pair of flowing white pants with a turquoise tunic. Her only jewelry is a pair of gold hoop earrings. She looks both elegant and casual, and I marvel at the ease and grace of her manner. "Addison," she says, smiling brightly as she pulls me into a hug, and I breathe in the scent of her perfume. "Come in, darling," she says, letting me go. As she closes the door, one of the folders falls from my hands.

"Sorry," I say, and bend down to retrieve it.

"Oh, great, Addison. You've brought the pictures. Thank you for bringing over some ideas."

"Of course, I was glad to."

"Grace has put out a lovely tray of shortbread cookies and chamomile tea in the sunroom for us," she says, leading the way.

Maybe I've been in a home this grand in the life I don't remember, but I'm still awestruck whenever I come to Gabriel's family home, a gracious stone building complete with a separate carriage house. One day, when we'd been seeing each other a few months, Gabriel took me on a tour of the house while his parents were away for the weekend, and my jaw dropped to see the rooms, each more beautiful than the last. The vast living room has three separate seating sections, a grand piano, and a wall of elegant French doors that lead to a terrace overlooking the swimming pool. The library is a reader's heaven, a quiet retreat with dark-green walls, floor-to-ceiling bookshelves, and oversize leather sofas and chairs. My favorite room, though, is the sunroom, a bright glass-walled space with a domed ceiling, filled with plants and flowers that make you feel like you're outdoors. It's a happy room, one I could stay in forever.

After she leads me in there, Blythe takes a seat at the glass table by the window and indicates the chair opposite for me. I sit and put the folders on the table, where I see she has already placed a binder, filled with printed lists and brochures.

"Now," she says, and smiles at me again. "Let's talk about what you have in mind."

I look at her remarkably unlined face, so pretty. "I was thinking," I begin, and then back up. "That is, Gabriel and I were thinking that we'd like something small, nothing too fancy. We even thought it might be fun to have a brief ceremony at the gallery and then dinner afterward at a restaurant, or even here at the house. Just the family and a few friends?"

I try to read her expression, but her face gives nothing away.

"I see," she says.

I hurry on. "We were hoping to have the ceremony sometime in November. It really shouldn't take too long to organize."

Blythe takes her time pouring two cups of tea and then hands one to me on a saucer. She offers me a cookie from a white plate, which I happily accept, but I notice she doesn't take one for herself. She takes a sip of tea, holds the cup for a moment, and then sets it down. Reaching across the table, she takes my hand in hers. "I understand that you'd like to keep things simple, and I hope you won't think me terribly old-fashioned, but may I ask you to hear me out?"

"Of course."

She takes her hand away and takes another sip of tea. "First of all, I want you to know that I see how happy Gabriel is with you, and I'm glad for that. Finding love is something to be celebrated, and I suppose I feel strongly that I want to share my son's happiness and this big step he's taking with all my family and friends. I want them all to meet you, Addison, and to be part of your and Gabriel's big day. Can you understand that?"

"Yes, I guess I can," I say, and already I feel myself losing ground.

"This is a milestone in both of your lives, and not something to be rushed through. We are fortunate enough to have the means to give you a lovely wedding with all the trimmings. You and Hailey and I will have so much fun shopping for a wedding dress. If you'd like, we can hold the ceremony and reception at the club. Or if there are other venues you'd like to explore, we can do that. Whatever you'd like, we'll do." She picks up the binder from the table and hands it to me. "Here, I put this together for you. It's information on venues, florists, photographers, and so on. You and Gabriel can look over everything at home. I'll make an appointment with Philippa Morgan to look at wedding dresses. We could even go to New York if you'd like."

She's making me dizzy with all the plans. It sounds daunting—the dress and fittings, menus, guest lists, and standing in front of tons of people as we say our vows. I slide the brochures into one of my folders. "I'll talk to Gabriel and see what he says."

A look of determination settles on her face. "Gabriel will do whatever you tell him you'd like."

So it's my call, I think. If I go against her, I'll start off married life with a strike against me. "You're right, Blythe. We'll look it all over and choose the venue. Then we can go from there." I pause, thinking. "It's almost the middle of September. Do you think we'll still be able to get it all together by November?"

"Oh no, darling. Events of this magnitude take long and careful planning." She inclines her head toward me. "But by this time next year, you will be dancing your first dance as husband and wife."

The first thing I do when I get in the car is call Hailey, who luckily picks up right away. "Hey, it's me. I'm just leaving your mom's."

"How did it go?" she asks.

"Not like I hoped. I went in thinking she'd go along with a small wedding, and I left agreeing to the event of the season."

I hear Hailey chuckle. "I could have told you that would happen. I adore my mom, but when she sets her mind on something, there's no use trying to change it." Then her tone becomes serious. "I know you don't want to be the center of attention for hordes of their friends, but listen—you and Gabriel will probably be so wrapped up in each other on your wedding day that you won't even notice anyone else."

"I don't know. Maybe," I say. "But having this huge thing means we'll have to wait a whole year."

"Hmm. I hadn't thought about that part. But I'm sure the time will fly by. And I'm telling you, it will be a beautiful day, and you'll have a great time. And whatever you need help with, I'm here. You know that."

"I know. Thanks, Hailey. I'm sure you're right," I say, although I'm still not completely convinced. "I'll call you tomorrow. Good night."

"Good night, sister," she says, and clicks off.

When I get home, I go to the bedroom to change from my linen pants and silk blouse into cozy sweats. I sigh as I sit down to look through the binder. I turn the cover and see dividers with their subjects written in Blythe's neat handwriting: BRIDESMAIDS & GROOMSMAN'S GIFTS, BANDS, FAVORS, FLOWERS, INVITATIONS, PHOTOGRAPHERS, VENUES. She's thought of everything. As I turn to the section on attendants' gifts, a leaden feeling descends in my stomach as I realize that the only person I feel close enough to ask to be a bridesmaid is Hailey. In two years in Philadelphia, I've yet to make any close friends outside of Gabriel and his family.

The first brochure is from Tiffany and has pictures of lovely bracelets, necklaces, earrings, and charms, the least expensive of which is $300. I don't make much at the photography store, so it's all way beyond my budget, and even though Blythe and Ted have offered to cover *everything*, I want to find a way to pay for this one part myself. There are more brochures from other stores, most I've never heard of. The last one features Lladró figurines of bridesmaids, brides, and grooms.

I flip to the back of the brochure, and my eyes are drawn to an image of two girls on a bench, one with her arm around the other's shoulder. My hand begins to tremble and I drop the pamphlet as a memory explodes in my brain. I'm sitting in a dark room and can only make out shadows around me. I'm next to someone, my arm around her, and her shoulders are shaking. "Shh, he'll hear you," I warn her, needing her to be quiet. "Don't do it," she whispers, "You can't do it." I disentangle myself from her, and then feel around under the mattress until my hand closes around something hard. A gun. I tighten my hand around it, and I hear a different voice, coming from somewhere else, saying, "Kill him, you have to kill him."

The sound of my phone ringing shocks me back to the present. I gasp for air, pushing a damp strand of hair from my forehead. In a daze, I get up and grab the phone from the kitchen counter. Gabriel's name is on the screen. I exhale and hit END. I can't talk to him right now. I close my eyes, trying to recapture the memory, but it's gone. The only thing that remains is a feeling of rage so strong that before I realize what I'm doing, I throw the phone against the wall with such force that I know before looking at it that the screen is completely smashed.

5
Julian

Julian set down the plate of sugar cookies in front of his daughter. He broke a piece from one and popped it into his mouth. He'd followed Cassandra's recipe, but they still didn't taste the same. Nothing was the same. Sighing, he grabbed his mineral water from the counter and leaned against the kitchen island.

"Thanks, Daddy," Valentina mumbled, her mouth full.

"It's finally stopped raining," he said. "Shall we do something special?"

Valentina looked at him, her eyes wide. "Can we go to the American Girl doll store? Please?"

He gave her an indulgent smile and nodded. He knew he spoiled her, but she was such a sweet child, and after everything she'd been through, he would do anything to make her happy. "Do you have a particular doll in mind?"

She gave him a solemn nod. "I want a Truly Me doll with green eyes like Mommy's and mine. And dark hair like we have. That way I won't forget her."

It took everything he had to conceal the pain her words caused him. He held his arms out, and she ran into them, hugging him tightly. When they pulled apart, he lifted her chin gently and looked into her eyes. "You won't forget Mommy, sweetie. I promise. We look at her picture every night before we say a prayer for her."

Valentina's lower lip trembled. "Why did she go away? Doesn't she love us?"

This was something new. Even though they had talked about Cassandra's disappearance many times, Valentina was precocious for seven, and the older she got, the more questions she asked.

"Of course she loves us. She's trying to get back to us. You just have to be patient and wait."

Valentina scowled. "Don't want to wait. It's not fair."

Julian had noticed that her usually sunny disposition had changed recently; she was becoming moody, even argumentative, at times. He squeezed her hand. "I know, princess."

He wondered if he was doing her more harm than

good by keeping hope alive. He still paid a detective a hefty monthly sum to keep looking. But he couldn't, he wouldn't, believe that Cassandra was dead. He would intuitively know if she were gone from this world. He wouldn't believe it unless he had proof. She was out there somewhere, and he would bring her home someday. He was sure of it.

. . .

After he put Valentina to bed that evening, Julian walked over to Cassandra's dressing table, opened the drawer, and took out her leather journal. He'd found it after she'd gone. The detailed log she'd kept of their lives together made him feel closer to her, and reading her words gave him comfort, as though she were still with him. He sank into the armchair next to the bed and opened it to the first page, which he'd read many times by now.

Julian asked me to marry him! He took me to Ricard's for dinner. He ordered their most expensive bottle of champagne. It only took a moment for me to see the diamond sparkling at the bottom of the crystal flute. The ring is a perfect fit— of course—just like Julian. It feels as though my life is finally taking a turn in the right direction. He's been my rock and my safe place these last few months, but I never dreamed he felt about me the way I do him. I'll finally have a real family of my own. We talked about children, and he told me he wants them as much as I do. It's time for me to leave the painful past where it belongs and look ahead to a bright future.

He sighed and closed the book, the tightness in his chest increasing. How beautiful she had looked that night. He'd spent weeks planning the proposal, down to the smallest detail. He hadn't known what she would say, but the look in her eyes when she saw the ring told him all he'd needed to know. And unlike that of so many couples he knew, their love hadn't diminished over time, but had only grown deeper with each passing year.

He stood and walked out of the bedroom and toward Valentina's room. Slowly opening the door, he peeked in to check that she was sleeping. Her raven hair fanned out on the pillow, her porcelain skin unblemished, even in sleep she looked so much like Cassandra. The resemblance was a comfort and a curse at the same time. He stepped quietly into the room and stood by the bed, gazing at her.

"Don't worry, my sweet. I'll bring her back. Everything is going to turn out fine, I promise."

6
Blythe

Blythe looked across the table at her son, the crushing love she felt for him washing over her. He'd come over for their customary Sunday dinner. From the time Gabriel and Hailey were small, she and Ted had made a commitment to keep Sunday sacrosanct. The weekdays may have found them running in a million different directions with sports, activities, and other commitments, but Sunday was reserved for family. Church in the morning, Sunday brunch at the club, and a home-cooked meal on Sunday evening, one that the children helped to prepare as they got older. The contentment that she usually felt sharing this meal with those she loved best in the world, though, was overshadowed by a nagging worry.

Her gaze traveled to Addison, and the familiar tug-of-war inside her resurfaced. She and Gabriel were clearly very much in love. He'd fallen hard and fast for her, and Blythe couldn't deny that she seemed kind and caring. She was a beautiful young woman, too, with her pale skin and eyes the color of fiery emeralds—the complete opposite of the blond, blue-eyed Darcy, who had been his serious girlfriend until he met Addison.

The fact that Addison's entire past was a mystery didn't seem to bother the rest of the family. Hailey adored Addison, claiming her as the sister she'd never had. And Ted seemed perfectly comfortable with his son marrying someone who was as much a stranger to herself as to them. But then again, Ted loved everyone. It wasn't that Blythe didn't have sympathy for her son's fiancée. After all, it wasn't Addison's fault that she had amnesia, as Gabriel made a point to remind her.

She'd seen that look in his eyes the day he came to tell Blythe about the new talent he'd discovered, the same look he used to get when he found a stray dog or lost kitten. He'd gone on and on in an excited rush about this beautiful and talented young woman who'd been rescued by kind strangers, and Blythe could tell he was a goner. If only Hailey had been the one to bring her into the family, Blythe reflected, she would have been happy to take her in as a surrogate daughter. What concerned her most was that one day Addison would remember who she was and go back to her own life. For all they knew, she already had a husband. Blythe had an ominous feeling that one day Addison was going to break her son's heart.

"Mother, did you hear me?"

"What?" she asked, startled out of her thoughts.

"Addy and I are going to see *Beautiful* next Thursday, you know, the Carole King musical. I thought maybe you and Dad would like to join us. We could grab dinner first."

"That sounds lovely. What do you say, Ted?" Even though she had a million and one things still left to do for Ted's birthday party next Saturday night, she was grateful for their desire to include her and Ted and didn't want to do anything to offend Addison. Especially as she knew that it had most likely been Addison's idea to invite them along. When Gabriel was dating Darcy, the two of them had gone to the theater all the time, and he'd seldom thought to ask her and Ted to join them—not that she would have expected him to. But since Addison's arrival on the scene, Gabriel had spent a lot more time with the family. She wanted to believe that it was because Addison yearned for a family, to be a part of something, but sometimes she couldn't help but wonder cynically if she was only currying favor. Blythe hated to think that way, but her own mother had ingrained in her the need for caution due to their wealth.

Ted smiled. "Sure, sounds great."

"I'm so glad you're going to join us," Addison said, giving them a warm smile.

When they finished eating, Addison jumped up and began to clear the dishes away. Blythe put a hand up. "Darling, it's okay. Grace will see to that." She tried to keep the annoyance out of her voice. This wasn't the first time Addison had dined with them, and Blythe was frustrated that she had to keep reminding her that they had help. Was her insistence on taking in her own plate a little form of rebellion against their lifestyle?

"Sorry," Addison said, turning red. "I guess maybe it's something that was instilled in me? I wish I knew."

Gabriel shot his mother a look, and she swallowed a sigh. "Of course," she said. "I didn't mean to make you uncomfortable. How about some coffee in the living room?"

He gave Blythe an approving nod, and she thought once again how fraught this situation was. If she showed the slightest hesitation about his commitment to Addison, he would only dig his heels in further. He had a heart of gold but a will of iron, and the only way he would ever change his mind would be on his own.

Blythe's protective instincts, however, gave her the

edge. Gabriel and Addison had acquiesced to her insistence on a year-long engagement so they could plan a proper wedding. That meant she had one year to find out everything she could about Addison, or whatever her real name was. She had already made an appointment with a detective to look into her. No matter how lovely and charming she appeared, there was simply no way Blythe would let Addison join this family until she knew who she really was.

7

Addison

We pull up the drive, and I'm struck again by the majesty of the Olivers' house. When Gabriel puts his Land Rover in park, a valet comes to the passenger side to open the door, then takes Gabriel's place behind the wheel and drives the car away. Ted is turning sixty, and tonight is the huge bash Blythe is putting on for him. Over one hundred guests. I'm always astounded at their enormous social circle and how often they entertain. Gabriel is as outgoing and social as his parents, and that is one of the things that worries me, as someone who is most comfortable with one-on-one relationships.

As soon as we walk in, I see Darcy near the dining room table, talking to Blythe. She looks pretty in a flowery slip dress and high strappy sandals, her white-blond hair loose and not in the usual low ponytail. Darcy strikes me as someone who is sure of herself and her place in the world. Her charm is rooted in the sense that she enjoys and is completely at ease with people.

Especially my future mother-in-law. They're leaning in toward each other, and their conversation looks lively and animated. I hate the fact that their closeness bothers me. I learned that his parents hoped, even expected, that Gabriel and Darcy would marry one day. The moment his mother looks up and sees us, she smiles and waves us over, and I feel my throat start to close.

"You're late, darling. What's the point of that new watch if you don't use it?" Blythe teases Gabriel and kisses him on the cheek.

She turns to me and takes my hand in hers. "I'm so glad you're here. You look lovely, Addison." Blythe is always gracious and kind to me, but she's lovely to everyone.

"Thank you," I say, and give her my best smile before turning to Darcy. "Hi, Darcy."

"Hello Addison, Gabriel." Darcy gives a slight nod. It's clearly awkward for her, but she is polite. She was raised to have good manners, and it shows. Still, I wonder if she hates me. Gabriel was seeing her when we met, and later told me that he ended it with her before we even went on our first date. He's honorable like that. She's still in love with him, though. I can tell from the way she looks at him, her smile getting very small and her eyes growing sad.

"Glad you could be here to help Dad celebrate," Gabriel says.

A brief and awkward silence follows, which Blythe thankfully breaks. "Darcy was just telling me some wonderful news," she says, putting her arm around Darcy's shoulder and drawing her closer. "She has a second audition next week with the Philadelphia Orchestra."

Gabriel breaks into a wide grin. "That's fantastic, Darcy. Wow. What position is it?"

"Second violin. I tried out with the auditions committee a few weeks ago, and they called me yesterday to come back."

"They'd be crazy not to choose you," he says sincerely. "You've been working toward this as long as I've known you."

Her face lights up. "Remember the shows we put on when we were kids? I'd play and you'd sing. Our poor parents, we'd make them sit and watch us perform for hours."

Blythe laughs. "I'd forgotten about that. You were good even then." She turns to Gabriel. "No offense, but I'm glad you didn't pursue a musical career."

He gives his mother a wry look. "Thanks a lot. Just for that I'll sing 'Happy Birthday' extra loud tonight."

They all laugh, and I stand there with a frozen smile, trying to hide how left out I feel. Does Darcy realize how lucky she is that she's known from the time she was a little girl what she wanted to do with her life? She is such a talented, accomplished musician that even though the violin is her instrument, she's great on the piano too. In fact, it seems to me that there is nothing that Darcy isn't good at. Tennis, sailing, horseback riding—you name it.

What I'm good at is taking photos, observing others. Is it because I'd rather watch than participate? Once again, I'm plagued with doubts and have the urge to run. But I can't run again. As Gigi keeps reminding me, in time I'll make more memories. Ten years, twenty years, I'll have a past again, and that's something worth fighting for. I have to get over the fact that Darcy has a lifetime of memories, and that her memories all include Gabriel. No matter what I tell myself, a part of me is waiting for him to come to his senses and tell me that he's going back to her—that I was just an interesting diversion, or a charity project that he's tired of.

I swallow hard and add my congratulations to Darcy, forcing away the intruding thoughts.

"Thanks," she says politely before excusing herself.

Blythe gives me a reassuring look, seeming to read my unease, but Gabriel is oblivious.

"Come on, let's go get a drink." He holds out a hand, and I take it as we walk deeper into the room, nodding hello at the sea of friends gathered in small circles. I make small talk with a couple who approach, old school friends of Gabriel's. I'm only half listening, though, as I scan the room, looking for Darcy. My stomach lurches when I see her approach Ted, and he wraps her in a bear hug. She hands him a small wrapped box, and I'm reminded of the long history between her and Gabriel's family. Gabriel follows my gaze and puts a hand on my arm.

"You okay?"

I nod, biting my lip.

"I love you," he whispers in my ear.

Why? I want to say, but instead I smile and tell him I love him too.

8
Julian

Julian ended the call and heaved a deep sigh. Another false lead, according to the detective. He just couldn't understand it. How could she have disappeared without any trace? Of course, after she disappeared, he'd checked all the local hospitals, as well as those in the surrounding areas, but there was nothing. He'd set Google alerts for a series of keywords pertaining to missing women or unidentified persons, but the hits he got were all dead ends. How was it possible to disappear in this age, when surveillance cameras made anonymity impossible and a bank machine could mark your location instantly? But of course, that had been one of the problems. Cassandra's bank card, along with her driver's license and credit cards, was in her Hermès wallet, which was in her Chanel purse, which was still in her bedroom closet upstairs. Her passport still rested in its leather holder in her top dresser drawer. No cash had been withdrawn from any of their accounts, and the thousand dollars' worth of cash that Julian kept in the house for emergencies had not been touched.

He picked up his wineglass and swirled the crimson liquid before taking a long swallow and picturing Cassandra sitting in the chair opposite him, the way she used to after they'd put Valentina to bed. They would talk about their day, catching each other up in the quiet of the evening hours. Ever since she'd left, he drank a glass of wine alone every night before he went to bed. And every night he fantasized that she was again sitting across from him, her eyes shining with happiness and her smile reserved for him.

After finishing tonight's wine and checking on Valentina, Julian retired to his room. He felt the pull of Cassandra's diary as soon as he walked in, and he picked it up, carrying it with him to the wing chair.

We're having a small wedding. Just a few close friends of Julian's, and his father, of course. I've lost contact with most of my friends from work, but Marion and I are still in touch, and she'll be my maid of honor. I'm nervous about meeting Julian's dad. He's some sort of famous doctor who's written a lot of books. Apparently, the name Grant Hunter is very well known in medical circles. He used to teach at Harvard, but now he lives in Arizona because the climate is good for his arthritis. I'm afraid that he'll think me too uneducated for his son. I went to work right out of high school. I always thought that one day I'd go back to school, work toward a degree in fashion, maybe. But it never happened. And now I'm twenty-seven, divorced, and about to marry the one person in the world who seems to really get me. I just hope I make a good impression on his father. Julian tells me I don't need to worry, that he loves me and nothing will change that. But I've heard the way his voice changes when he's on the phone with his father. He gets a strained, polite tone, and he clutches the phone tightly in his hand. He's uptight for hours after those phone calls, and it's only after a few glasses of wine and soothing on my part that his good humor is restored.

Julian shut the journal and leaned back, closing his eyes. He'd read these words before, but they still gave him a shock. He understood now that Cassandra had seen so much more than she let on. He hadn't realized that she could tell how much his father upset him. His father was a hard man, remote and unemotional, and Julian never felt that he could live up to his exacting standards. Even Julian's acceptance to Stanford had been met with "I suppose if you're more interested in a laid-back environment, then choose Palo Alto over Cambridge." Whether his father had minded that Julian hadn't chosen his own alma mater or truly felt that Harvard was superior, Julian had no idea. He just wanted to get as far away from Boston as he could. The only reason he'd come back and done his residency at Mass General was because by then his father had moved to Arizona.

Cassandra had been right to worry about how Julian's father would receive her. He hadn't even tried to hide his disapproval of his son's bride, and it had greatly upset her. It had taken everything in Julian's power to calm her down and convince her that Grant's opinion didn't matter to him. In the end, ironically enough, Grant *had* come to love her, especially after she'd given him a granddaughter.

9
Addison

The sound of water running in the shower wakes me, and I turn over groggily to look at the clock on the night table in Gabriel's bedroom. Six a.m. Why is he up so early on a Saturday morning? The gallery doesn't open until eleven, and he normally sleeps in on the weekend. I hear the water stop, and a minute later Gabriel walks out of the bathroom, a towel around his waist. A few beads of water still glisten on his chest as he moves toward the bed and leans over to kiss me. I reach up and run my hands along his torso and around his neck, pulling him onto the bed with a laugh.

"What are you doing out of bed so early?" I say, nuzzling his ear.

"Couldn't sleep," he says, and gives me a long kiss

on the lips. He slides an arm around my waist and presses his body to mine. "On second thought, I think I'll come back to bed."

As we make love, I relish the feel of his body— tall, strong, and athletic—against mine, feeling safe and protected in his arms. When we finish, we stay in bed, tangled up together, and he drifts off to sleep. In this moment I feel peaceful and connected, something I couldn't have conceived of six months ago. Gabriel changed everything the day he walked into Exposed, the photography store where I work. There was something appealing about the way he casually strolled around, looking at camera equipment, or maybe it was his warm and generous smile when he came up to the counter.

"Hi there," he said.

"Hi. Can I help you with something?"

"Yeah. I'm looking for a new camera. A mirrorless DSLR."

"Follow me," I said.

He examined several models in the case and chose a Sony A-7. As we headed back to the register, I asked him what he was going to use the camera for. I didn't usually attempt small talk with customers, but something about him was so approachable.

"I'm photographing some artwork, actually. I manage my family's gallery, and I have to shoot a painting for a prospective buyer in California, and my old camera wasn't cutting it."

"I understand," I said. "Would I know the gallery?"

"Maybe—the Oliver on Second Street?" he said.

"I've been there. You have wonderful pieces."

He looked right at me then, and I noticed how perfect his face was—the dark brown eyes and full lips. I felt my face flush and quickly looked down at the credit card machine.

"I must not have been there when you came," he said. "I'm sure I would have remembered you."

I shrugged, giving him an I-don't-know look, too flustered to speak.

"Are you a photographer?" he asked.

To my utter horror, my face grew hot again. "Not really. I mean, not professionally. It's just something I love to do." I pointed to a wall of landscapes. "Those are some of mine."

Gabriel walked over and stood there for a while, seeming to take in every picture, and then turning to me. "These are amazing, what you've captured."

"They remind me of a fresh start. Going from one place to another. That's what I see when I look through the camera lens."

He looked at me a long minute, and I saw something in his expression change. "Are you doing anything for lunch today, Miss . . . what is your name?"

"Addison. Addison Hope. And I'm not doing anything for lunch."

That was the start, and I'd be lying if I said I wasn't scared to death at the beginning. Gabriel was the first man I'd dated since coming to Philadelphia. What was I supposed to tell him about myself? That I was a woman with no past, a woman who knew nothing at all about herself or her family? I was sure he'd think I was some kind of freak and run as fast as he could. But that isn't at all how it happened. After our lunch that day, where I'd been able to steer clear of personal topics, we made plans to go to dinner on Saturday night. I knew I'd have to tell him then.

He took me to an old-world French restaurant with soft lighting and small tables. The candles on the table, the wine, the handsome man sitting across from me, all made for the most romantic night of my life, although I realize that I have no actual basis for comparison.

I can recall our conversation that evening almost word for word, and when I told him I remembered nothing about my life before the last two years, he looked completely confused.

"I'm not sure I understand," he said. "You have no idea who you are?"

"Yes, exactly."

"But your name. You remember your name."

"No. Um . . . I made up a name," I lied. "It's Addison Hope."

"I like it. And the last name. Hope. You're struggling, but you have hope." He reached across the table and squeezed my hand.

His hand felt strong and comforting. "I do. It's hard, though. There are times I feel overwhelmed, like I'm all alone in the world, connected to nothing. I try to imagine what it must be like to have a mother and father, siblings maybe, to belong to someone. And then I think maybe they're out there somewhere, my family, wondering where I am and what happened to me. I'm not a whole person, and I'll never be until I know my real identity." I slid my hand out from under his.

"You'll find out someday, I'm sure. I can't imagine going through this, but whoever you are, really are, that's in here." He pointed to his heart and then leaned forward. "I know you're a good person. I can just tell."

"How can you know that?"

"I sense it. And you know what else? I think we were supposed to meet."

I raised my eyebrows.

He took my hand again. "I felt a connection the minute I came into the store. I don't usually go there, and I only did because my regular camera store had been broken into the night before and was closed. It was no accident that I walked in that day. It was meant to be."

I shut my eyes and rubbed my temples. Thoughts spun around in my head until I felt like it would explode. What was happening here? As I steadied myself, my thoughts turned sober. "You know nothing about me, of the family I come from or what I might have done in the past. Who knows what I could have been? Maybe even a criminal. I'm not sure you could cope with that. It's hard enough for me."

"It doesn't matter. What matters is who you are now. And who you are now is beautiful, intelligent, and kind. That's all I need to know. Don't run away from me. Let me be the someone you're connected to."

So I gave in to him and the whirlwind romance. We spent almost every day together after that. The first time I went over to his condo, which is in a restored nineteenth-century building in Fishtown, I couldn't get over the peculiar name of his neighborhood. He explained it was named after the early settlers, who were fishermen, and I soon discovered a vibrant and hip area filled with bistros, great restaurants, and a terrific art and music scene. When we started spending more time in his home, I appreciated how he understood that I needed to take things slow. The idea of sex was terrifying at first. Would I even know what to do? And what about the scars I'd no longer be able to hide? But he was gentle and patient, and the first time it happened, all my fears were allayed. It felt so natural, and he made me feel safe and cherished.

After we became engaged, he asked me to move in with him, but I couldn't, though I often spent the night instead of making the trip back to Gigi and Ed's house in Northeast. I loved being with him in that idyllic space, with its warm red brick walls and wood-beamed ceilings, but I wasn't ready to give up my own space, to leave the surrogate parents who meant so much to me. Gigi and Ed's house was the only home I'd known, and they were the only security I had. It's another reason that I now feel grateful that Blythe pushed for a year-long engagement. It will give me the time to adjust, to get myself ready to live with Gabriel and be with him every day and every night. To trust him enough to let him hear the screams that tear from my throat when the nightmares come, the ones with all the blood and dead bodies.

Are they nightmares, or memories? I'm trying to believe in a happy ending for myself, but in the back of my mind always lurks the fear of what I left behind in that other life. It's like crossing a bridge and having no idea what you left on the other side of the river. What will happen when I remember what was I running from?

10

Blythe

Blythe put on her pearl studs and regarded herself in the dressing table mirror. The fine lines at the corners of her eyes and the slight frown line between her brows were a little more obvious than last year, harbingers of the aging that in a few years would make her the proverbial older woman who "must have been a real beauty when she was young." Lots of her friends were getting Botox and fillers. That was fine for them, but it wasn't something she was interested in. She'd been blessed with great skin, and wore no makeup beyond a touch of bronzer, a sheer pink lip gloss, and on special occasions, a coat of mascara. There was a certain lightness about her, reflected in the natural fibers she favored, her loose, wavy hair, which never looked "done," and her lithe, athletic body. Here, this all said, was a woman who was comfortable in her own skin, who made other people comfortable when they were with her. It was one of the things Ted had always loved about her, he said.

Blythe glanced at her watch and saw that they had to leave in a few minutes. She called up the stairs to Hailey, who had spent the night at the house. "Are you almost ready, honey?"

"Coming," her daughter called back.

They'd arranged to meet Addison at Chantal Morgan Couture for their 10:00 a.m. appointment. When Blythe first proposed the outing, Addison had demurred, saying she didn't want to spend a lot of money on a wedding gown she'd wear once and mentioning that a coworker had suggested she check out Rent the Runway. It wasn't that Blythe turned her nose up at frugality, and she knew a lot of young women used and loved Rent the Runway. Fine. But a wedding dress was special, and she hated the idea of Addison renting one when Blythe was willing to buy her any dress she wanted.

Hailey came bounding down the stairs, her short blond hair still damp. She was tall and slim, like her mother, and wore a navy-blue jumpsuit that accentuated her height even more.

Blythe grabbed her handbag from the hall table and headed out the door. "Let's go. Don't want to be late."

"This is so exciting." Hailey settled into the car and buckled her seat belt. "I can't wait to see what dress she picks."

"I wish Addison had even a quarter of your enthusiasm," Blythe said as she pulled out of the driveway.

Hailey turned to look at her mother. "Addison doesn't let her emotions show much, Mom. You know that. It doesn't mean she's not enthusiastic."

"I guess I don't understand. This is supposed to be one of the happiest times in a young woman's life. She should be brimming with excitement. Certainly Darcy would be," Blythe said, keeping her eyes fixed on the road.

"Mom." Hailey said the word like a reprimand. "You have to stop this. Gabriel's not marrying Darcy. He's in love with Addison. I don't know why you're having such a hard time with that."

Blythe flexed her fingers on the steering wheel but said nothing. Hailey was right about Addison. She might not have had Darcy's joie de vivre, but why would she, given all that she'd had to overcome? If Blythe were being honest, she had to admit that Addison possessed an inner strength, a courage even, that was admirable. It was unfair to compare her to Darcy.

"Have you and Addison talked about *your* dress?" she asked, changing the subject.

"She just said to pick something I'd be happy to wear again. Not a froufrou bridesmaid dress, thank goodness. But I'll wait and let her choose hers first."

Blythe didn't reply. Hailey was to be Addison's only attendant. It bothered Blythe that in the two years Addison had lived in Philadelphia, she hadn't gotten close enough to anyone else to include in the wedding. She wondered what that said about Addison's ability to connect with people.

Blythe was able to avoid sensitive topics for the rest of the short drive, and when they walked into the salon, she was pleased to see that Addison was already there and talking to Philippa Morgan, the owner.

"Ah, here they are," Philippa said as she and Addison turned to welcome them. "Hello, Mrs. Oliver. Addison and I were just talking about what kind of style she has in mind."

"Please call me Blythe. This is my daughter, Hailey." She stepped forward to give Addison a quick hug. "Hello, my dear."

"Thank you for arranging this, Blythe," Addison said. "I appreciate it."

"Wonderful," Philippa gushed. "May I get you coffee or tea? Perhaps some water?"

"Nothing for me," Addison said.

Blythe waved her hand. "Maybe later. Why don't we get started?"

"Perfect. Well, as I was saying, Addison and I had a few minutes to talk about the styles she's interested in seeing, so why don't you and Hailey have a seat while I take the bride-to-be to the dressing room?" The owner turned to Addison. "All long-sleeved, right?" She waited for Addison's nod and then said to Blythe, "She'll be out in a jiffy to model for you."

After a few minutes Philippa swept back into the room with a flourish. "Here is the first dress for you to see."

When Addison stepped up onto the dais in a Carolina Herrera silk gown with a cascading train in the back, both mother and daughter gasped. She looked stunningly beautiful in the elegant, form-fitting dress.

"Oh my," Blythe finally said. "I'm not sure she needs to try on anything else."

"It's fabulous," Hailey chimed in. "You look amazing."

"I . . . I don't know," Addison said, turning around and looking at her reflection from different angles. She stepped down from the pedestal and went to Blythe. "It's so expensive," she said softly. "I didn't even want to try it on, but Philippa insisted."

"She was right. It's perfect for you."

"But it's almost nine thousand dollars," Addison said, looking stricken. "I'm not sure I'd be comfortable wearing a dress that cost so much."

It was a struggle to contain her frustration, but Blythe did her best. "I understand," she said, and turned to Philippa. "I think we're interested in seeing some gowns that are more in the one-or two-thousand-dollar range." She looked at Addison. "How does that sound?"

"I'm sorry. I hope you don't think I'm ungrateful, because I'm not. You and Ted have been wonderful. It's just . . ." She looked at the floor, and Blythe could tell that she was trying not to cry.

"It's fine, Addison. We'll find a dress you love and then have a nice lunch. Don't worry."

"Thank you," Addison said, still looking upset.

After trying on eleven more gowns, Addison finally settled on a similar style at a much-reduced price. She looked lovely in it, because she would look wonderful in anything, Blythe thought, but it had none of the elegance and sophistication of the Carolina Herrera gown.

"It's really pretty, Addy. I like it," Hailey said, rising and stepping up on the platform to get a closer look.

"You do?"

Hailey smiled, taking both of Addison's hands in hers and holding them out as if to get a better look at the dress. "Absolutely. It's perfect for you."

Blythe sat quietly and watched the two of them. They seemed to have a great deal in common, not least of which was their shared love of animals, and Hailey had recruited Addison to volunteer with her at the SPCA. It was clear that they had the kind of connection that Blythe had so far failed to achieve with her prospective daughter-in-law, and that bothered her. She adored both of her children and had always envisioned a close relationship with whoever they married, and she knew she'd have had that with Darcy, who was so warm and affectionate. Addison seemed—*aloof* was the wrong word—more like fearful of revealing too much, of getting too close. Blythe sighed, inwardly chastising herself for being so critical. Maybe in time things would improve.

She watched as Hailey touched the row of satin buttons on one of the dress's sleeves. As the fabric shifted slightly, Addison jerked her hand away, but it was too late. Both Hailey and Blythe had seen the jagged scar starting at her wrist. Dear God, Blythe thought. What terrible things are hiding in this young woman's past?

11
Addison

I tap lightly on the screen door and lean closer to look for Gigi in the kitchen. "Anybody home?" I call, and open the door. As I enter, Gigi rushes into the room.

"Hi. Come and sit. How'd it go yesterday? Did you pick a dress? I'm so sorry I had to work. I wish I could have gone with you."

"Me too. We chose the dress. But I was careless."

Gigi frowns. "Careless? What do you mean?"

"Blythe and Hailey saw the scar on my arm," I tell her.

Gigi sits back in her chair and purses her lips. "What did Blythe say?"

"Nothing." I bite my lip and look at the floor. "But I saw the expression on her face." I look back up at Gigi.

"I know she's leery of me. I can't really blame her. I'm leery of me too. I know eventually I'll have to tell her about my scars—I can't wear long sleeves forever. But I really wanted to wait until she knew me better and would be apt to give me the benefit of the doubt."

"I don't believe she would ever hold this against you, Addy," Gigi says kindly. "She seems like a good person."

"She is. And I give her a lot of credit that despite her inevitable reservations, she's doing her best to make me feel welcome. The least I can do is try to show her that I appreciate all she wants to do for us. It's the reason that I'm going along with this big wedding, even though all that attention is the last thing I want."

Gigi cocks her head. "Try to think of it simply as a day when the people who love and care about you and Gabriel want to support you and share your happiness."

I get up and pour myself a glass of water, then lean against the counter to face her. "Some days I don't know why I even agreed to marry Gabriel. He's a great guy. Good-looking, kind, funny. I love him, or at least I think I do. But do I even know what love really is?"

"There you go again. Overthinking. You don't have to dissect love and put it under a microscope."

"But why is that a bad thing to do? It's all I have, really. I can't look back over my life and judge what

I've done right and what I've done wrong, what choices I've made." What I don't say is that I feel like an impostor who has taken up life in a body that used to belong to someone else. I can't stop agonizing over what could have caused me to try and take my life. Or maybe it's possible that someone else is responsible for the slashes. That question keeps me up nights, and the fact that it doesn't keep Gabriel up keeps me up even longer.

I got so lucky when Ed picked me up. When I think about it, that situation could have ended in a very different way. A young woman with no identification and no memory, hitchhiking. And I think of how Gigi's medical knowledge might have saved my life, too. When we arrived at the house, it felt like a hammer was pounding on my head, but I was more afraid of being taken to a psych ward somewhere than dying. Gigi put an arm around my waist, and as we walked to the car, she kept repeating that everything was going to be fine and that she wouldn't let anything bad happen to me. I still remember how her voice sounded in my ear, so gentle and reassuring.

At the hospital they gave me every test imaginable: MRI, CT scan, blood tests to check for infection, an electroencephalogram for possible seizure activity, even a gynecological examination. A psychiatrist asked me lots of questions, some of which I could answer but most of which I couldn't. I felt so afraid and lost as I was wheeled from one test room to another, put inside clanging machines in dark spaces. It was terrifying. And then the diagnosis, which I could have told them myself: retrograde amnesia, the inability to recall any events that occurred before the development of the amnesia. Memory wiped clean.

I went home with them as soon as I was released and stayed in the guest room the first few months. Gigi is so wise. I think she realized that I couldn't be alone at the beginning, but as I gained confidence, it would be good to have autonomy and a little space.

"I was thinking that you might like to have a place of your own," she said one morning at breakfast.

My body got cold suddenly, and it felt like my stomach was dropping through my feet. Were they kicking me out?

I suspect Gigi saw the look of panic on my face. "What I mean," she hurried on, "is that we have a nice one-bedroom apartment above the garage. You could stay there if you like and have a little privacy and room to move around as you please. It even has a kitchen, if you want to cook." She paused here and gave me a look. "I guess you might not remember if you like to cook or not. But anyway, you're still welcome to have every single meal with us. What do you think? Would you like to take a look at it?"

"Sure," I said a little tentatively. The thought of leaving the safe comfort of their house was a little daunting.

Together we walked up the stairs to the small apartment, which was sparsely furnished but adequate for my needs. There was a small galley kitchen and a wooden table with two straight-backed chairs that took up half of the living space. The other half had a two-seat sofa of dark green velour, next to a round end table with a mock kerosene lamp. There was one picture on the wall—a marshland scene, featuring a black-and-white-spotted dog with a bird in its mouth. I turned to Gigi. "It's a really nice place."

"Oh, poppycock." She laughed. "This furniture? Can you tell Ed picked everything out? It was going to be his man den, but even he thought it was awful." She laughed again. "Come see the bedroom."

It was a large room, and totally empty. "What happened to the bedroom furniture?"

"Ed never got around to that. Why would he sleep here when he had our nice warm bed in the house?" She laughed again. "He made this space into a one-bedroom in case we might want to rent it out someday."

"I see," I said, wondering how I was going to get money to buy a bed. I desperately needed to get a real job, but that was impossible. Up until now, I'd done odd jobs around the neighborhood—dog-sitting, and that sort of thing.

"I can see your wheels turning," Gigi said. "Now listen, you and I are going to go shopping and do this place up. We'll make it pretty and comfy, and it will be your own little refuge. Like I said, you can spend all the time you like at the house. You know we love having you there. But I think you need to take this step if you're going to move forward." She gave me the Gigi smile that I loved, the one that made me feel like I was being wrapped in loving arms.

"I can't let you spend all that money, Gigi. It's not right. I need to get a job somehow."

"One thing at a time. And don't tell me how I can or cannot spend my money. Ed and I both earn pretty darn good money, and we have no other family to leave it to. So I say we should spend it now. And it will give me great pleasure, not to mention a lot of fun, to go on a nice little shopping spree."

My eyes filled. How had I been so lucky to wind up with these incredible people?

We spent the next week shopping and setting up the apartment. I even hung a few of my photographs, the ones I took the day Ed and Gigi took me to Marsh Creek Lake for the day. The night before I was going to move in all my things, we sat together at dinner. Ed had just gotten back from a long-haul assignment, so we felt a little celebratory. Gigi poured a glass of wine for each of us and made a toast to me and my new digs.

"You guys have been amazing to me. I'll never be able to thank you enough for all you've done." I put my glass down and pressed my lips together. "But I can't keep taking from you. I have to figure out a way to earn some real money."

The problem was that I was a nonperson. With no social security number, no driver's license or birth certificate, no kind of ID whatsoever, I couldn't get any kind of job besides odd ones. And when I went to state agencies to ask what I could do, they just looked at me with blank expressions and said, "Nothing. There's nothing you can do." What kind of crap was that? How was I supposed to support myself, or drive a car, or open a bank account, or get a credit card? At first it was frustrating, but I'd passed frustrating a long time before. Now it just seemed like a plot against me.

"Well," Ed said. "I think I may have solved your problem." They were both smiling like they shared a secret.

I waited.

"I took a small detour from my route. Went to visit some beautiful cemeteries in Georgia and Tennessee."

"What?"

"Some of those tombstones are very sad. Babies dying just days after they're born."

"Are you saying what I think . . ." I trailed off.

"You need a birth certificate. The only choice they've given you is to use someone else's. Someone who was born around the time you were and died right away. I figured you're around twenty-four or twenty-five, so I looked for a match," he said, pulling a paper from his shirt pocket. "And I found one."

He handed me the paper, which I unfolded. *Addison Hope. Born August 28, 1994, died September 3, 1994.* I raised my eyebrows and looked back at Ed. "Are you saying I am going to pretend to be this Addison Hope? I don't understand."

"No, not pretend to be her. You're just going to take her name. We have a name and date of birth now. I know someone who can have a driver's license made for you in that name with your photograph. Once we have the license, I can get her birth certificate from the state vital records office. Once we get that, the rest is easy. Social security card, etcetera. Presto. You are now in the system."

"How on earth do you know about this stuff?" I asked. "And a guy who can make a fake license?"

"You'd be surprised at the things truckers run across."

I thought for a minute, chewing on the inside of my cheek. "But is that legal?"

"No. It's highly illegal. But what's the alternative?" Ed said, and I heard Gigi sigh.

He was right. There *was* no alternative. So I became Addison Hope and told myself it was only temporary, until I remembered my real name. But despite all my work with neurologists, psychiatrists, psychologists, and even hypnotherapists over the last two years, I'm still unable to recall a cohesive past. When I say I don't remember *anything*, though, that's not entirely true. If you consider the flashes that come at unexpected times to be memories, then I have a few—blood-spattered faces, flesh torn away from bones, eyes open and staring at me, lifeless and condemning. So many bodies.

12
Julian

Julian took a sip from his mug of coffee. He sat down on the sofa and began to read from Cassandra's diary.

Valentina is the most perfect baby I could have ever dreamed of. At four months, she's already sleeping through the night, and the only time she cries is if she's hungry or needs to be changed. I could sit and stare at her all day. Julian is as besotted as I am, and we practically argue over who gets to hold her. Julian was so sweet and hired a part-time nanny to come and help now that he's gone back to work full-time so that I can have some time to myself, go back to a yoga class here and there.

He took a month off to help me when Valentina was first born. I have friends whose mothers came to stay with them, but of course that's not an option for me, and I think Julian sensed how alone I felt. Over the years I've yearned for my parents, especially my mother, but never as much as when I became a mother myself. Julian pampered me that first month, made all my meals, made sure I rested in between feedings, massaged my back. He's made up for all the misery and loneliness in my life before I found him.

Julian set down the book. It was too painful to read anymore. A part of him knew that eventually he would have to move on, to accept that Cassandra's absence was permanent, but he couldn't yet. Even if he could forget, he had a duty to his daughter to bring her mother back home. And he remained very concerned about his wife's mental state. In the months before she disappeared, she'd been confused, forgetful. She'd started taking a heavy dose of antianxiety and depression meds, all left behind. After she'd disappeared, the detective kept pushing him, implying that maybe she had just decided to leave on her own. All he'd had to do was show him that her purse, her phone, and all her IDs were still at the house. What woman starts a new life with no money, identification, anything?

More importantly, she would have never left their daughter. No, Julian was convinced that something had happened to cause her to forget who she was. To forget him and Valentina. But they would never forget her. He wouldn't ever stop looking until she was back home where she belonged.

13
Blythe

Blythe hadn't slept well the night after the bridal appointment. The scar on Addison's arm was unmistakably from a suicide attempt. Once she thought about it, she realized that Addison always had her arms covered. She thought back to the numerous times over the summer she had invited Addison to the club for tennis or swimming, and Addison always had an excuse for why she couldn't make it. Even at their engagement party, on a ninety-degree day, Addison had been in long sleeves.

When Blythe got home from the fitting, she'd called Gabriel to confront him. He'd admitted that Addison had a matching scar on the other arm, and that she assumed she'd tried to take her own life. But he was quick to add that she had no recollection of it.

Blythe had been furious. "You didn't think to tell us? Gabriel, this is very serious."

There was a long moment of silence on the other end of the line. "What do you want me to say? I didn't tell you because I knew this is exactly how you would react."

"How do you expect me to react? God only knows what's in her past, and now this—"

"Mom. Stop. I don't care. I only care about her future. Our future. Maybe she'll remember one day, and maybe she won't. In either case, I'll be with her every step of the way."

She'd bitten her tongue, knowing that if she didn't, she'd go too far and push him further away. "We'll talk about this later."

Now she headed to the kitchen, where Ted was sitting with the paper and his coffee. She leaned down to give him a peck on the lips.

"Based on the way you tossed and turned all night, I presume you're still upset," he said.

She took a seat across from him and pushed her hair back behind her ear. "Yes, of course. Aren't you?"

He sighed. "I'm not thrilled to learn that she did something so desperate. But we don't know why."

She arched an eyebrow. "Does 'why' really matter? Clearly she was unbalanced. You don't slice your wrists up to your elbows unless you're serious about ending your life."

"I know, sweetheart, but there's nothing to be done about it. Gabriel has made up his mind."

She rose from her seat and started pacing. "I'm aware. He gets that stubborn streak from you."

He laughed good-naturedly. "You can't pin this one on me. Weren't you the one always praising him for his empathy?"

She wasn't in the mood. "Of course I'm glad he's kind, but he doesn't have to throw his life away trying to save a wounded bird. It's too much. She's so closed-off, Ted. I try. I try so hard, but it's like hitting a brick wall."

He gave her a sympathetic nod, then stood. "Everything will work out. I'm going to head over to the gallery after I stop at the bank. You coming in?"

"Later. I'm meeting Darcy at the club for lunch first."

"Is that a good idea?"

"She asked if she could get my advice on something. And just because Gabriel and she are no longer a couple, that doesn't mean she isn't still a part of our lives."

He put his hands up in surrender. "Fair enough."

Darcy had called the night before, asking if she'd meet her at the club because she wanted to get her take on something. Blythe had hesitated only a moment before agreeing. While she realized that it might seem disloyal to Addison, they'd been close with Darcy's family for years, and her mother had been one of Blythe's best friends until her devastating sudden death from a heart defect two years before. Gabriel and Darcy had dated since high school, spending summers and school holidays together when they attended colleges in different states. Blythe wasn't about to turn her back on her now.

The truth was that before Addison came along, Gabriel had seemed happy enough with Darcy. When he decided to end things, Blythe was both surprised and upset. There'd been no warning, nothing to suggest that he wanted out of the relationship. In fact, the following week they were all supposed to head to the Olivers' Palm Beach house for a long weekend.

Blythe remembered the day her son told her. She'd been in her studio, working on her latest sculpture, when he poked his head in. "Mom, I know you don't like to be disturbed when you're working, but can I talk to you for a minute?"

His expression was serious, and she worried that something was wrong. "Of course, come in. What is it? Are you okay?" she asked, her heart in her throat, as he took the seat opposite hers.

"Yes, I'm actually great. I've met the woman I'm going to marry."

Blythe's mouth had dropped open. "What are you talking about?"

His eyes sparkled in a way she realized she hadn't seen for a long time. "Mom, she's amazing. Her name's Addison. She's an artist like you. A photographer. I walked into Exposed, and there she was." He smiled again. "We had coffee and talked nonstop for hours. I can't stop thinking about her."

"But . . . what about Darcy?"

He grimaced. "Darcy's great, but I think I've always known deep down that I'm not in love with her. I guess I went along with it because I liked her and we had a good time together, and it made our families happy. She's a great person, but this is different."

Blythe was quiet, trying to gather her thoughts.

Gabriel leaned forward and, resting his elbows on his knees, looked intently at her. "It's like what Dad always says about you, that he knew the minute he laid eyes on you that he'd marry you."

If she'd known her son would foolishly believe that was how love worked, she'd have told Ted never to share that story. Yes, he'd felt that way, but they'd had friends in common, shared a professional interest in art. She wasn't some stranger he met on the street.

She reached out a hand and put it on his. "Darling, slow down. What do you know about this girl?"

"Only that I want to know more. We're going out to dinner Saturday night. But in the meantime, I have to let Darcy know that it's over. I don't want to hurt her, but I can't go on a date while I'm still in a relationship."

She didn't want him acting rashly. "But you don't really know this Addison. At least wait until after Saturday night before you make a decision you might regret. You and Darcy have been together a long time, and friends for your whole lives. What if you discover this is just an attraction, nothing more?"

He shook his head. "You're asking me to hedge my bets. You raised me to have integrity. I can't in good conscience go out with her without ending things with Darcy."

Blythe had sighed. "Well, then I guess you'd better go talk to her."

So he had, and it had gone as well as could be expected. Darcy had taken the news like a lady and wished him the best. And after Gabriel's date that Saturday night, it was clear to Blythe that he was completely infatuated with Addison.

Blythe dressed, and an hour later got behind the wheel of her silver Infiniti and drove to the club. As she pulled into a parking space at the Cricket Club's

Wissahickon Clubhouse, Darcy's red BMW pulled up next to her.

They embraced in the parking lot, then walked in together and were seated right away. After the waiter had taken their drink order, Darcy turned to Blythe. "Thank you so much for meeting me on such short notice."

"Of course, I was happy I was free. So what's going on?"

"I heard back from the symphony."

Blythe leaned forward. "And?"

"I didn't get it."

"Oh, Darcy, I'm so sorry."

Darcy shrugged. "It's okay. It was an honor to get as far as I did. It came down to just the two of us, and the woman they chose is a brilliant violinist. Anyway, the good news is that I do have another opportunity, and I wanted your thoughts on it."

"Go on."

"I've been offered a teaching position at the Royal Academy of Music."

Blythe was delighted. "How wonderful! Wow, London."

"I know. So far away. But I don't know about leaving my dad, now that Mom's gone."

"Sweetheart, that's very sweet, but your dad's still

a young man. You can't live your life for him. Have you spoken to him about it?"

"Yes. Of course he's encouraging me to go." She sighed and twisted her napkin in her lap, then looked at Blythe. "If I'm being honest, it's not really my father I don't want to leave. He's been spending a lot of time with Charlotte Bekins, and I'll know he'll be fine. But, Blythe, do you really think Gabriel is going to go through with it?"

Blythe's brow creased. "You mean marry Addison?"

"Yes," she whispered.

Blythe reached out and took Darcy's hand in hers. "Yes, darling. I do. I'm so sorry that my son hurt you. And you know how I feel about you, but it's time you moved on. As hard as that is."

"I know, you're right. But . . . I just worry about him. I want him to be happy. I mean, yes, I was hurt, but he's always been honest with me, and I can't fault him for his feelings. But I think he's fallen for an illusion. She's like this mystery. How can he build a life with someone who doesn't even know who she is?"

Blythe didn't disagree, but she couldn't voice those concerns to Darcy; it would be disloyal. No matter how much she cared for Darcy, Addison was going to be family.

"I'm not comfortable discussing Addison with you.

She's going to be my daughter-in-law, and she's been nothing but lovely. I understand your concerns, but Gabriel has made a new life, and it's time you do the same. If he's the only thing holding you here . . ."

Darcy's eyes filled, and she expelled a breath. "You're right. I'll take the position."

"When do they want you to start?"

"Next month."

"I think it's a really exciting opportunity for you. But I'll miss you," Blythe said, and she meant it. But this would be better in the long run. Darcy would have constant reminders of her heartbreak if she stayed in Philadelphia. Their circle was too tight, and she'd be constantly faced with Gabriel and Addison at every social event. Blythe only wished that she were as optimistic about the marriage as she pretended to be. In truth, she wished that Addison were the one moving across the ocean.

14
Addison

"I don't think your mom was very happy with the dress I chose," I tell Gabriel, nestling in the crook of his arm as we lounge on his living room sofa.

"Really? She told me it was beautiful."

I straighten up, turning to face him. "She said that?"

He gives me a funny look. "Yeah, she said that. Why do you look so surprised?"

"Gabriel, does your mom talk about me to you often?"

"You're not still worried about that remark she made about your engagement ring, are you?"

I wave my hand. "No, no. It's not that. I know you explained to her that I can't wear it when my eczema flares up."

He's still stretched out and relaxed on the couch,

but his brows draw together in a frown. "What do you mean, then?"

I twist a strand of hair around my finger. "I don't know. Sometimes I feel like she doesn't like me."

Gabriel stiffens and starts to say something, but I speak before he can. "Wait. I don't mean it that way. Your mom is always nice to me. She's never said or done anything that was unkind. But there's this distance between us, and I don't know if it's me or what."

"She's as eager to be close to you as you are to her, I promise," he says. "I wasn't going to say anything, but she did ask me about the scars."

I jump up and stand in front of him, feeling the heat rise in my neck. "What? Why didn't you tell me?"

"I didn't want to upset you. She's just concerned, that's all."

Aside from Ed and Gigi, Gabriel is the only other person I've let see my scars. It was exhausting at first, having to always remember not to push my sleeves up, choosing shirts that would cover them. But I couldn't figure out any way that we were going to be able to make love without him seeing them.

One night, I sat him down and told him I needed to talk to him.

His face clouded over. "Is something wrong?"

I shook my head. "I just need to share something with you. I'm nervous."

"Have you remembered something?"

"Not exactly. But I think I tried to hurt myself . . . before."

His brow furrowed. "What do you mean?"

I pushed up my sleeve and showed him my arm.

He stared at me, saying nothing at first. "Addison . . . I'm so sorry."

I tried to hold back the tears as I stood, backing away from him. "I don't remember. But obviously I was damaged, or crazy, or something."

He jumped up and pulled me to him, hugging me tight. "You're not damaged or crazy. You don't know how it happened. It might not have even been you."

I looked at him in shock. "Of course it was me. Look." I thrust out my arms again. "These are self-inflicted wounds. Something happened, and I didn't want to live anymore. What could have been so horrible that I tried to kill myself?"

"I don't know, Addy. Maybe that's why you were on the road that day. Trying to get away from something. You're a survivor. You didn't die, and I'm going to keep you safe."

"You don't know what you're saying. Doesn't this scare you?"

"Of course it does. And it infuriates me to think that somebody hurt you enough to make you want to take your life. But that's over. You're safe now. What scares me more is losing you. I love you, Addison."

"You do?"

"Yes, I do."

For the first time I felt someone saw me, the real me. If he could look past my scars, my blank spaces, all the things that terrified me, and still love me, then I loved him.

I look at him now, wondering if Blythe seeing the scars might have caused him to have new reservations.

"She must think I'm crazy. Be honest with me—I already have enough secrets in my life. She wishes we weren't getting married, doesn't she?"

He sits back down and pulls me with him. "Okay, okay. At first, she did caution me. Told me we were moving too fast. And she is concerned that you might one day remember a whole life, another family, that you'll go back to. But I don't care what anyone else thinks. It's my life."

Lately I've begun to worry the same thing, too, that maybe I'm already married. Do I really have the right to start my life over without knowing what I've left behind? But I don't tell Gabriel about these reservations.

"How did you leave it with her after she asked about the scars?"

"I told her that you don't remember, but that whatever happened in the past is in the past, and if you do remember, we'll figure it out together."

I still can't let it go. "She must have been horrified, though."

He puts a hand on my shoulder. "If she was horrified, it was at what you've gone through, not at you. But I have a new topic," he says, picking up a folder from the coffee table and handing it to me. "I was thinking we might want to move into something larger than my condo. Look at this restored town house. It's got the original hardwood floors and moldings. We'd still be in Fishtown, but we'd have lots more room. I was thinking we could go to the open house this weekend."

I flip open to the first page of the pamphlet and look through the photographs. My eyes rest on a picture of the living room with its light-gray rug, and suddenly my body begins to shake violently, uncontrollably. A picture flashes through my mind. A woman's body is sprawled on the floor in a pool of blood that has spread to turn the gray carpet a dark black. Half of the woman's face is gone, and her brains are splattered around her. Clutched in one of her hands is a broken lamp. As fast as the image appears, it's gone. My heart is pounding, and sweat runs down my face even though I'm shivering with cold. Gabriel's hands are clenched around my shoulders, and I can hear him saying my name, but it's hard for me to focus on his face.

"Addy, Addy, what is it?"

Finally my breathing slows. "I . . . I don't know. I just got dizzy for a moment." I can't tell him what I saw until I know what it means. It was so real. Like something I'd seen firsthand. Did *I* hurt that woman? I close my eyes and try to summon the picture again, but it's no use.

"Are you sure you're okay? You're shaking."

I open my eyes, take a deep breath, and swallow. "Can you get me some water?"

He looks back at me as he walks to the kitchen, and I force a smile to my lips to assure him I'm okay. But the truth is, I'm terrified. I remember the lamp—its base is made from two golf clubs crisscrossing. It hits me with absolute certainty then. I've been in that room before. I saw her like that. The question is, did I kill her?

15
Addison

Gigi is sitting on the front porch when I walk over from the garage. I frown as I get closer and see that she's crying. I pick up my pace and run to her.

"What's wrong?"

Gigi looks up. "Today's the anniversary."

September 25th. I can't believe I forgot. "Oh Gigi, I'm so sorry. What can I do for you?"

She pats the empty space next to her on the porch swing. "Come and sit. Just be with me."

I sit down, and we rock back and forth in silence. I don't know a lot about their daughter, Beth, but what I do know is that ten years ago she ran away after a huge fight with them over her boyfriend, who they'd disapproved of from the very beginning. It was after ten when they discovered that she'd snuck out of the house and tried to hitch a ride to his apartment. The man who picked her up was a convicted rapist who had just been released. He graduated to murder the night Beth got into his car.

The swing sways gently as we sit in silence. I can feel Gigi's grief as if it's a tangible thing. "I'm so sorry," I repeat.

"You know?" Gigi says. "They say that some good comes out of everything. I never did see what good could ever come from Beth being murdered." She folds and refolds the tissue in her hands. "There is one thing, though. Maybe her death has kept another girl safe."

I knew that this was the reason Ed had made it his mission to be the savior of female hitchhikers. He will never pass one without stopping and always warns them of the danger and tries to get them help, though I'm the first one who's actually come to live with them. Gigi told me that he once picked up a girl who turned out to be a trafficking victim, so he became an active member of Truckers Against Trafficking, an organization dedicated to combating human trafficking. I think it's the reason they were so willing to take me in. I don't believe that I can in any way replace Beth, but I think it makes them feel good to set the table for three again.

After a while, Gigi turns to me. "She would have been twenty-six by now."

I don't know what to say, so I just nod. It's so rare that Gigi opens up about Beth, and I never want to cause her more pain by asking too many questions, so I just try to listen now.

"He only got twenty years, you know," she continues. "He'll be forty-seven. Still young enough to do it again." She shakes her head. "I can only hope something happens to change him."

"That's terrible. He should have been put to death," I say, infuriated at the injustice of it all.

Gigi gives me a strange look. "No, child. We are not God. We don't get to decide who lives and dies."

I'm quiet because I don't agree. I think he should be made to suffer the way Beth suffered, the way Ed and Gigi suffered. It makes my blood boil knowing that he's still allowed to breathe the air that he deprived Beth of, and I don't understand how Gigi can stand the thought of him living while her daughter is long dead and gone. I guess that's something else I'm discovering about myself—I'm not very forgiving.

"Tell me more about her," I say, despite my previous hesitation. She seems to want to talk about Beth, even need to talk about her, today.

Gigi smiles now. "A spitfire. Always knew what she wanted, and nothing was going to get in her way or stop her. Oh, the blowups she and Ed used to have! But just as passionate as she was about her ideals, that's how passionate she was about her family. I'll never forget, one time we were having coffee after church and a man was giving Ed a hard time about the allocation of funds for the building committee—they were both on the board. This man started raising his voice to Ed, and Beth, who was only ten years old at the time, came stomping up and told him he'd better speak to her father with respect. Told him he was not being a good Christian example at all." Gigi laughs. "That shut him up, I'll tell you."

I swallow the lump in my throat, trying not to imagine Beth's last moments on earth fighting off a rapist.

Lost in her memories, Gigi continues. "We had high hopes for her. She wanted to be a lawyer, and she would have done it too. She always was one for the underdog." She sighs. "I don't know. I'll always wonder if we were too hard on her. She was seeing a boy who was nineteen, and we thought he was too old. If we'd known she was going to go off on her own like that . . ."

I reach out and hold her hand. "It's not your fault. Of course you couldn't have known. Terrible things happen sometimes. I wish they didn't. But please don't blame yourself." I stop, suddenly worried I've gone too far, but her expression is still kind.

"You're such a sweet young woman, Addy. Thank

you. For the most part, I forgave myself a long time ago. The truth is, he *was* too old for her, and none of us could have known what would happen. But Ed, I think Ed still feels like he failed her. You know, a father feels he should be able to protect his daughter." She pats my hand. "I'm glad he found you. Since you've come to us, a little bit of the spark is back in his eyes."

I take her hand in mine and hold on to it, but inside I'm afraid. It's wonderful having people care about you, and I know how lucky I am to have Ed and Gigi. But what will happen if it turns out that the sweet young woman they think I am is really anything but?

16
Blythe

The waiting room of the private detective's office suite looked a lot like how Blythe had imagined it. Gray walls with peeling paint, generic framed art hanging on them, and a wooden coffee table piled with out-of-date magazines. There was no receptionist, and a sign on the inner door announced "With Client."

Blythe hadn't known who to ask for a referral until she remembered that her friend Elaine had hired someone to follow her husband, whom she suspected—correctly, as it turned out—of cheating. Jim Fallow had provided Elaine with enough proof to negotiate a favorable divorce settlement, and she'd assured Blythe that Fallow was as good at his job as he was discreet.

The door opened, and a woman wearing dark sunglasses walked past Blythe. Suspicious wives must be this guy's specialty. When Fallow came out, she was surprised by how well-turned out he was. She chided herself for buying into the stereotype of too many old movies. No rumpled, ill-fitting suit for this detective; he wore pressed black dress slacks, a white button-down shirt, and a well-tailored camel jacket that appeared to be cashmere. He was handsome, with salt-and-pepper hair, and seemed to be in his early forties. Whatever money he saved on the modest office, he obviously didn't spare on his personal appearance.

"I'm Jim. You must be Mrs. Oliver." He shook her hand warmly and motioned for her to come inside.

"Blythe, please. Nice to meet you."

In his much more stylish interior office, he led her to a small round table with two comfortable chairs and invited her to sit.

"Can I get you anything to drink? I've got coffee, tea, sparkling water."

"I'm fine, thanks."

He leaned back and gave her an appraising look. "What can I do for you?"

"I'd like you to look into someone for me."

He waited for her to continue. She shifted in her seat. "The thing is, my son is engaged, and his fiancée claims to have amnesia."

"Claims to?"

Blythe shrugged. "I don't mean to be suspicious, but I've learned over the years that you can't always take everyone at face value. Our family is quite wealthy, and there have been a few occasions on which people have tried to get close to my children for that very reason."

"And you think that's what this woman is doing?"

She shook her head. "No, not really. I think she is likely sincere in her affection and she probably does have amnesia . . . which is a problem unto itself. I guess I'm saying either she has something to hide, in which case she's pretending not to remember, or she really doesn't remember, which means somewhere there are people missing her. Maybe a husband, a child. I'd rather find out before my son becomes legally bound to her."

"I understand." He wrote something on the pad and then looked at Blythe. "If she does in fact have amnesia, and if she isn't able to recall anything at all, we can still discover plenty using only her name and hometown."

"We don't know any of that."

"So you don't even know her real name?"

"No, that's the problem," Blythe said. "She goes by Addison Hope, but she doesn't know her real name."

Blythe filled him in on what Gabriel had told her about Ed and Gigi and the illegal documents Ed had obtained. She still wasn't sure how she felt about this, but she knew it bothered her.

Fallow cocked his head and raised his brows in surprise. "Wow. They could get in deep trouble for that." He made another note. "So, this Ed and Gigi. They've known her now for two years? What's your sense of their credibility?"

Blythe thought back to the night when they'd had dinner together at Ed and Gigi's, a sort of meet-the-parents gathering. Blythe had instantly liked them both—Gigi was warm and kind, and Ed seemed like a good down-to-earth guy. That these people had taken Addison in and clearly gotten to know her so well had allayed some of her fears.

After dinner, Gigi had taken Blythe aside to speak privately. "Addison was nervous about tonight," she said. "She has a lot of insecurities because of her memory loss. It's hard for her."

Blythe appreciated her directness. "I have to admit it's a bit worrying to me. It's moved very fast."

"I can understand why you would feel that way, but I want to tell you that Addison is one of the finest young women you'll ever meet. I don't know what happened in her past, but if she wasn't always a caring and compassionate young woman, she turned into one along the way. I'm sure that's what Gabriel sees in her too."

"I'm glad to hear you say that, and I look forward to getting to know her better."

Gigi's eyes had grown soft. "Do give her a chance, Blythe. She deserves that."

Shaking Gigi's words from her head, Blythe exhaled. She looked across the desk at the private detective. "They're nice enough. I do know they lost a daughter years ago, so how much that's informed their attachment to Addison, I don't know. But her whole story, about Ed finding her hitchhiking along a highway in New Jersey, with no ID, no money, no credit cards, nothing, has always sounded a little fishy to me. Shouldn't someone be looking for her? And wouldn't it be easy to find her?"

He stopped writing and frowned. "That depends. If she's from somewhere far away and has changed her name, it might not be easy for someone to locate her. But we're getting ahead of ourselves. What about a phone? Did she have one with her?"

"No. As I said, she had nothing besides the clothes on her back." She cleared her throat. "Actually, I would love some water after all."

He walked over to the refrigerator and brought her a bottle of Evian and a tall glass.

"Thanks," she said as she poured it. Then something occurred to her. "There's one more thing."

"Yes?"

"She has long scars on her wrists and forearms, all the way up to her elbows. A serious suicide attempt."

He raised an eyebrow. "Okay. Since she was picked up in New Jersey going south, I'll have the picture you emailed to me circulated to some connections I have in law enforcement there as well as in New York. I'll cross-reference the missing persons databases and also hospitals with attempted suicide admissions in the past ten years." He leaned forward. "Do you only want her background checked, or do you want her followed, too?"

Blythe considered this. "I'm not sure there's much you'd discover that way. She spends pretty much all her time either working at the photography store or with my son."

"You'd be surprised," Fallow said.

"If you think it would be helpful, that's fine. I don't want to spare any expense."

"I have someone in mind. We'll watch her for the next week and see what we see. In the meantime, can you take a glass or utensil she uses, put it in a plastic bag, and bring it to me? I'll take a DNA sample."

"Yes, of course."

"I've got enough to get started now," he assured her. "Let me do some digging, and I'll let you know my progress."

She rose. "By the way, I'd like to make sure this all stays between us. Can you make sure you only use my cell to contact me?"

He gave her his word, and she shook his hand and left. When she got to her car, she added him to her contacts under "Marie Fallow," so it would look like just another tennis friend of hers if Ted or Gabriel saw it come up on her phone.

As she drove home, she felt a peace descend over her. Now at least she was doing something concrete. Gabriel would be upset if he knew, but in the end, he'd understand, be grateful even. That was her job, after all, to protect her children.

17
Addison

As I give the gate attendant my boarding pass, my stomach tightens. This is the first time I've flown with fake credentials. I'm always half expecting that the fact that I'm using a dead girl's identity will be discovered, and the police will show up and take me away. But the attendant scans the pass and waves me in after a quick beep. We walk down the Jetway to the plane, and Gabriel puts our suitcases in the overhead bin. We're headed to Florida for a few days so that he can meet with a potential new client.

"Aisle or window?" he asks.

"I'll take the window, thanks."

I'm about to sit when the cockpit opens, and the pilot walks out to greet the first-class passengers with a friendly hello. Suddenly I can't speak. I'm freezing, and my hands are shaking. I stumble over my purse as I grab the side of the seat and fall into it, trying to even my breathing, hearing that horrible voice in my head again. *Shut up, shut your stupid mouth before I shut it for you.* I want to scream and hit something. Rage envelops me, and I clench my fists so tightly that my nails dig into my hands.

"Addison, what is it?" Gabriel leans down, concern in his eyes.

"Leave me alone," I snap.

His expression is hurt, but I don't care. I stand up, pushing past him, and pull open the door to the lavatory. Locking it, I put my hands to my mouth to stifle the scream that fights to explode. I grab the roll of toilet paper and pull it, shredding the tissue as violently as I can. All I want to do is punch the wall, but even in my agitated state, I know better than to attract attention to myself. After a few minutes my breathing slows. I splash water on my face and leave the bathroom. When I sit down beside him, Gabriel doesn't say anything, just waits for me to talk.

"I'm sorry. I don't know what got into me. Some sort of flashback. I didn't mean to be short with you."

"That's okay," he says kindly. "What did you remember?"

"I don't know, it was too fast, but it wasn't pleasant. I don't want to talk about it."

I've thought about seeing someone again to to try to make some headway with these flashbacks, but I tried that route before and all it did was frustrate me. The therapist I was seeing through social services tried her best to help me remember, and after six months we were no further along than when we'd started. The neurologist was no help either. I have to rely on myself to get better.

We're quiet for the rest of the plane ride, my excitement about the trip doused by the darkness of the images in my mind.

. . .

When we arrive in Palm Beach, we drive straight to his family's house, which turns out to be a beautiful place on the water with views of the sea from every window and porch. It's not nearly as imposing as their home in Philadelphia, but I like the casual beachy feel of this house so much better. It's filled with framed family photographs. I pick up a picture of Gabriel and Hailey, the two of them on their hands and knees building a sandcastle on the beach, their sun-browned shoulders touching. I glance at the other photos, chronicling their growing up years. Gabriel's only sixteen months older than his sister, and as teenagers they almost look like they could be twins. They've always been close, and even now Gabriel's condo in the city is less than a mile from Hailey's. I set the photo back on the table next to one of the whole family. They're sitting around a table in a restaurant. Gabriel's arm is around Hailey, and she is leaning close to him, both of them with happy grins on their faces. The loneliness that follows me around every day feels even more crushing as I examine picture after picture.

While Gabriel is at his meeting, I spend the morning looking for seashells along the beach and sipping from a to-go mug of coffee. I feel such freedom, and a curious sense of familiarity that I haven't had anywhere for the last two years. Did I have some special connection to the beach and the ocean in my other life?

When Gabriel gets back to the house in the early afternoon, he looks happy. His meeting went well, and that will result in a nice sale for the gallery. We've planned a day of gallery-hopping in Miami for tomorrow, including a visit to the Art Deco District in South Beach and the one I'm most looking forward to— Dot Fiftyone Gallery, with its incredible photography exhibitions.

Before dinner, we drive the forty-five minutes to Fort Lauderdale to visit the Jamali Gallery, spending a couple of hours examining the exquisite paintings, which look like they are from another time and place.

The colors are extraordinary, but still when I discover the price on one that I especially love, I'm surprised at the six figures, even though I've seen some pretty expensive works go in and out of Ted and Blythe's gallery.

At seven we head to our reservation at the Tradewinds, where I'm awed by the stunning ocean views. Once we're settled in, Gabriel looks across at me and raises his glass. "Here's to us," he says, and we both drink. "I've been thinking. What if we find someone who maybe specializes in helping people remember?"

I shake my head. "I've tried. Nothing has worked. Retrograde amnesia is a neurological—"

"I know, I know," Gabriel cuts in. "You've explained that to me. But, Addy, sometimes I can tell that you're remembering something, even if it's just for a few seconds. What if you started writing down all these little things and talked to someone who could maybe help you string them together and come up with something?"

"Maybe," I say, though I'm not ready to tell anyone about the terrifying images I see, even a therapist. I'm not sure I want to know what they reveal about my past.

"Okay. Enough said," Gabriel says, and takes the conversation in another direction. "What do you think about coming back to Miami in December for Art Basel?"

"Oh my gosh, I would love that. It would be amazing."

I feel on much more solid ground as we talk all through dinner about the art fair and all the galleries we would get to visit then. I'm learning so much about art from Gabriel. I hang on every word, trying to concentrate, but every now and then my eyes wander to a man sitting at a big group table near us who keeps staring at me. It's disconcerting, but I make up my mind to ignore him. I shift position to get him out of my sight line.

"This has been such a great day, Gabriel," I say. "I've loved every minute of it."

He reaches across the table and takes my hand in his. "Me too. And we have so much more ahead of us. I love you, and I always will."

Always. What do any of us know about always? "I hope so," I say.

"You think I'm in deep and don't know what I'm doing, but you're wrong. You can wonder about who you are all you like, Addy, but I don't need to know your past to know the kind of woman you are. I want to spend my life with you, whether you ever remember anything or not."

His words hit me in a powerful way, and I feel like I'm going to cry. I don't deserve him. I can't continue to sit in these feelings, so I rise from my seat. "I have to use the ladies' room. I'll be right back."

I go in and take a few deep breaths, then walk back out. I have to stop questioning whether or not I'm good enough to have this remarkable man in my life.

There's a man standing a few feet outside the door, the man who has been watching me throughout dinner. His stomach hangs over his pants, and his face is pock-marked. He could be anywhere from thirty to forty-five. I try to pass, but he puts a hand out to stop me.

"Hey, babe, it's been a long time," he says with a lecherous smile. "Still dancing somewhere? Let me know, 'cause I'd pay a lot to get a look at that hot body again."

I recoil from him in revulsion. "I don't know what you're talking about."

He laughs. "Okay, I get it. Mr. Suave doesn't know you dance naked?" He takes a card from his inside jacket pocket and hands it to me. "Here's my number. Call me sometime." He pats my backside and walks away, leaving me openmouthed and shaking.

When I return to our table, I see that Gabriel has settled the bill and ordered two after-dinner drinks,

Kahlua and coffee. I down mine in one long gulp, feeling a slight burn as the liquid glides down my throat.

"Let's head back to the house and finish what we started," Gabriel says.

We stand to leave, and I notice that the table where the man and his friends were sitting is now empty. Gabriel and I leave the restaurant hand in hand, the card burning a hole in my pocket.

18
Julian

Julian's cell phone rang just as he pulled into his marked parking spot at the hospital. He hurried to answer when he saw that the call was from Valentina's school.

"Dr. Hunter speaking, is Valentina all right?" It all came out in a rush.

"Yes, yes. This is Dr. Sommerville. Valentina's fine, but there's been an incident. Can you come to the school?"

He was already reversing his Jaguar and heading back on Storrow Drive. "Of course. What kind of incident?"

"I'd rather discuss it in person. I can assure you, there is no need to panic."

His mind raced as he drove the twenty minutes from the hospital to his daughter's private school in Brookline. What kind of trouble could a second-grader get into? He parked the car and sprinted up to the school entrance, hitting the door intercom impatiently. A guard buzzed him in and, after looking at his license, pulled him up on the computer and printed out a visitor's badge.

The woman at the reception desk was on the phone; he tapped his foot while waiting for her to finish. She hung up and looked at him.

"May I help you?"

"Yes, I'm Dr. Hunter. Here to see the headmistress."

She lifted her phone and spoke quietly, then looked back at him. "Have a seat, she'll be right out."

He sighed and sat in one of the pleather chairs, his impatience getting the better of him. After a few more minutes, the headmistress came out and shook his hand. She led him back to her office, where she closed the door, took a seat behind her desk, and folded her hands.

"Dr. Hunter, I want you to know that we're sympathetic to Valentina's situation. We thought that she was adjusting finally, doing better. But today she hit another child."

"What?" Valentina was such a sweet child, he couldn't imagine what would prompt her to become violent. "Why? What happened?"

"According to her teacher, they were outside for recess, and one of the children asked her who she was going to bring for the mother/daughter breakfast next week."

Julian felt the heat rise to his face. "Do you think her teacher might have alerted me to the fact that this breakfast was taking place? How insensitive can she be?"

She put a hand up. "Let me finish, please. A note was going home today, and it's actually a female empowerment day, so the children can bring any woman they look up to. Many are bringing their mothers, and so Emma phrased it that way to Valentina."

"Okay, so what did my daughter say?"

"Valentina told her she was going to bring you, and Emma said she couldn't because you're not a woman." Dr. Sommerville paused. "And then she said that Valentina was stupid, and that was probably why her mother left. That's when Valentina slapped her in the face."

Julian's mouth dropped open. No wonder his poor little girl had acted out. "I'm not condoning violence, but certainly you can see she was provoked. I hope you're also going to speak to Emma's parents about her bullying." The little sociopath, he wanted to add.

"Yes, of course. We don't condone bullying, and Emma will be dealt with. But I'm afraid, despite the circumstances, we cannot tolerate any physical violence in our school community. I'm sure you understand that the safety of students must come first."

"Are you expelling Valentina?"

She leaned forward. "No. Normally we would, but because you've been such a good friend to the school and because of Valentina's unique circumstances, we're only suspending her for the rest of the week. We would also like her to speak with our school psychologist before she comes back."

Julian looked at her like she'd lost her mind. There's no way he was letting some school shrink get inside his child's head. It was outrageous. He took a deep breath, willing himself to remain calm. "Valentina was cruelly provoked, and she's just a child. Children are impulsive, and what she did, while wrong, was not pathological. I won't have her made to think that something's wrong with her. Furthermore, I know nothing about the credentials of your psychologist, but I've seen her, and she looks about twelve. I'd be shocked if she's been out of school a year."

"Well, I er, that's . . . ," Dr. Sommerville stammered.

Julian shook his head. "I'll speak to Valentina, and I'll let her pediatrician know what happened. If he feels examination by a mental health specialist is warranted, then I'll take her to one of my choosing. In either case I'll have him send you his recommendation. Will that be sufficient?"

"I suppose that will have to do."

He was still fuming when he left the meeting and picked up Valentina from the nurse's office.

"Daddy," she said, "I'm sorry for being a bad girl."

He scooped her up in his arms. "Who said you were a bad girl?"

She sniffled. "My teacher."

Julian would have to follow up on this, but right now his daughter's well-being was most important. He put her down and knelt on one knee, looking her in the eye. "Listen to me. You are not a bad girl. What you did was wrong, but it doesn't make you bad. I'm sorry that Emma said those mean things to you. Do you want to tell me your side of the story?"

They walked hand in hand to the car, and Valentina gave him her account, which was much the same as the one the headmistress had given. "I couldn't help it. I was so mad. I just wanted her to be quiet. She kept saying I was stupid, and that Mommy left because of me." She started to cry again. "Is that true?"

"No, baby. Of course not. I told you. Mommy didn't mean to leave, and I'm going to do everything I can to find her. But we need to talk about the hitting. How did it make you feel when you did that?"

She put her head down. "Emma started crying real loud, and I felt bad. I didn't mean to hurt her."

"I'm sure you didn't. What could you have done instead of hitting?"

She looked up, biting her lip as she thought about it. "I could have told my teacher."

"Yes, that would have been a good thing to do. If something like this ever happens again, tell your teacher." Though he wondered if someone who'd clearly demonstrated such bad judgment could be trusted with this.

"Okay, Daddy."

His heart swelled with love for her, this child for whom he would lay down his life. She was suffering, and he didn't know how much longer they could go on this way. Two years was a long time to wait. As much as he hated to admit it, maybe it *was* time to move on, for Valentina's sake. If she thought her mother was dead, she wouldn't feel abandoned. It would hurt, yes, but not as much as thinking that her mother didn't love her. And the detective hadn't come up with even a single lead. Julian had to admit that it was a real possibility that Cassandra was dead.

Valentina's birthday was three weeks away. He'd wait a little while after that, maybe another week, and then he'd tell her that her mother was gone. And they'd figure out how to begin anew.

19
Blythe

Jim Fallow didn't bother with any preamble. "Your girl's a ghost," he told her.

Blythe's stomach sank. "You weren't able to find anything?"

"Nothing on her background. My friend at the FBI ran the DNA through CODIS. No criminal record. No missing persons photos matching hers, nothing on any facial recognition software picked up from CCTV. Nothing."

Blythe sighed in frustration. "So what now?"

"I'm going to go to New Jersey, since that's where we know she was. I'll show her photo around, talk to folks and see if I turn anything up. I'm also using a facial recognition program that works with social media to see if she had any profiles out there." He pursed his lips. "There is one update from our surveillance. As you predicted, her life is pretty routine. Back and forth to work, to your son's apartment, etc. But she took a long walk one day at Pennypack Park. My guy said that she started talking, and he thought she was on the phone. When he sped up to pass her, he realized she was talking to herself. She sounded quite upset, apparently."

Blythe felt herself go cold. "What was she saying?"

"Just two words, over and over. 'Go away.'"

Blythe was silent, trying to process what this meant. Was Addison mentally ill? "Um, thanks. Have your man keep watching her, please."

"Will do."

"Okay, I appreciate the update." She ended the call and walked back into the bedroom, where Ted was already in bed, reading.

He looked up from his book, peering over his glasses. "Who was that?"

She waved her hand. "Just an update from one of the projects I'm working on for the club." She felt bad lying to him, but she didn't want to hear him lecture her on letting the kids live their own lives. What was it with men? They were so much more capable of turning their worry off than women. She knew that Ted would tell her to just let things play out, that she couldn't control everything, yada, yada, yada. She was no more capable of doing that than he was of giving birth.

She slid under the covers next to him and touched her foot to his. He jumped.

"Woman, your feet are like ice cubes."

"So warm them up."

He smiled and moved closer to her, taking her in his arms. They made love, and afterward she snuggled against him, feeling contented and relaxed. They had a good marriage, and she was grateful for it. Not that it had all been rosy. They'd had their share of ups and downs, times of closeness and times of distance. But he was a good man, and she'd never doubted his loyalty or fidelity. They had a shared history, families who knew each other, and similar values. Was it so wrong for her to want the same thing for her children?

She lay awake long after Ted had fallen asleep, tossing restlessly. At five a.m., she gave up and went to her studio, where she escaped all uneasiness for the next few hours, concentrating fully on her clasped-hands sculpture. Finally, arching to stretch her back, she put down her tools and surveyed the piece from every angle, slowly turning it around. She'd gone as far as she could this session. Turning out the lights, she went back to the house. Ted was up and dressed, sitting at the kitchen table with the morning paper and a cup of coffee.

"Mm. Coffee smells good," she said, pouring a cup for herself.

"You were up early." Ted folded the newspaper and placed it next to him on the kitchen table. "Did you have trouble sleeping?"

Blythe sat down at the table. "I did. I figured I might as well use the time to do some more work on the hands."

"You haven't been yourself lately. Distracted. Troubled. Do you want to talk about it?"

"It's nothing. Really."

He shrugged. "If you say so."

Blythe could see that he wasn't convinced, but she said nothing. When the landline rang, it startled both of them.

"I'll get it." Blythe rose and picked it up. "Hello?"

"Hi, Mom. Okay if I stop by? I have some good news."

A smile spread across Blythe's face. "Yes. Come for lunch. I'll see you then."

Ted looked at her, eyebrows raised.

"Hailey. She has some news."

"Ah. You'll let me know?" He got up to leave. "I'll

be home early." He gave her a longer kiss than their usual morning one. "Shall we go out to dinner tonight, have a romantic evening, just the two of us?"

"I'd love that. I'll make a reservation."

Blythe finished her coffee after he'd gone, but it did nothing to ward off her exhaustion. She tried to read the paper, but her eyes grew heavy. She went to the sunroom and lay down on the sofa. The soft cushions and warmth of the sun shining through the windows put her to sleep instantly.

"Mom," Hailey said, her hand on her mother's shoulder.

Blythe opened her eyes, getting her bearings. "Oh my gosh. I must have fallen asleep. What time is it?"

"Twelve thirty. Are you all right?"

"Yes, yes. I just didn't have a very good night's sleep, so I decided to lie down for a bit. I didn't mean to sleep so long." She ran her fingers through her hair as she rose from the sofa and hugged her daughter. "So, tell me your news. Sit."

"Well, I was with Barbie yesterday, and she's broken off her engagement to Nathan."

"Oh my, I'm sorry to hear that," Blythe said, not understanding why Hailey had come over to tell her this. "What happened?"

"It was a mutual decision, not some big terrible

fight. I guess they were both questioning if they were ready to make such a big commitment."

"That's very sensible. If they have any doubts, they've made the right decision."

"I agree. But here's the thing, Mom. They had the club booked for January. That's four months away. And now that date is open." Hailey was grinning.

"And?" Blythe had a sinking feeling in her stomach.

"We can grab that date for Gabriel and Addy. Then they wouldn't have to wait a whole year."

"I don't know, Hailey. We already have the plans in place, and Gabriel and Addison are fine with them."

"No. I told Gabriel about the club opening, and he jumped at it. He'd love to move up the date and have a winter wedding."

Blythe's body grew rigid. "And you told Addison too?"

"Not yet, but I'm sure Gabriel has."

When Blythe remained silent, Hailey continued. "Why should they wait, Mom? Just think. You and Dad could have a grandchild by next year." She winked.

How was she going to get out of this one? Blythe wondered. She desperately needed that detective to come up with something, anything, to reassure her or give her ammunition. And she hoped it would be soon.

20
Addison

"I need your advice," I tell Gigi. We're sitting together on her porch, a pitcher of iced tea on the table between us.

It's been a week since Gabriel and I got back from Florida, and I can't count the number of times I've looked at that damn card. I know the man's phone number and email address by heart, and his name, Frank Margolis, tumbles around in my head day and night. Every time I pick up the phone to call him, I lose my nerve and hang up, telling myself he must be wrong, that he's mistaken me for someone else. But I know I'm kidding myself. Could he really have known me from a Fort Lauderdale bar or strip club? It just doesn't feel possible. First of all, I've learned

I'm a terrible dancer—stiff and a little awkward on the dance floor—which Gabriel loves to kid me about. And I hate being the center of attention. I can't imagine dancing on a stage with a bunch of strangers staring at me.

But I've done some research on whether I could have been such a different person before amnesia, and the answer is not reassuring. The fact is, it's highly possible that amnesia affects a person's propensities and natural tendencies. There's every reason to believe I might not be at all like the old Addison. Or whatever my name was.

I haven't told Gabriel about it. I can't yet. I wasn't going to tell anyone, but the encounter with that horrible man is all I can think about. If I don't talk about it to someone, I'll go crazy.

"Now," Gigi says, "what is it you want to talk about? You've seemed a little off since your trip. Did you two have a fight?"

Her question takes me by surprise. Gabriel and I have never had a fight. "No, not at all. It's something else." And I tell her, in halting sentences, about the man in the restaurant. "Do you think it's possible that I might have been a dancer in some sleazy bar in my past life?"

"Just because some old geezer tells you that, it doesn't

mean it's true. Did you recognize *him*? Did he look familiar to you?"

"No, but that doesn't mean anything. I have no memories at all, remember?" I don't mean to sound sarcastic, but that's how it comes out.

Gigi gets that don't-get-smart-with-me look on her face and wags her finger. "You can't take some idiot's comments as truth. I'm not saying he's lying, but you can't construct a past life for yourself based on what he said."

"What do you suggest I do?"

Gigi sits back in her chair, looking out at her garden. The September weather is warm, but the steaming heat of August is past, and the colorful blooms in her flower beds look happy and rejuvenated. "Have you looked him up online?"

"I have. He's a sales rep for a brewery, according to LinkedIn. And single, it seems from Facebook, so I guess it's a point in his favor that he's not ignoring his wife to leer at dancers."

She nods and picks at the cuticle on her index finger like she always does when she's thinking. We hear the front screen door slam. Gigi looks at me. "That's Ed. Can we tell him?"

I nod. Embarrassed as I am, Ed has always been a source of support.

Ed comes sauntering outside. "What's up, ladies?" he says, smoothing his mustache with his hand. "Mind if I join you?"

"Sit down, honey," Gigi says, lifting her face up to him for a kiss.

He takes a chair and folds his tall body into it. "You ladies look mighty serious. Something wrong?"

Gigi refills her glass and hands it to him. "Addy has a little story to tell you."

I repeat to Ed what I told Gigi, and he never takes his eyes from mine. "Hmm. That guy sounds like a real asshole."

"Yeah, he is. But that's not the point. What if I *am* the girl he was talking about?"

"Only one way to find out," Ed says. "Someone's got to go talk to him."

"I can't do that," I tell him, already feeling my stomach twisting in knots.

"Of course you can't," Ed says. "I mean me. I'll go."

I agree to the plan, but now that there's a chance I might find out the truth, I feel even worse. I don't really want to know that I was an exotic dancer before my memory was wiped out. And what if Ed does find out that it's true? Will he and Gigi kick me out? What will Gabriel say? And even if he doesn't care, what if his family discovers the truth?

21
Addison

We've just left the Pennsylvania Academy of Fine Arts and Gabriel and I are walking along a crowded street. I contort my body to avoid being jostled by passersby, who all seem to be in a hurry, feeling as though the throngs are closing in on me. We have only a few more blocks before we reach the restaurant where we're meeting Ted, Blythe, and Hailey for dinner. It's Hailey's birthday, and she wanted to spend it together. She has so many friends who would love to celebrate with her, so I was more than touched when she said she wanted to be with us instead.

Gabriel offered to grab a cab for us, but I insisted on walking. Now I'm sorry. I feel like I'm wilting from the humid air and the crush of people surrounding me. I hold the gift bag close to me. I enlarged my favorite photo of Hailey and me, taken at the beginning of the summer. We're sitting beside each other, laughing, our shoulders touching, and there is a shimmering lake in the background. I've attached the photograph to one leaf of a velvet-covered binder, and on the other inside leaf is a letter I've written to her. It's not something I made for display, but something for her alone. Something to let Hailey know that she is a sister to me, and that I love her.

It's time to cross the street, and we wait for the signal to walk. Cars are whizzing by nonstop, and I wonder again at the sheer number of people in the city today. A woman's annoyed voice gets my attention. She is trying to juggle her packages while holding on to her two young children's hands. She bends over to pick up a dropped box, and at the same time the young boy's balloon escapes from his grip.

"Come back!" she yells as he runs straight into the street and into the path of an oncoming car.

Before I can think, I dash out and grab him, pulling him into my arms as the car screeches to a stop just inches away from us. Horns blare, and all traffic comes to a halt as I run back to the sidewalk with the child. Gabriel's face is white, and the mother, crying now, thanks me and clutches her son to her chest.

"You scared the hell out of me." Gabriel's voice is

ragged. "But that was really brave. You saved that boy's life." He takes my hand and moves me out of the middle of the sidewalk. We lean against a building. "Take a minute to collect yourself," he says.

I let out a large breath, realizing that my legs are shaking. "I saw him, and I just reacted. Thank God he's okay." As the words leave my lips, I wonder suddenly if I even believe in God. I think I do, actually. It seems right. But who knows what beliefs the old me held? That's how I'm now thinking of myself. New me, old me. I've started keeping a journal as well. It helps me to organize my thoughts, but the other reason I keep it is one I don't like to admit even to myself. It will serve as my memory if something happens again, and I am back at square one, my life a blank page.

"Addison, Addy . . ."

"What?"

"Where'd you go? You haven't heard a word I said."

"Sorry."

"I don't think we should keep walking. I'm going to hail a cab."

I nod wordlessly, waiting where I am until he calls me over a few minutes later. We're at the restaurant in less than ten minutes, but my heart is still racing.

Gabriel's parents and Hailey are already seated when we arrive, and Gabriel tells them in a long rush what just transpired. Blythe is on her feet immediately. She folds me in her arms. "I'm so glad you weren't hurt! How are you doing? Sit. Sit."

Ted pulls out a chair, and I take it, still not quite feeling myself. They're all asking questions at once, and I can't focus. There's a glass of water in front of me, and I reach for it thirstily but knock it over instead. I watch, horrified, as the water spreads across the table. "I'm sorry! I didn't mean it!" I push back from my chair before any liquid reaches me.

The waiter is there in seconds and has the tablecloth changed while everyone stares at me. How could I be so stupid? I made a huge mess and ruined everything.

You're so clumsy! says a voice in my head. *You idiot! You can't do anything right.*

22
Addison

I can hear my heart hammering in my ears as Ed unfolds a piece of paper and puts it on the table in front of us. He returned from Florida this morning, and I'm afraid to hear what he has to say.

"What did you find out?" I ask him.

His lips pursed together, he shakes his head. "Not much, I'm sorry to say. I did find your guy Frank Margolis. I caught him outside his office building after work. He didn't want to talk to me at first."

"Was he hostile? Or afraid?" Gigi asks.

"No. None of that. I think people are just cautious, you know? Some stranger comes up to you asking questions, you feel threatened."

I laugh. "I'm sure it doesn't help that you're six-four and look like you could take him in a fight."

"Yeah, I figured that too." He leans back in the chair and crosses one leg over his knee. "He was a little leery at first, but I think I convinced him that I wasn't looking to make any trouble for him and that whatever he told me would be just between us. Anyway, we went to a bar down the street from his office, and he was pretty open with me."

"But you made it sound like he wasn't much help."

"Well, that depends. I told him the truth. That I was trying to help a girl who has amnesia. I showed him your picture and said you'd run into him last week at the Tradewinds. He remembered you and said he hadn't seen you in five or six years, since you were a dancer at a place called the Blue Mirror."

"Did he remember my name?"

Ed shook his head again. "Said he never knew your real name, but the name you used at the club was Juniper. Does that ring a bell?"

My face is hot. I'm mortified for Ed and Gigi to discover this about me. "Juniper." I turn the name over in my mouth. "No. It means nothing to me."

"What about the club—did you get to see if they remembered her there?" Gigi asks.

Ed shook his head. "It closed four years ago."

Another dead end.

"Maybe we can find out who owned it. Get in touch with them and get employee names," I suggest, although I know it's a long shot.

"Well, that's the thing. I had the same idea, so I did a little research," Ed says, and I can tell he has more bad news. "The guy who owned the bar was a Connor Gibbs. He owed a lot of people a lot of money when he closed the place, and I don't think they were very nice people." He stops and strokes his mustache again. "Seems he had a bad car accident after that. He died a day later."

"So we know nothing. Except that I was a stripper and worked for a gangster. I'm sorry I ever ran into that guy in the restaurant." I put my elbows on the table and rest my head in my hands.

Gigi comes around to my side of the table and puts her arms around me. "Don't worry, honey. This isn't the end. We're going to find out more, I promise."

"I don't want to know anything else," I cry into my hands. "I don't want to know."

She shakes me gently. "Look at me."

I put down my hands and face her.

"This might not be you. And if it is, so what? What's wrong with being a dancer? You needed to earn a living. That doesn't mean you're a bad person."

"I know that. But honestly, Gigi, can you imagine the reaction Gabriel's parents will have when they find out?"

I'm serious, but she starts to giggle, and then Ed joins in, and soon we're all in hysterics at the thought of the proper Olivers reacting to the news. As tears of exhaustion and mirth fill my eyes, I look at Ed and Gigi and think how much I love them.

"Okay," Gigi says, "let's get cooking. We're having breakfast for dinner."

Gigi mixes up the pancake batter while Ed lines the bacon up in a baking pan, and I crack the eggs into a large glass bowl. I love how Ed always pitches in, even when he's been on the road for a long stretch. Gigi's a terrific cook, and he acts as sous chef/comedian/ practical joker. She pretends to get annoyed when he's too rambunctious, but I think she secretly loves it. I set the table while Ed and Gigi stand at the stove together, talking and giggling like kids, and I wonder if the time will ever come when I'm that lighthearted. Theirs is the kind of marriage I so want to have, but I'm not sure I'll ever be able to be that kind of partner for Gabriel.

"Bacon's done," Ed says. "I'll do the eggs now." He pours them into the frying pan and grabs a wooden spoon from the utensil holder.

Gigi hands me the dish with bacon to take to the

table. As she brings over the pancakes, Ed's phone rings.

"I'll get this in the other room," he says, looking at the number. "You want to take over, sweetie?" He tosses the wooden spoon to Gigi before he turns to go.

It's like the spoon is moving through the air in slow motion. I scream, cowering, and put my hands up to protect my face and head. I see a man in my mind. His eyes are narrowed, his cheeks a fiery red. He's yelling, his face contorted in rage, just inches from mine, his black eyes blazing as he bangs the spoon on my head over and over and screams, *You stupid bitch! How many times do I have to tell you I don't like runny eggs? Why can't you get that through your thick head? I don't know why I don't just kill you.*

"Addison!" Gigi shouts, and I feel her hands on my shoulders, shaking me. "What is it?"

I look at her, and for a moment I don't know where I am. "I . . . uh." I drop onto a chair, still seeing that face in my mind. Who is that man?

"Honey?" Gigi pulls a chair out and sits next to me. "What happened? Did you remember something?"

"Oh, Gigi, I'm so scared."

"It's going to be okay," she says, trying to comfort me.

It's never going to be okay, I think, and look down at my wrists. Is this man the reason I tried to kill myself?

23
Addison

The closer the exhibition at the gallery gets, the more apprehensive I feel. The photographs I've chosen tell the story of where my life has been for the last two years, ever since I came to Philadelphia. The more I explored the city, the more I came to love the grand old buildings and beautiful green spaces. One night, as I strolled through Fairmount Park, I looked up to see the Strawberry Mansion Bridge in the distance, colorfully lit up, its lights shimmering on the waters of the Schuylkill River. It took my breath away, and all I could think of was how I wished I had my camera with me. The very next night I set up my tripod and with my wide-angle lens began my nighttime odyssey, over the next month moving on to other bridges that span the Delaware River as well. I titled the exhibition *Journey into Light* because crossing a bridge *is* a journey from one shore to another, and if you're traveling in the dark, you can't know where you are going or what is on the other side, but the lights—the lights are what keep you safe and show you the way. It hasn't escaped my attention that the bridges are a metaphor for my life—traveling from an old shore to a new one. One day, I hope, I'll remember how to make the return trip.

I recently read an article about the great photographer Dorothea Lange that described so perfectly what I want people to see when they look at my photographs. The camera is an instrument, she said, that teaches people how to see without one.

Gabriel and I have made plans to meet for lunch at the country club, and I arrive first. The maître d' seats me at a table by the window, overlooking the golf course. I order an iced tea and look around the room. The dining room is almost full, and there's a loud buzz of conversation. When I see Gabriel coming toward me, the familiar fluttering in my stomach reminds me of how attracted I am to him. He smiles as he passes family friends and neighbors at other tables, the epitome of charm and good manners. When he approaches our table, his lips widen in the smile reserved only for me. Leaning over, he gives me a peck on the lips.

"Hi, gorgeous," he says.

"Hello yourself," I tease.

The waiter takes Gabriel's drink order, and he leans back in his chair and sighs. "Busy morning. I was barely able to get away. How's your day off been?"

"Productive. I finished my last piece for the show . . . but I actually wanted to talk to you about that."

The space between his brows creases as he waits for me to continue.

"I'm not sure about the show, Gabe. All these people looking at my work, judging me. And putting a price tag on my work feels odd. I should have thought it through before I agreed to do it."

He reaches across the table and takes my hand in his. "Babe, I get it. But most artists I've worked with feel that way before their first show. Even the ones who were dying for a show get the jitters beforehand. It's natural."

I shift in my seat, anxious to get all my thoughts out. "It's not just the jitters. I never wanted a show. I mean, I was perfectly happy just having my photos hanging in the shop. I don't need to sell them."

"Addy, I know that. But art is meant to be shared. You have an amazing talent—a unique eye. Don't you want others to be able to enjoy that?"

I feel myself getting annoyed. It's not like I'm withholding the cure to a disease. "Are you saying I have an obligation to share my work? Those photos are a part of me. Maybe I don't want to trade them for money."

He puts his hands up. "I'm sorry. I guess it's easy for me to sit here and tell you what to do when I'm not the one putting a piece of myself out there. All I'm saying is that having cold feet is normal, and I'd hate for you to lose the opportunity to share your work because you're afraid."

I think about that for a moment. Maybe he's right, and this *is* just jitters. "It might just be fear. I don't know." An idea comes to me. "What if I donate part of my sales to the homeless shelter on Prince Street?"

His face lights up. "That's a great idea. I'll talk to Mom and Dad and see if they'll donate part of the gallery's commission as well."

I shake my head. "You don't have to do that. The gallery has costs—this is just something I want to do for me."

Suddenly a shriek pierces the room, and I startle. I turn to see a little girl trying to pull a stuffed animal from another child's arms, yelling "Give it back!" Her mother jumps from her chair and takes them both by the hand and leads them out of the room. My heart begins to race, and I feel like I can't get a deep breath. A little girl with dark curls flashes in my mind. She's holding her arms out and asking for her stuffed Ellie.

Who is she? A sense of despair overcomes me—a feeling of longing and loss. I try to remember, thinking, thinking, but her face fades and she's gone.

"Addison, are you okay? You're white as a sheet."

I take a large gulp of water. "Fine. I'm just hungry," I sidestep, unsuccessfully trying to retrieve the girl's face. "Haven't eaten all day."

For the first time, I feel sure that I've left people I love behind. I have to find out who I am. Florida is the only real clue I have. I'm going to have to go there myself and see what I can turn up. Even if the bar where I supposedly worked is gone, if I lived there once, there must be other people who know me. I would have had an address somewhere, gone to school, eaten in restaurants, had friends.

When I was first examined, the doctor told me that there was no evidence that I'd ever been pregnant or given birth, so I never worried that I'd left a child. But now I wonder. Am I remembering someone? Maybe I adopted or had a foster child or stepdaughter. Either way, I need to know.

An idea starts coming together in my mind: I'll do the show next week as planned, and leave for Florida the next morning. I look across the table at my sweet Gabriel. Should I tell him what I'm thinking? A little voice warns me to wait.

24
Julian

The flight from Boston to Philadelphia had given Julian ample time to go over his notes for the next day's symposium, and he grabbed a taxi outside the airport and directed the driver to the Warwick Hotel in Rittenhouse Square. It was a sunny October day, and not as chilly as it had been at home. Good weather for strolling around, and from the hotel he'd be able to walk the mile and a half to the Philadelphia Museum of Art and the Barnes, the reason he'd chosen the Warwick in the first place. That and the fact that he never stayed at the conference venue. It was one thing to spend his daytime hours with so many humorless and puffed-up colleagues, but quite another to subject himself to their pontifications over a scotch and soda in the evenings. No. If he hadn't had a paper to present, he wouldn't have come at all. He hated leaving his daughter with the nanny overnight. When Valentina cried and asked him to promise he was coming back, it had broken his heart.

He had a panel that evening, and his talk was scheduled for the next morning. As soon as he finished the talk, he would fly back home. In the meantime he checked in, deposited his overnight bag and briefcase in the room, and walked along the boulevard to the museum. As he neared the entrance, with its classical Greek columns, his mind went to the visits they used to make to the Museum of Fine Arts in Boston. He could still hear his daughter's oohs as she looked up in awe at the imposing building, and then the excitement in her voice as she said "Mommy, look at the big baby heads!" when they showed her the huge sculptures. Julian's favorites were the old masters, but Cassandra was always drawn to the photographs in the Ritts Gallery. She especially loved the work of Alfred Stieglitz and would stand transfixed before his photos, studying the nuances of light and form.

Julian sighed, feeling the familiar wave of melancholy as he climbed the flights of stairs leading to the Impressionism Gallery. As he stood before one painting after another, all of them slightly out of focus, an indistinct image of the real thing, almost dreamlike, he realized that they were exactly what his life had felt like for the last two years. He sat on one of the long, padded benches in the gallery and let himself feel the genius and pain of the artists surrounding him. Claude Monet, whose wife died tragically young at the age of thirty-two. Edgar Degas, blind and destitute at the end of his life. Sometimes it helped Julian to remember that he was not the only one who'd experienced suffering and heartbreak. They were, after all, hallmarks of the human condition.

Pulling back his coat cuff, Julian checked his watch. He should head back to the hotel for his briefcase if he was going to get to the panel on time. He put his hands on his knees and looked around for another minute before rising and exiting the gallery. As he walked outside, he buttoned his coat and quickened his gait. The wind had picked up. When he reached the curb, he waited for the Walk sign to appear. A young woman approached him and held out a flyer. He shook his head and waved her away, but she smiled and said, "I saw you come out of the museum. Tomorrow is First Friday in the Old City. All new exhibits." Julian took the paper just to be polite, but after she'd walked away, he crumpled it up and put it in his pocket. He'd throw it away when he got back to the hotel. Julian hated litterbugs.

The title of his panel was Pediatrics and the Well-Developed Child, and Julian had been flattered to be included. Dr. Graham Parker, a brilliant researcher in the field, was the moderator, and the four other panelists were equally respected. The panel itself went well and lasted only fifty minutes, but the Q&A afterward drew it out for another forty minutes, and Julian was getting antsy. All he wanted to do was get back to the hotel and relax before tomorrow's session. As they filed out of the room, Graham put a hand on his back. "How about a drink at the bar? It's been a long time since I've seen you."

"I have plans tonight," Julian told him. "Heading over to Old City to check some of the local galleries," he elaborated, thinking of the flyer in his pocket.

Graham's face broke into a smile. "That sounds interesting. Mind if I join you?"

Great, Julian thought. He would rather have gone back to his room, and if he really planned to visit the galleries, he'd prefer to do it on his own, but what could he say without sounding like a jerk? "Not at all," he said.

Julian was pleasantly surprised at the depth of Graham's knowledge and appreciation of art as they talked companionably, walking from one gallery to the next.

After about an hour and a half, though, the events of the day began to catch up with him, and he felt his energy flagging. His stomach, too, was reminding him that he had skipped dinner. "I think it's time for me to call it a night," he said to Graham, and they said good night and headed in opposite directions.

Most of the galleries along Second Street were dark as Julian walked past. There were posters in many of the gallery windows advertising the exhibits that would be opening the next day for First Friday. Toward the end of the block and across the street, he saw a large poster hanging in the window of one of the galleries, with a photograph of a woman. He did a double take, squinting to bring it into focus. Finally he crossed the street to get a closer look. As he moved nearer to the window, his heart beat so fast it felt like it would break through his ribs and explode. It couldn't be, could it? He put his palms against the window and leaned his forehead against the glass. His mouth dropped open. It *was* her. He had found Cassandra.

Julian fixed his eyes on the poster. The Oliver Gallery. How had she wound up in Philadelphia? he wondered. Had she been here the whole time? What had she been doing? There was no question, however, that the face on the poster was Cassandra's. Finally the nightmare was over. He'd bring her back where she belonged, and everything would be all right again. He pressed his hand against the glass and stood still, as if letting her know that he was there. And that he would finally take her home.

25
Addison

After we finish hanging the photographs at the gallery, Gabriel, Hailey, and I sit on the floor, eating cold pizza from Pizzeria Beddia. It's after midnight, and we've been working here four hours. When Gabriel first brought up the idea of the exhibition, I had no idea of all that would be involved. But he and Hailey have worked patiently with me for the last month, choosing the photos, determining the size of each one and whether to frame it.

Gabriel pulls his sweater off and drops it on the floor next to him. "Hot," he says, and runs a hand through his wavy hair. We've kept the door to this exhibit room closed so the light won't shine into the front of the gallery, which closed at eight.

"Cold pizza and warm ginger ale. That should cool

you off," Hailey says, taking a bite of a limp-looking slice, and we all laugh.

I look at both of them and feel such a rush of gratitude and love that it chokes me. "I can never thank you guys enough for all your help."

"Of course." Hailey squeezes my shoulder. "We're family."

I look at her—this fresh-faced woman who will soon be my sister-in-law—and think how much like her brother she is. She's welcomed me without reservation, and I can relax with her in a way that feels so easy and natural. A few months ago we started a new tradition—a girls' night every Thursday. She introduces me to a different restaurant each week so we can discover what I like. We've done Thai, Indian, Chinese, Italian, Greek, Mexican, French, Spanish. I've discovered that I actually enjoy all different kinds of cuisine, but my current favorite is Thai, with Indian a close second. Hailey makes it fun to try and figure out my predilections, and never makes me feel odd in any way. She's one of those people with the rare ability to bring out the best in people, and even though I have missing parts, she makes me feel whole.

We've almost finished the drooping pizza when Blythe and Ted come in with two large cartons.

"Wine delivery," Ted calls out, and Gabriel jumps to his feet and takes the box from his mother.

"This is great. Thanks, Mom."

"You're welcome. This is the white. Why don't you take it back to the refrigerator?"

"I'll put the other one here." Ted places it on the floor and looks around. "How's it going? All finished yet?"

"Come on, take a look," Gabriel says to his dad, and Hailey and I both get up to follow them.

We stand there, the five of us, at the back of the small room and look without speaking. I know Gabriel and Hailey are looking at the exhibit with pride. They've both had such a big hand in it from beginning to end that I know it feels like it's their exhibit too, and I'm glad for that. I'm not quite sure about Ted. He strikes me as a man who doesn't rush to judgment but takes his time, careful not to jump to conclusions. If he doesn't know what to make of me yet, I think he is giving me the benefit of the doubt unless I prove him wrong. The outlier is Blythe, of course. She has actually pitched in to help with the exhibit, but without the gusto of the rest of the family. There's always a little bit she withholds.

"It looks amazing," Gabriel says, coming to put his arm around me.

Blythe nods. "The photographs are beautiful, Addison. I've seen these bridges for years, but your camera has turned them into a thing of wonder. Thank you for trusting us with your work."

I feel a rush of gratitude. Her approval means more to me than I care to admit. Dare I believe that she's come a little bit closer to accepting me?

"Thank you, Blythe. It's really something to see them displayed like this. It's more than I ever dreamed of."

"I have a feeling that after tonight your name is going to be spoken of in a lot of art circles," Gabriel says with a huge smile.

For some reason the thought makes me nervous. I'm comfortable in the small little world I've created. I think about the ticket I've booked to Florida. Who knows what might happen if that world opens up too wide?

26
Julian

Julian fumbled as he removed his wallet from his inside jacket pocket, and his hand shook as he pulled the photograph from the covered flap. Cassandra with her arm around Valentina, both of them grinning at the camera. He looked from the picture to the poster and back again. Some of the light had gone out of her eyes, he thought sadly, but it was without a doubt his Cassandra. He read the information under her photograph.

First Friday: Journey into Light
Photographs by Addison Hope
Oliver Gallery 5:00–10:00 p.m.

She'd changed her name. Julian frowned. The only possible explanation was that she didn't know who she was. He'd been right. Something had happened to make her forget. How on earth had she wound up so far away from home? He took a picture of the poster and hailed a cab back to his hotel, feeling a weight lifting from his shoulders.

As soon as he got back to his room, he called the airline and canceled his flight back to Boston. Then he phoned the house to let the housekeeper and nanny know that he would be delayed in Philadelphia. Next he opened his laptop and searched online for Addison Hope, but she had no social media presence he could find. He leaned back in his chair and sighed heavily, thinking about next steps. He thought about calling the detective but decided against it. Instead he picked up his phone and tapped the Photos app, scrolling through the hundreds of photos he had of Cassandra and him, as well as some shots with Valentina in them. Tomorrow night he would go to the gallery. When he showed her the pictures, they would finally reunite.

By the time he finally got into bed, it was after two, but despite the late hour he barely slept. At five he gave up and threw back the covers, rising to shower and shave. He looked like hell, he noted. Too little sleep and too much tension. His stomach rumbled with hunger as he slid into the taxi, but there was no way he could hold down breakfast. He nervously tapped his foot on the floor of the cab until they finally reached the symposium hotel, where he bolted into the lobby. A group of participants were clustered outside the meeting room, and he nodded as he walked briskly past them, hastily placing his notes on the podium in the room and opening a bottle of water that had been left for him.

As the audience filtered in, he felt himself grow edgier. How was he supposed to get through the eight hours before he could see Cassandra again?

. . .

It was a relief to get back to his room and be alone at last. The hours of waiting had been agonizing. There were times during the day when he'd actually been rude to some of his colleagues, his impatience and anxiety getting the better of him. Now he had a little time to think about what to say and what to do when he saw her. It was going to be a very delicate thing. Unpredictable. But he was trained for unpredictability, he reassured himself.

Julian changed out of the shirt and tie he'd worn to the symposium. Cassandra used to tell him he always overpacked—more like a woman than a man—but as he buttoned a fresh blue Brooks Brothers shirt, he was grateful that he had brought extras. A little after five he left the hotel and walked to the Oliver Gallery. He ran his moist palms along the sides of his jacket as he approached the building. He was finding it hard to take a deep breath. Then he was standing in front of the gallery with his hand on the doorknob. He hesitated, and someone behind him said, "Going in, buddy?"

"Sorry," Julian said, startled, and pushed open the door.

Only a few people were wandering about in the main room of the gallery, where glasses of wine and trays of cheese and crackers sat on two high round tables in the middle of the floor. Julian walked around, still trying unsuccessfully to get a full breath of air into his lungs. He swept his gaze across the entire gallery and saw that one of the two side rooms looked more crowded than the other. That must be where her exhibit was, he thought, and strode over to its entrance.

Suddenly he saw her across the room. The hammering in his chest began again, just like the night before, when he thought he wouldn't be able to keep his beating heart from crashing through his chest. She looked beautiful in a simple black dress, her long hair touching her shoulders and her eyes shining with excitement. She held a glass of white wine in her hand as she chatted with a few guests. Julian stood rooted to the spot as a good-looking guy with a mop of curly brown hair walked over to her and put his arm around her waist. Cassandra looked up at him, smiling, and Julian clenched his jaw. He flexed his fingers, forcing the blood to circulate, and walked purposefully toward her, never taking his gaze from her.

He waited until the man had stepped away to approach her. She extended her hand, not seeming to know him. "Hello, I'm Addison Hope. Thank you so much for coming tonight."

Julian shook her hand, staring into her eyes, and she continued to smile blandly at him. No flicker of recognition. "Hello. I'm Julian Hunter. I'm here from Boston for a medical conference, and I saw the sign for your exhibit last night." He watched her face carefully as he spoke. Nothing.

"Well, I hope you enjoy the exhibit and your time in Philadelphia," she said, turning away to greet someone else.

"Wait," he said, touching her arm.

She turned around to him, frowning slightly. "Yes?"

"There's something I'd like to show you. Would you mind if we moved to a quieter corner of the room for a moment?"

She cocked her head and gave him a quizzical look.

"Please. Just for a moment."

They walked to the edge of the room, and Julian took the picture from his wallet and handed it to her. "Take a look at this," he said.

She stared at the picture, her brows knitting as she held it up for a closer look. When she looked back at Julian, her eyes were clouded. "That's me." She glanced at the photograph again. "Who *are* you?"

He had to tread lightly. "Addison. That's not your real name, is it?"

She took a small step back from him, and he saw fear in her eyes.

"I'm not here to hurt you. I'm here to help you." He hoped his tone was reassuring. "You don't remember anything about your past, do you?"

"Do you know me?" she asked, and Julian thought he saw a flicker of something like hope in her eyes.

"I do." He looked past her to see the curly-haired man approaching.

"Everything all right here?" he asked, looking from Cassandra to Julian.

"This man knows me." Cassandra's voice shook. "He knows who I am. He has a picture of me. From before."

"Let me see," the man said, and Julian handed the picture to him. Then he brought out his phone and pulled up all the photos of Cassandra.

"Take a look at these, too," he said, giving the phone to Cassandra.

"Oh my God," she whispered, leaning against the wall as she scrolled through.

The man next to her stared at Julian. "Just who are you?" he asked.

"Her husband. I'm her husband."

27

Addison

I lean against the wall as I try to make sense of what I'm seeing. It is me, that much is obvious, but I don't recognize the man or the child with me. *Husband.* The word reverberates in my mind. I try and connect to it, but there's nothing. I look up at him, trying to place his face. His looks are the opposite of Gabriel's. Thick blond hair, crystal-blue eyes, and a strong jawline. He's handsome, almost too handsome. He looks like he might be in his late thirties or early forties, tall and slender and elegantly dressed. I glance at his hand and see the gold wedding band on his finger. Why can't I remember him?

I look down at the phone again, my heart beating so loud I'm sure everyone can hear it. I stop scrolling when I get to a photo of a little girl. She's beautiful. Long dark hair, alabaster skin, and emerald-green eyes. Eyes like mine. The memory of the little girl crying comes crashing back to me. *I want Ellie.* Was it her I was remembering?

I turn to the stranger who says he's my husband. "Is this . . . is she . . ."

He smiles at me. "That's Valentina. Our daughter. Do you remember her?"

I shake my head. "No. I was told I've never been pregnant."

"That's right, you haven't. She's your daughter, but we used a surrogate. I can explain more, but first, tell me. I've been looking for you for two years. What happened? Where did you go?"

Suddenly I feel dizzy. A surrogate? What is he talking about? I put a hand on Gabriel's arm to steady myself. Blythe sweeps over and takes charge.

"Let's take this in the back where we can have some privacy. Follow me, everyone." She takes my arm, and I stumble along in a daze, just needing to get somewhere quiet and sit.

All of us go back to the private lounge area. I sink onto the sofa, hugging myself, my gaze fixed on the floor. While I scream inside my head, Blythe tells everyone to take a seat, brings over water, and gets everyone settled. Gabriel starts toward me, but I give him a look to telegraph to him that I need space. I'm about to find out who I really am, and I should be ecstatic, but I just feel numb. My eyes travel around the room, the faces blurring. A hand touches my shoulder, and I look up. Blythe.

"Darling, it's okay. Take a minute. Breathe in through your nose."

She models it for me, and I squeeze her hand and try to inhale. I close my eyes and then open them again. I look over at Julian, who's sitting in a chair across from me.

I may as well start at the beginning. "What's my name?"

"Cassandra. Cassandra Hunter. You were Cassandra Dryer when we first met. We've been married for ten years."

Ten years? That seems impossible. "How old am I?"

"Thirty-seven."

Blythe gasps, and the others turn to look at me in shock. Gabriel is only thirty, and I'd assumed that I was in my late twenties.

"But . . ."

Julian looks at his hands. "You've had some plastic surgery. That's why you look younger."

Hot shame goes through me. Why would I have gotten cosmetic surgery so young? What kind of a person *am* I? There are a million questions I want to ask, not the least of which is how I got the scars on my wrists. But not here, in front of everyone. I feel naked, embarrassed. All I want to do is go to my room, crawl under the covers, and close my eyes.

The door opens, and Gigi and Ed come in. I stand up shakily and run into Gigi's arms.

Ed's voice booms across the room. "What's going on? We turned around, and all of you were gone."

I hear Ted talking fast, explaining. I can't seem to let go of Gigi, and she doesn't pull away. After a few minutes I do let go, and Ed comes over to put an arm around me.

"Are you all right, honey? This must be quite a shock."

I shake my head, not able to find my voice. He looks at Hailey. "Why don't you sit with Addison? I'd like to talk to this gentleman." Gabriel stands up and comes toward me, but Blythe puts a hand on his arm, and he sits back down next to her.

Hailey squeezes my hand. "Are you okay?" she whispers.

I squeeze back and say nothing.

Julian extends a hand to Ed. "I'm Julian Hunter. And you are?"

"Ed Gordon. Addison's been living with my wife

and me for the past two years. So you claim to be her husband. Do you have any proof of that?"

Julian nods. "Of course. Not with me, though. I had no idea I'd find Cassandra here. But I have pictures." He hands the phone to Ed, who looks through them, frowning, then hands the phone back. "I suppose that's a start. Where do you live?"

"Boston," Julian answers, his tone even.

"How did you find her?" Ed asks.

Now they're talking about me like I'm not even here. "Please, please. Everyone. I can't do this right now. I need some time." I rise and look at Gigi. "Please take me home."

"Cassandra—," Julian says, coming nearer.

"Stop calling me that! I don't know you. I can't . . . just give me a minute."

Ed steps between the two of us, blocking Julian. "I suggest you go back and get some paperwork to prove what you say. Come back in a day or two, and we can talk about everything. This is too much for her to process all at once."

Julian gives him a penetrating look, then sighs. "I understand. But *you* have to understand how difficult it is for me to walk away after I've been searching all this time. We have a child together. A life."

Ed puts a hand up. "I know, I know. Just a couple of days." He takes out a card and scribbles on it. "Here's our address."

Julian looks at Gabriel then. "Exactly who are you to my wife?"

Gabriel's chin juts out, and his eyes narrow. "Her fiancé."

The two men appraise each other, and I feel like my heart is breaking into a thousand pieces. I want to reach out and tell Gabriel that it will be okay. That I love him and need him. But I think of the little girl in the picture, and my mouth goes dry.

"Julian," I say, his name feeling strange in my mouth. "Is Valentina okay?"

He gives me a sad look. "She misses you terribly. But she's okay. I've done my best. She's going to be so happy to have her mommy home."

My hand goes to my stomach reflexively, and then I remember what he said about a surrogate. Even so, how could I forget that I have a child? It seems so impossible, but yet it must be true. Again, I wonder about the person I am. What kind of mother leaves her child? "We'll talk again soon," I say to Julian. Then I take Gigi's hand, and we leave the room and the gallery. As I walk out, I keep my eyes fixed in front of me, unable to look at Gabriel or his family. No matter what kind of pain I've caused them, I can't concentrate on them right now. I have to find my way back to my old life and finally discover what I was running from.

28
Addison

Gigi drives my car home from the gallery, Ed following closely behind us. I'm straining to think, to remember something—anything—but there's nothing. My head feels like mush. I can't think straight, and my stomach feels hollow. We pull into the side driveway, the one that goes directly to my apartment, and Gigi turns off the engine. When I open the car door, Ed reaches in and takes my hand. "You shouldn't be alone. Why don't the three of us go upstairs?"

I grip his hand tightly as we walk up the stairs to my apartment, and I still haven't let go when we sit together on the small love seat. Gigi sits across from us in the orange IKEA recliner that I love to sit in when I read. On the table next to it is my current stack of books. I know I must look shell-shocked, because that's exactly how I'm feeling right now.

"It's going to be okay, Addy. We'll get some answers now. That's what you've been wanting," Gigi says.

The panic builds in me again. "I'm scared, Gigi. What if the answers are something terrible?"

"Of course you're frightened. It would be strange if you weren't. But you can take things slowly. One step at a time."

I nod at her and then turn to Ed. "I keep thinking about all the things he said. If I lived in Boston, how did I wind up on the highway in New Jersey? It doesn't make sense."

"I don't know, Addy. Maybe you'd gotten a ride there from Boston and something went awry."

"Maybe," I say, contemplating that. "But how could I not remember that I'd had a child? He said we used a surrogate, which would mean I couldn't get pregnant. If we went to that kind of extreme, it must mean that I really wanted a child. So how could I forget her?" I search Gigi's face for answers.

"I'm not an expert on amnesia, but I believe an amnesiac could forget even having a child."

I chew on the inside of my lip. I'm trying to pull my thoughts together when the door opens to reveal Gabriel standing there. I'm both relieved and concerned to see him. "You left so fast. We need to talk," he says, not moving, his hand on the doorknob.

Both Gigi and Ed get up. "We'll give you two some time alone," she says. "If you want to come over later, we'll be up."

Gabriel moves out of their way, and as they leave, I hear him thank them. Once we're alone, we stare at each other, saying nothing for what feels like a long time. This is the man I love and want to marry. How am I supposed to give him up? If Julian comes back with incontrovertible proof, what am I going to do? I don't know him at all. How do I go live with someone who's a complete stranger to me? What if I never regain my memory? Am I going to have to spend the rest of my life with someone I can't remember?

Gabriel comes over and sits beside me. "He might be lying. Or he could have you confused with someone else who looks like you."

My gut tells me that theory is unlikely, but I nod. "Maybe."

"We need to check him out, Addy. We'll do an online search, or even have him investigated. Who knows what kind of scam this could be? We can't just take his word at face value." I can hear the desperation in his voice, and I feel it too.

I shake my head. "I think that's a bad idea. If I read

up on him, I might have a hard time distinguishing between what I remember and what I've just learned. I don't want to take that chance." I touch his cheek. "You understand that, don't you?"

"I guess." He gets up and begins pacing the small room like an animal ready to strike. I hate what this is doing to him. I never wanted to hurt him, but all along I've had the sickening feeling that in the end I would.

"I want to be here when he comes back," Gabriel says, looking at me expectantly.

I think about it for a long moment. "I don't think that's a good—"

"I can't just let him come in and take you away," he interrupts. "We still don't know anything about him."

"Ed and Gigi will be with me. He's going to be bringing proof. This isn't something you can do with me, and I think you know that."

He stops suddenly and spins around to look at me, his face animated. "I have an idea. We'll leave tonight. Go somewhere no one will find us and elope."

It's so sweet and crazy that I almost laugh. I get up and hug him, holding him to me as I say, "I want with all my heart to marry you, but you know we can't do that." I pull away and take his hands in mine. "What would we do, hide from your family and never see them again? I would never let you hurt your parents and sister that way. Besides, if I'm already married to Julian, I would be committing bigamy."

He looks at me helplessly. I think of the little girl again. "And if I have a daughter, I can't leave her again."

His face clouds over. "You need to insist on a DNA test. That surrogate business sounds fishy to me. You have to get proof."

My head is spinning. "Please, Gabriel. Let me figure this all out."

"I can't lose you, Addy. I just can't." He pulls me into his arms, and we stay that way, feeling the beating of each other's hearts. I can't lose you either, I think, but I know it's too late. He's already lost.

29
Julian

The elation Julian felt when he'd found Cassandra had completely evaporated by the time he left the gallery. She hadn't recognized him, nor remembered Valentina—she had no recollection of her life before her existence as Addison whatever-her-last-name-was. As he traveled back to the hotel, he tried to tamp down his anxiety. He couldn't believe that she'd started an entirely new life in just two years. He'd put his own life on hold while he searched and waited, but when he thought about it, he realized how foolish it had been of him to assume that time would stand still for her as it had for him. All he could do now was go home and gather the evidence to show her and the people around her that she belonged with him.

When Julian reached the hotel, he strode quickly

through the quiet lobby to the elevators. The first thing he did when he got to his room was to open a scotch from the minibar and drink it in one long gulp. Then he opened his laptop and booked the earliest available flight to Boston for the next day. He needed as much time as possible at home to take care of everything. He'd make arrangements for Valentina, and have his assistant reschedule all of the coming week's patients. After that he'd gather anything that might help prove to Cassandra that he was telling the truth.

There was a split second when he considered bringing Valentina back with him to Philadelphia, but he quickly dispensed with that idea. It would be reckless to reveal anything to their little girl until he was sure Cassandra was coming home. Valentina had been hurt enough in her young life. No, it was a time for careful planning, not a time to act rashly. He would ask their nanny, a woman he trusted implicitly, to take the child to her house for a few days, until he deemed it the right time for Cassandra and Valentina to reunite. On Sunday he would drive back to Philadelphia and meet with Cassandra. If all went according to plan, he'd drive back to Boston with her on Monday.

Julian closed the laptop and grabbed another scotch from the minibar. He sat in the dark and replayed the scene in the back room of the gallery that night. The older woman had taken gracious but firm control of the situation, and he'd realized immediately that she was someone to be reckoned with. Somewhere in her late fifties or early sixties, he estimated, she possessed a natural elegance and beauty. He thought he'd heard one of them call her Blythe. The fiancé's mother. Gabriel. It was clear that Gabriel was in love with Cassandra, from the possessive way he'd put his hand on her arm and the horror on his face when Julian announced who he was. The question was, did Cassandra love Gabriel? He sat still with that thought, letting his feelings sink in. It angered him; there was no question. He hadn't so much as looked at another woman since Cassandra went missing. His primary concern had been for their daughter, and so he'd put all of his love and time into Valentina. It had been enough for him while he waited.

He knew he had to put any jealousy or judgment aside if this was going to work. He would have to be gentle with Cassandra and give her time. Patience, he repeated to himself. This was going to be hard for Cassandra too. It was not a time to be selfish and dwell on his own feelings. No, this needed to be a very careful reentry into their married life. If he pushed her too quickly or made a wrong move out of impatience, it could very possibly end in disaster. Slow and steady was the way forward. First, she had to feel safe and even comfortable with him. That was the reason he'd decided they would drive the five hours to Boston together rather than fly back. He knew that many people felt more comfortable talking in a car, where there was a relaxed informality—the lack of eye contact lowered inhibitions, making it easier to speak honestly.

Julian rested his chin on his steepled fingers. He felt some optimism, the first in a long time. Yes, he knew Cassandra would be torn about leaving the life she'd built, and he might have to deal with the anger that he'd seen in Gabriel. It also hadn't taken Julian long to recognize the deep bond Cassandra shared with the man and woman—their names eluded him—who'd taken her in. But he was confident of his ability to overcome any obstacles all of this might present. Time would take care of the emotional toll for her and the people in her life at parting.

The thing that nagged at him, though, was how much to tell Cassandra about her past. She'd made such great progress with therapy and putting the horror behind her. He'd have to take it slowly, assess her state of mind, the extent of her fragility. He assumed she was off her meds, since she had no memory of who she was. It was a miracle that she'd been doing so well without them. He didn't want to alarm her by telling her right away that she'd been on a potent combination of anti-

depressants and antianxiety drugs, but it was impera-
tive that she get back on her protocol, especially once
she came home. He couldn't risk her doing anything to
hurt Valentina. One day at a time, he told himself. He'd
figure it out one day at a time.

30
Blythe

The atmosphere in the room bordered on funereal, Blythe thought as she carried in the tray with four coffee mugs. Ted sat at one end of the sofa facing the fireplace, and Gabriel had taken a seat at the other end. Hailey, in sweatpants and an oversize turtleneck sweater, was curled up in an armchair with her bare feet tucked underneath her. She looked like she had just lost her best friend, which in a way she had. Hailey and Addison had grown almost as close as sisters, and that had worried Blythe. But of course the whole situation had worried her. Now that she had been proved right, though, she didn't find any sense of satisfaction in it, just loss.

Gabriel was the only one who had seen Addison since the scene the night before at the gallery. Blythe understood that Addison needed time to try to come to terms with everything before confronting Gabriel's whole family, but her main concern right now was her son. He was a wreck, alternating between misery, anger, pessimism, and hope.

"What's the latest you've heard, son?" Ted asked.

Blythe put down the tray and sat, looking from her husband to her son. They'd always been close. From the time Gabriel was small, Ted had played ball with him and taught him tennis, and when he was older, some of their favorite times had been fly-fishing trips to Penns Creek. They'd even learned to tie their own flies. She knew not all father-son relationships were as good, especially when they worked together like Gabriel and Ted did.

"He's gone back to Boston. Supposedly he's going to bring back proof for her."

"Supposedly?" Blythe said.

Gabriel sat with an ankle crossed over his knee, his foot bouncing with agitation. "Who knows if it's even true, Mom? He could be making it all up."

"But there were photographs of her with a child," Blythe said.

"With a child she supposedly had via surrogate? What a load of crap. Besides, photographs can be altered. You know that as well as I do. It doesn't prove anything."

"No, it doesn't prove anything, but it does raise questions. The woman in those photos was definitely Addison. What motive could that man possibly have to lie?" Blythe tried to keep her tone neutral. It was patently clear that Gabriel was unwilling to give one shred of credence to Julian Hunter's story. When they'd gotten home last night and Blythe had gone online to search for Julian, she found that he was a respected doctor in Boston with an impressive background—an MD from Stanford, after which he'd moved to Boston for his residency. And despite the difficult and painful situation in which Julian had clearly found himself, he'd seemed gentle and understanding with Addison. Blythe had noted his tasteful attire, his polished good looks, his kind demeanor. In fact, she had found him quite likable, and all of this together made her feel that he was telling the truth. The one thing that had struck her as odd was that she could find no news articles about him, nothing mentioning a missing wife. Blythe had always been one to cross every *t* and dot every *i*, however. Before she'd gone to bed, she'd texted his name to Jim Fallow on the off chance that there was more to Dr. Julian Hunter than met the eye.

Now, Blythe waited to hear what Gabriel had to say, but he was silent, crossing and uncrossing his legs and drumming his fingers on the arm of the sofa. She had no illusions about how this was going to end up. Gabriel would continue to stay in his world of denial until it was impossible not to confront the truth, and that worried her more than anything. Her son was in pain, and she couldn't bear the thought that he would hurt for a long time to come.

"I think your mother has a point, Gabriel," Ted said. "Why would this man lie about Addison? What would he have to gain by doing that?"

"I don't know. All I know is we shouldn't jump to conclusions until there is undeniable proof. And so far, we haven't seen it. And that bullshit about Addy having cosmetic surgery and being thirty-seven. There's no way."

Hailey uncurled her legs from under her and sat up straight. "I've been thinking about something else. Maybe this guy *is* telling the truth, and they're married. But what if she was unhappy? Or afraid of him? Maybe she deliberately ran away. He could even be the reason she tried to kill herself."

That possibility had occurred to Blythe, too, and the prospect worried her deeply. She knew how quickly Gabriel would take on the role of superhero and protector. If Julian Hunter were violent, her son could be in danger. She knew it was selfish of her to think first of her son, when Addison could also be a target, but she was his mother first.

Gabriel leaned forward, planting both feet firmly on the floor. "Yeah, that makes total sense. We all knew she was running away from something. It had to be him. What other explanation could there be?" He was suddenly animated, as if he'd been thrown a lifeline.

"At this point, all of this is conjecture," Ted said. "We can create all the scenarios we choose and suppose all we want, but there's no point in guessing until we have all the facts. And the one who will make the final decision as to what is or isn't true will be Addison. Perhaps she will regain some memory of exactly what happened or who she was. We just need to wait and see."

Blythe could have kissed her husband. He had always been the calm voice of reason and common sense, the one who often diffused a family disagreement.

"All right, then," she said. "Let's stop taking shots in the dark and getting upset over things that may not turn out to be true. Agreed?"

Hailey nodded, unsmiling, but Blythe could see that Gabriel wasn't convinced. He leveled a look at her. "I need to ask you something."

She waited.

"Are you planning to call Darcy? To tell her what's happened?"

For the first time since Julian Hunter appeared, she felt anger toward her son. Was he so obsessed with Addison that he questioned his mother's integrity? "Of course not. How can you even ask me that?"

"Let's be honest, Mom. You were never crazy about the idea of Addison and me getting married."

Blythe's face felt like it was on fire. "Only because I was afraid you'd get hurt," she said, and then added hotly, "Just as you have been."

"All right, all right," Ted said. "Let's all sit back and calm down. Attacking each other isn't helping anything."

Gabriel looked at the ceiling, silent. Then, returning his gaze to Blythe, he said, "I'm sorry. I . . . I don't know. I can't even think straight right now."

She went to the sofa and put her arm around her son, drawing him near. "It's all right. I understand. I'm so sorry for what you're going through."

He leaned into her, and she felt his body shake as he cried against her shoulder, the way he had when he was just a little boy and cut his knee or broke a toy. This time, though, a bandage or tube of glue wouldn't fix it. This time Gabriel's heart was breaking. At that moment all Blythe wished was that her son had never met the woman who called herself Addison Hope.

31
Addison

A black Jaguar pulls into the driveway, and I watch from the window as Julian gets out of it. I'm struck again by his good looks, although they don't engender any feeling in me. My heart still belongs to Gabriel. I move from the window and go to the door, opening it before he knocks.

He gives me a broad smile. "Hi."

"Hi," I say, feeling suddenly shy.

He raises one eyebrow. "Is it okay if I come in?"

A nervous laugh escapes my lips. "Of course. Please." I open the door wide, and he walks inside. Gigi and Ed are in the living room, having convinced me to allow them to stay, and she's put out a tray with coffee and pastries.

"Please come and sit. I hope you understand, but Ed

and Gigi would like to talk to you, too. They've become like parents to me," I explain.

A look passes over his face, but I can't tell what it means. "Of course."

He's carrying a briefcase, which he places on the floor next to his chair before pulling out a folder from it. "Here's your birth certificate, license, and passport." He hands the folder to me, and I examine each carefully. There's my photo, and my birthday, which still shocks me. June 8, 1984.

He retrieves another document from the briefcase. "Valentina's birth certificate." I take it from him, my hand shaking. "Cassandra Hunter" under "Mother."

"Well, I guess this proves who I am. So can you tell me what happened the day I disappeared?"

He clears his throat. "I came home from the hospital, and the front door was wide open. It was around seven, and already dark outside. Your purse and phone were sitting on the console table, but you were gone."

"Was there a sign of a struggle, anything out of place?" Ed asks.

Julian shakes his head. "No, and none of the neighbors saw anything. Of course, our house is pretty secluded. But the detective on the case questioned everyone in the area, and there were no witnesses. It was like you simply vanished."

It makes no sense to me. "Maybe I let someone in, and they kidnapped me? Then I got away? I still don't understand why I don't remember, though."

"We've been trying to figure out what happened for two years. But there is something you should know." He sighs. "You were on medication for depression and anxiety."

"What?" I say.

"I don't want to overwhelm you with too much at once, but you didn't have the easiest childhood. There was a lot of . . . trauma."

Trauma? That's the first thing I'm hearing that makes sense to me. I can feel it in my body, and I know I've been through something terrible. It also explains the things that come back to me and scare me so. "Tell me. I need to know. You don't have to sugarcoat it for me."

Julian pauses a moment, looking at each of us. "Your parents were killed in a car accident when you were twelve. You had no other family, and so you were put into foster care. You were moved around quite a bit, and unfortunately you suffered abuse in some of the homes. You were working on it in therapy when I met you."

"Is that why I . . ." I look down at my wrists.

"It's not an easy question to answer, but you battled

depression as a result of your past. I thought you had it under control, but after Valentina was born, it got a hold of you again. That's when you—" He stopped and expelled a deep breath. "Do you really want to get into that right now?"

I'm relieved that he's given me an out. I'd rather hear about this one-on-one. "No, I'd rather not, actually. Maybe I can speak to my therapist about it all . . . assuming he or she is still available?"

"Yes. I was also going to suggest that you try to do some hypnosis work to try and recover your memories. It's worked for you before," he tells me. "You had suppressed certain childhood memories—understandably, of course."

The thought fills me with equal parts hope and dread. Recovering my past, being a real person and filling in all the blanks, is something I'd started to lose hope of ever happening. But I'm filled with dread as I realize that those memories will come with untold measures of grief over those I've lost and what I've endured.

"Why did she have plastic surgery?" Gigi asks. "Was she in an accident?"

He nods. "A car crash. She drove into a concrete wall. Her face was badly damaged."

I am stunned into silence. The picture that's forming

in my mind of Cassandra, of me, is scaring me. "How did it happen?"

Julian hesitates. "We have time to go into all of it."

I feel sick to my stomach. "Did I do it on purpose? Are you saying that I hurt myself more than once?" I push my sleeves up and expose my arms, challenging him.

"Yes, but we got you help."

"What in the world did you see in me?" I ask before I can stop myself.

Julian looks taken aback. "What do you mean?"

I stand up, my face warm from the anger surging through me. "I sound like a basket case. Depressed, anxious, unstable. Two suicide attempts! Did I have any redeeming qualities?"

"Addy!" Gigi interjects.

I look at her. "Well, seriously. What am I supposed to think?"

"Of course you have redeeming qualities. You're the most loving and tender person I've ever met. You care deeply about others. You're a wonderful mother, and you take amazing care of me and our daughter," Julian says.

I don't know whether or not I believe him. "What do I like to do? Do I have any hobbies?"

He nods. "You love to cook, and read, and you're a

terrific photographer. But you know that already." He rises, taking a tentative step toward me, and extends his hand. "Could I just give you a hug?"

His eyes are so plaintive that I can't say no. I move toward him and let him put his arms around me. His touch is gentle, and as the scent of sandalwood wafts over me, a feeling of familiarity stuns me. I close my eyes. I know this cologne. I have another flash of kissing someone, his hands tangled in my hair, and mine running through his blond locks. I'm dizzy again, feeling a buzzing in my ears. It's too much information at once. I pull away and fall back onto the chair, putting my head between my knees.

"I think she needs a little break," Gigi says.

"Yes, of course."

Ed clears his throat. "Why don't you and I go take a walk," he says to Julian, "and let them have a moment?"

After the door closes, I say to Gigi, "This is so strange, hearing him tell me about me. I don't feel any sense of familiarity with the woman he's describing." I run a hand through my hair. "I don't want to become that woman."

Gigi gives me a stern look. "Now you listen to me. Even if you do remember, you are not going to morph into a stranger. You are you now. Your experiences of the last two years have changed you again. If you don't like the woman you were, you don't have to become her. And you don't have to go back to Boston. You can stay here. Maybe find a new therapist here to help you remember."

"No—I have a daughter, remember? I have to go back." I hesitate a moment. "Besides, I think I remembered him when he hugged me."

She raises an eyebrow.

"It was a pleasant memory," I say.

"Well, that's good. That bodes well, don't you think?"

"I guess."

"Regardless, just know that you can always come back here. And I want you to check in with me every day. I need to know that you're safe."

I nod. But I'm not worried about my physical safety. I'm uneasy about what I'm going to find if this cryptic tapestry called my mind is finally unraveled.

32
Julian

Julian loaded Cassandra's suitcases into the trunk and then slid into the driver's seat. After her emotional goodbye with Ed and Gigi, they were on their way, and he was relieved to finally be alone with her. He'd been anxious to get away from their prying eyes and begin to reestablish a relationship with Cassandra on his own terms.

"There are some cans of raspberry LaCroix in the cooler in the back, as well as KIND bars and bags of almonds." He'd brought her favorite snacks and beverages with him—or at least, the things that used to be her favorites.

She spoke without turning to look at him. "Thanks, but I'm fine."

They were quiet as he drove, and he decided to let

them sit in the silence with the hope that some of the awkwardness would dissipate. He pressed the stereo button, and the sound of classical music filled the car.

"I've got Sirius, so if there's something else you'd like to listen to, feel free to change the channel."

"This is fine," she said, staring out the window.

He fought the urge to say more, to try and coax conversation from her. As the miles passed, he thought ahead to what would happen when they reached the house. He'd offer to put her in the guest room, of course. No matter how much he wanted her to feel immediately at ease and come back to their bedroom, he knew she needed time.

"How did we meet?" she asked, turning to look at him.

"At O'Hare airport, of all places—waiting for a flight to Boston. You'd gone to a training session in Chicago and were returning home. I was coming from visiting my father in Arizona. My connection was Chicago." He paused. "Sadly, he's gone now."

"I'm sorry about your father. Is your mother alive?"

"No, she died a long time ago. I'm afraid you, me, and Valentina are the only family we have left in the world." He could feel her eyes on him, as if she were pondering this new information.

"You must have felt very alone after I left."

He was gratified to see that she was still empathetic. "You have no idea."

She was quiet again, and when he glanced over, she was leaning back on the headrest with her eyes closed. *Penny for your thoughts?* he wanted to blurt out, but he knew that would only serve to make her withdraw more. They drove for another half hour without speaking. Just as he was questioning the wisdom of his decision to drive instead of fly, she turned to look at him. "You said I was in Chicago for training. What kind of job did I have when I met you?"

"You were working at a department store. An assistant buyer. You were training to get your boss's job, but your real dream was to become a professional photographer." Julian took his eyes from the road for a second and smiled. "But once we had Valentina, you wanted nothing more than to be a mother." He paused. "And a wife," he added.

"Tell me about Valentina." She leaned her head back again.

"She's a wonderful girl. She looks like you, Cassandra, just like you. She loves school. She's seven now, in second grade this year, and an outstanding student. Reading is her favorite subject. That's because of you. You would read to her every night, and you taught her to read when she was four."

"You really love her, don't you?"

Julian nodded, pressing his lips together and blinking back tears.

"Do you think she'll remember me?"

"Of course she will. We talk about you every day, and she keeps a picture of you on her bedside table."

"And does she know I'm coming home?"

"No. I wanted to be sure first. I couldn't take the chance that something might go wrong and hurt her all over again."

"I understand. That sounds like the right call." She unbuckled her seat belt, leaned over to the cooler on the back seat, and pulled out a cold LaCroix. "Would you like one?"

He shook his head, and she flipped open the tab on hers and drank. "I need you to know how afraid I am. I'm not sure anyone can truly understand how it feels to know nothing about yourself. Do you have any idea how terrifying it is to know that I have a daughter I don't remember? How does a mother forget her own child?"

This is good, Julian thought. She was opening up to him, telling him what she was feeling. Trusting him. "I don't know how that feels, you're right. But I do know that it must be awful for you. I want you to know that you can be honest with me about your feelings, whether you're scared, or angry, or sad, or whatever. I want us to put our life back together the way it used to be. And for that to happen, we have to be open and honest with each other."

In a small voice, she said, "Thank you."

Julian drove on, not speaking and keeping to the promise he'd made to himself to let her be the one to start any conversation. The silence was less awkward now, however, and he felt himself becoming more relaxed. They were just over an hour and a half from the house when she asked if he would mind pulling into the next rest stop.

Julian parked the car, and they headed in together. Once inside, she went to the restroom, and he waited in front of a display of sunglasses, wondering who would be foolish enough to buy these designer knockoffs.

Cassandra walked over to him and picked up a pair of aviator frames from the carousel. He was about to tell her he'd buy her the real thing when her hand began to shake and she dropped the sunglasses like they were a piece of hot coal.

"What is it?" Julian asked, alarmed.

"I . . . I don't know. Something. I saw something bad. In my head. But it was so fast. Too fast." She was backing away from him and turning to the exit. "Please, let's go. I have to get out of here."

She was almost running, and Julian caught up with her as they neared the glass doors to the parking lot. When they got into the car, he started the engine but didn't pull out. He was disturbed by what had happened. She'd had some sort of flashback to a trauma in her past, that much was clear. There was so much he hadn't told her, so much she didn't know yet. What if it all came crashing back at once? The confidence he'd begun to feel slowly evaporated. He knew now what might lie ahead, and it wasn't good.

PART II

33

Addison

I'm awakened by Julian's voice, telling me we've arrived. I must have fallen asleep after we left the rest stop. Yawning, I rub my eyes and try to bring the world into focus. I look over at Julian, who still looks fresh and rested, his blue eyes clear, his hair perfect. It's a quiet road we're on, where high walls and hedges block any views of the houses behind them. This is definitely not your average middle-class neighborhood. Julian turns left into the next driveway, which winds quite a way up a hill to reveal a massive dwelling of red brick three stories high. My mouth drops open. It's wide enough to fit four houses the size of Ed and Gigi's inside it. There must be over fifteen windows in the front, the ones across the first floor tall and gracefully arched at the top. When Julian stops the car in front,

I sit there and try to take it all in. If the late-model Jaguar with its plush interior was a clue that Julian was comfortable, this house says he is much more than comfortable. It says he is rich.

He turns off the engine, and we're encased in tomb-like silence inside this luxury vehicle. "You got some rest. How are you feeling?" His face shows concern, and I'm touched by his kindness.

"Better," I say. "The house. It's so . . . it's so big."

He laughs. It's a nice laugh, I think, and I smile in spite of the apprehension I'm feeling right now. He tells me that our house is in Brookline, which I've never heard of. He explains that it's next to Boston, but the quiet streets feel far removed from the city noise.

"I'll get your things from the trunk, and we'll go inside. Okay?" He opens the car door.

I follow him up the three wide steps that lead to elaborate double doors. A woman who looks to be in her forties opens the door as we reach the top step. She's petite, with dark hair, clad in black pants and a plain smock. "Welcome home, Dr. Hunter," she says, and then turns to me. "Hello, Mrs. Hunter. I'm so happy you're home." She smiles like she's thrilled to see me, and I feel horrible that I have no idea who she is. I look to Julian and raise my eyebrows.

"Cassandra, this is Nancy, our housekeeper."

I put my hand out to shake hers. "Thank you for your warm welcome, Nancy."

She beckons me in, opening the door to its full width. "So nice to see you, Mrs. Hunter."

With some hesitation I enter the hallway, with its dark wood floors and wood-paneled walls. The domed ceiling is two stories high, and the walls are dotted with oil paintings. Despite the lofty space, the room is dark, and it feels confining and stiffly formal.

"I'll take these upstairs to the bedroom." Julian carries my bags to the staircase. "Would you like to change and have a little rest before dinner?"

I don't move, unsure of what to do. The word *bedroom* has made me anxious and nervous. As if reading my mind, Julian says, "I've moved a few of your old things to the guest room, and that's where I'll take your suitcases. There's a nice balcony that overlooks the pool and gardens." He gives me a look of assurance and understanding. Relieved, I follow him up the long flight of stairs to my room. He puts the cases down, gives me a little nod, and walks to the door. "There's a pull rope next to the headboard. Just tug on it if you need anything." He turns to leave, then stops and takes something from his pocket. It's an iPhone. "I got you a new phone and had all your data uploaded from your old one. I charged it for you too. Maybe looking through it will jog something for you. Your password is our anniversary, eleven eighteen."

I click the side button, and when the screen lights up, I enter the password. The wallpaper is a picture of Julian, Valentina, and me at the beach. We're at the water's edge; I'm in a cover-up, Julian has board shorts on, and Valentina is wearing a polka-dotted pink bikini. I'm curious to see what apps I have, but the first page consists mostly of the preloaded kind. I touch the Photos icon and begin to scroll through. There are loads of landscapes and water scenes. There are no pictures of any of us, but then I think maybe it's because I've shot most of them with other cameras. Next I go to my calendar. I'm surprised to find nothing there—for the past two years I've put everything in my phone. Maybe the old me preferred a paper calendar. There's a Kindle app, and I open it, curious to see what I used to read. There are lots of books here, most of them with dark covers and titles that indicate they are horror. Some of the authors I recognize right away—Edgar Allan Poe, Stephen King, Dean Koontz—while others are new to me. Scrolling down, I see some nonfiction: books about dealing with anxiety and depression, ways to improve self-esteem, and what to do when you're suicidal. My heart sinks, and I close the app. I continue looking through everything, but there's nothing else of interest. Suddenly I feel overwhelmed. I'm grateful that Julian arranged for Valentina to be away for a few days; I'm not ready to see her yet. I stand up, needing to busy myself with something, and begin to unpack, putting underwear and sweaters in the armoire drawers. When I open the closet to finish putting away the rest, I see the things Julian mentioned hanging there: a floor-length cotton nightgown, white with embroidery on the edge of the long sleeves and a cozy-looking fleece robe. Two pairs of pants, one linen and one corduroy, hang next to a white cotton shirt, a navy pullover, and a green-and-blue flannel shirt. I imagine Julian trying to decide what to choose. He's picked wisely; there is nothing suggestive or sexy about the clothing he's left. Nothing with an underlying meaning. To me the clothes say, *I am not rushing you. My only concern is that you be comfortable and feel safe.*

After I've unpacked everything, I take a moment to absorb my surroundings. The room is large and uncluttered, with dark green walls and heavy curtains. The only furniture is a four-poster bed, its thick posts ornately carved, a low mahogany bureau, and a matching bedside table. A weighty black-and-gray quilt with a geometric design covers the bed. Darkness seems to pervade this house. I wonder what drew Julian to it. Next to the bed, on the nightstand, is a book, *Rebecca* by Daphne du Maurier. When I open it, I see my name in black ink on the inside cover, written in my hand. Maybe it is not Julian who is drawn to darkness. Maybe it's me.

34
Addison

I am alone in the house—Julian was called out on some sort of emergency. He apologized profusely for leaving me on my first day here but promised to be back as soon as he could. I'm actually relieved; it gives me a chance to explore the house unobserved. The door to his bedroom is closed. I turn the doorknob, half expecting it to be locked. I step inside, onto the cool wood floor. A king-size bed sits in the middle of the room, on top of a beautiful Oriental rug in golds and greens. There are photos on the walls, beautifully framed pictures of boats and bodies of water. The photos seem hopeful, even happy.

After I've examined the photos, I walk to the dressing table and sit tentatively, feeling like I'm trespassing. It's the only old-fashioned piece of furniture in the room, dark wood with a velvet stool and a large beveled mirror above it. Picking up a bottle of Clive Christian, I spritz some on my wrist and inhale. The effect is immediate. Loud music. Arms holding me tight and swirling me around. I'm dancing. A face, Julian's, smiling, leaning down and kissing me. The kiss is intoxicating. I put the bottle down with a shaking hand. I think I must have been happy. In love. I search my memory for more, but as quickly as it came, the memory is gone.

I stand up and walk into the attached bathroom. I step inside the huge walk-in shower. Shampoo and soap on one shelf. A pink razor and shaving cream on the other—clearly belonging to a woman. I frown. Are they mine? Certainly if Julian had had another woman here, he would have cleared out her things. But it seems odd to me, if they are mine, that he's left them here for two years. Every time he took a shower, he'd have seen them. I swallow hard and rush out of the room.

When I go to the kitchen, I see a note on the counter next to the coffee machine: "Coffee all teed up. Just hit start when you're ready.—J." I press the button, and the machine comes to life. I wonder if he's always this thoughtful, or if he's just trying extra hard because of the circumstances. I search the cabinets until I find the mugs. My breath catches when I see the one on the top shelf—a homemade mug, the kind kids make in preschool. There's a childish drawing printed on it of a woman holding a little girl's hand, and the words "I love Mommy." I reach for it, but it's too high. Dragging a chair over, I stand up and take it from the shelf, running my finger over the words. Suddenly feeling like an impostor, I put it back and get down, pulling a plain white mug from the first shelf.

I take my coffee and walk around the downstairs, looking around at everything. I don't know how much time I have before Nancy returns from grocery shopping, and I don't want to have her watching my every move. The living room is tastefully decorated in what looks like antique furniture, in a much more formal style than I like now. I wonder if I had a hand in it, or if Julian oversaw the design. Over the fireplace is a twelve-by-twelve photo from our wedding. I move closer to study it. We're standing in front of a wedding cake, his hand over mine, which is on the knife. I have a wide smile on my face, as does Julian. We look in love. I don't particularly like my wedding dress, which makes me look a little plump. I also wonder at the choice of such a casual photo in this formal room. Who chose it? I'll have to ask Julian.

I move into the den, where the decor is a bit less formal: a fluffy blue sofa with two plush chairs on either side, with matching ottomans; a long table running the width of the windows on one wall, holding framed photographs. I pick up the first one, a shot of Julian and me on the beach. We're holding hands, smiling, and the wind is blowing my hair. We both look happy and relaxed. I can't tell where the photo was taken, except that the sand is smooth, and it looks like the ocean but I have no idea if it's on the East or West Coast. I put it down and pick up the next: Valentina sitting on my lap, a birthday cake in front of her. There are five candles on the cake. In this shot, I'm not smiling but look lost in thought. Was I depressed? I go down the line, more photos of the three of us in various domestic settings. They yield no clues other than the passage of time. I suddenly realize that I haven't seen any other wedding photos.

Putting my coffee mug in the dishwasher, I hear my cell phone ring. I pick it up and look at the caller ID. Gabriel.

"Hey," I answer.

"Hey," he says, his voice sad. "How are you?"

"I'm hanging in there. How are you?"

"Shitty. I miss you. I still can't believe this."

I hate what this is doing to us. "I'm sorry. I don't know what to say."

"I'm worried. I hate the idea that you're miles away in a house with a man we know nothing about."

"I know how hard this is, Gabriel, but please try not to worry. There are pictures of me everywhere. I look like I was happy. And he's been nothing but kind. I'm really not in any danger. We have to give this some time."

I hear him sigh. "Just stay in touch. I need to know you're okay."

"Of course I will."

"I miss you, Addy. I miss you so much."

"I miss you too."

I hear the chime of the front door opening. "I have to go, love you." I click off just as Julian comes into the kitchen.

He smiles when he sees me. "Cassandra."

I stiffen, still not used to being called by that name, but force myself to smile back. I suppose I'll have to start getting used to it. "How's your patient?"

"Doing better, thanks. What have you been up to?"

I shrug. "Just looking around and getting my bearings. I didn't see a wedding album, but I noticed the photo in the living room. Are there other pictures? Did we take any that were more formal?"

He hesitates a moment. "Well, um . . . I had to get rid of the wedding album. The photo over the fireplace is the only one you liked."

"Why?"

He points to a chair. "Let's sit, Cassandra. You've always been more comfortable behind the camera than in front of it. You tend to be very critical of your looks."

"What do you mean?"

"You didn't like the way you looked in pictures. You would say you looked ugly or fat. After a while you started throwing pictures away, even defacing some."

I feel my insides curl. The woman he's describing sounds insane.

"Defacing?"

"Putting an X on your face."

What the hell? "So there is no wedding album? No other photos?"

He stands up and goes upstairs, returning a few minutes later. He hands me a framed eleven-by-thirteen photo of the two of us standing together, his arm around me. "This was the only one I got to in time. I had it framed and hid it. I've had it on my dresser since you've been gone." He hands it to me as he sits down beside me.

I look at the photo again, zeroing in on the pearl necklace. I remember that necklace. My mother's. It was the only thing I had left of hers. My hand goes to my neck.

"The pearls. My mother's?"

He gives me an encouraging smile. "Yes. You're remembering."

I don't have a visual memory, but now, looking at the pearls, I remember that I wore my mother's pearls to my wedding. I look at him. "The psychiatrists told me that if I could find my way back home, being in familiar surroundings might help me remember. I thought they were just giving me false hope, but maybe they were right."

Feeling the excitement build in me, I screw up the courage to ask him the one question I still desperately need an answer to. "Julian, why did I try to kill myself?"

He sighs. "Are you sure you want to get into that right now? Maybe try to acclimate to everything first?"

I shake my head. "I need to know."

He crosses one leg over the other and presses his lips together. "You've had your ups and downs over the years. As I told you, when we met, you were in therapy. You were in an abusive marriage."

I look at him in astonishment. "What? I was married before?"

35
Addison

Julian's expression is somber. "Yes, you were married for five years. Your husband was not a good man, Cassandra. He was mentally and physically abusive." He gives me a long look, and I see pity in his eyes. "It happens sometimes. You'd been abused in foster care, and it was what you knew. But you got better. By the time you and I got married, you had put all of that behind you and wanted to start fresh."

A feeling of panic washes over me. I'm not sure I really want to know all the answers just yet. I press on anyway. "Where is my ex-husband?" I suddenly wonder if this ex-husband had something to do with my memory loss. Maybe he came after me.

He waves a hand. "He left town years ago, thankfully.

I have no idea where he is now, but I'm just grateful he got out of your life and left you alone."

I had a husband before Julian? It seems impossible, as if I'm listening to a story of someone else's life. Is my ex-husband the violent faceless person who comes into my mind in flashes that feel like a vicious invasion?

"We wanted to start a family, but your medical history was an impediment. You'd had several miscarriages during your first marriage, and it was determined that you had an incompetent uterus." He leans in and gives me a sympathetic look. "Are you sure you want to hear all of this now?"

My nails are digging into my hands, and I lick my upper lip, tasting the salty perspiration that has formed there. The word *incompetent* rings in my head like a braying taunt. An incompetent brain. An incompetent uterus. Can my body do anything right? "Yes, go on."

"That's why we hired a surrogate to carry Valentina."

I lean back. I think of Gabriel's insistence that I ask for a DNA test. "It was my egg, right? Not the surrogate's?"

His eyes widen in surprise, and he cocks his head. "Yes. We used your egg and my sperm. But you were very jealous of the woman who carried her. Began to believe I was in love with her. That we were plotting against you. That's when you started on medication."

My mind is going in a million different directions, and I can't keep up with the images bombarding me. I'm imagining another husband somewhere, a blank face, a woman carrying my child. It's too much. I put a hand up. "Please, stop. You're right. I need some time to process this." I put my head in my hands, trying to stem the nausea I feel. After a few deep breaths I look at Julian again. "Does the surrogate have contact with Valentina?"

He raises his chin and gives me a look that scares me. "No."

"Where is she?"

He stands and walks to the window. "This isn't doing you any good right now. Let's take things one step at a time." He turns to look at me. "I'm going to ask Valentina's nanny Lucy to keep her a few days more. I think it's too soon to bring her home. You need a little more time."

I look down at my hands, clasped together in my lap. Without raising my eyes, I say, "What happened to the surrogate, Julian?"

He continues to stare out the window. "When you're ready. I promise I'll tell you everything when you're ready."

I think about this. "What if I'm never ready?"

He walks back to where I'm sitting and stoops in front of me, placing a hand on my knee. "I think it would be better if you could try to remember on your own rather than my telling you everything. Sometimes hypnosis helps. When you feel ready, we can try that."

I straighten my back and look him in the eye. "I'm ready to start. It's been two years. I don't want to waste another day."

36
Addison

Nothing here is familiar. I keep waiting for something, anything, to trigger my memory, but that hasn't happened. I've gone through photo albums, looking at Valentina, the daughter I don't remember. Her nanny will bring her home this afternoon, and I will see her for the first time since I've arrived. I'm nervous, worried she'll realize that she's a stranger to me. Julian assures me that the therapy I'll begin next week will help me to recover my memories, which is why he hasn't tried to fill in all the blanks for me. I agree with him that it's more important for me to try and remember the rest on my own than to have him narrate every detail of my life. It's the only way I'll be able to determine if my memories are accurate or if I'm thinking I'm remembering details based on what he tells me. I'm grateful, though, to have a short reprieve before I discover things that I suspect will be very difficult to handle.

I've become more comfortable in the house now, and my favorite room is the library. Mahogany bookcases filled with beautiful leather-bound classics line the walls, and a burgundy Oriental carpet covers the floor. I could sit for hours in the peace and quiet of this grand room, burrowing into one of the deep leather chairs with a downy throw around my legs. When I am here, the memory of what I've left behind in Philadelphia is a tiny bit less painful.

Even though it's only been a few weeks since I arrived, it feels like years. I miss Gabriel so much I feel like I can't breathe at times. When he called me last night, Julian didn't say anything, but I could tell by his manner that he would prefer him to leave me alone. If the future holds a life here with my husband and child, the time to break all ties with Gabriel will have to come, but I'm not yet ready to do that. Before we hung up, I told him that I loved him and always would. And that I hated myself for the hurt I've caused him.

Julian has been wonderful, though. He's more than patient, and he goes out of his way to make sure I have everything I need. The more I'm around him, the more I can see what must have attracted me in the first place.

I realize it's been only a short time that I've "known" him and that no one is perfect, but he definitely possesses more than his fair share of charm. If I weren't in love with Gabriel, maybe I would be able to entertain the thought of being a wife to Julian in every sense of the word, but I can't go there yet.

I place the marker on the page and close the book I'm reading. Julian's last patient is at four thirty, and so he won't be home until after five. I decide to call Gigi. Her phone rings four times, and just as I am ready to hang up, she answers. "Addison! How are you?"

"I'm okay. I'm sad, but I'm okay, Gigi."

"Oh, honey. This is so rotten, what you're going through. I wish I could do something to make it better."

"I already feel better hearing your voice. I miss you," I say, trying not to cry.

"I miss you too. This whole place feels so empty without you here." She stops, and I hear what sounds like a stifled sob.

"Gigi," I begin. "You and Ed, you're like family to me. The only family I've known. You'll always be part of my life, no matter what."

"I hope so, Addy. I would hate to lose you." I know she's thinking of her own daughter too. "Tell me, have you been able to remember anything?"

"No, not really, but some things do seem familiar

in a way. Julian's been good to me, not rushing me, so that's really helped."

We talk for another fifteen minutes or so, and even laugh, and when we hang up, I feel better, more grounded. Gigi has always been able to do that for me. I pick up the book from my lap and try to read, but I'm unable to concentrate. I think about Valentina again. I'm grateful that Julian gave me time to adjust before bringing her home, although I'm sure it's been difficult for both of them to be apart these extra three days. We talked about how much I should tell her. We don't want to frighten her; she's too young to be able to grasp the concept of amnesia. At first, he suggested we devise some sort of fantastical story to explain why I left and stayed away. Some of the scenarios he came up with sounded like fairy tales. But the more we discussed it, the more we came to the same conclusion. We want to tell her the truth in a way that is simple enough for her to understand, and will assure her that I didn't deliberately abandon her.

I go back to my book, but soon my eyelids are heavy. I lower the book to my lap and close them.

. . .

My phone alarm goes off at five o'clock, startling me from sleep, and the book falls to the floor. The sun is beginning to lower in the sky, and the library has grown darker. I sit up straight in the chair, stretching and yawning at the same time, then rise and switch on a lamp. There's a crimp in my back from sleeping in the deep-seated chair. Julian will be home any time now, and the nanny will be here in less than an hour with Valentina. As I climb the stairs to my room to brush my hair and freshen up, the thumping in my chest begins, and my armpits are damp. I'm as nervous as a deer in the crosshairs. I take my sweatshirt off, throwing it into the hamper, and pull a white cable-knit sweater on over my jeans. When I sit at the vanity, my eyes look tired in the mirror. I press the inner corners of my eyelids, hoping to correct it, and apply a peachy gloss to my lips. I wonder if Valentina will think I've changed since she last saw me.

Sighing at my reflection I reluctantly get up and head downstairs. My stomach feels like it's twisting around itself, as if all of my insides are battling with each other. When I reach the bottom of the stairs, Julian is standing there.

"You're home. I'm so nervous, Julian." My hand grips the bannister.

"Don't worry. It will be fine, I promise," he says, and his quiet confidence and deep voice help to soothe me.

"Right. It's going to be fine," I repeat.

"Come," Julian says, taking my hand. "She'll be here any time now."

Just as we reach the foyer, the front door opens, and Valentina enters with her nanny. I'm struck by how small and innocent she looks. She stands still, continuing to clutch her nanny's hand, and stares at me, her eyes as big as saucers. Then she looks up at the older woman, who nods and smiles at Valentina.

"Sweetheart," Julian says, rushing toward her and swooping her into his arms. "Mommy is home. Just like I told you." He puts her down and then places a hand on Valentina's back, gently moving her toward me.

As she comes closer, I kneel so that we are face to face. I can see myself in her green eyes and thick black hair. She looks much more like me than she does Julian. When she is close enough, I take her little hands in mine. "Valentina. I'm so happy to see you. I've missed you."

Her face is solemn, and her lower lip trembles. "Why did you leave me?"

I hesitate just a moment, wondering how she will react to my story.

"Let's go sit in the living room with your father, and I'll tell you everything that happened."

Valentina nods once, her face still somber.

Julian settles into the large wing chair opposite me.

I sit on the sofa and pat the cushion next to me. "Will you sit with me, Valentina?"

Valentina looks at me and then at Julian, who gives her an encouraging nod. She scrambles onto the sofa but leaves a space between us. I try to imagine how she must be feeling to see the mother who's been gone all this time, leaving no explanation. Her reticence tells me she's probably angry and afraid. If I could leave her once, she must be thinking, I could leave her again.

"Valentina." I lock eyes with hers. "I'm going to tell you what happened that day two years ago, when I got hurt."

Her eyebrows go up, and her eyes widen with surprise. "Who hurt you?"

I clear my throat. "No one hurt me, sweetheart. I went downtown to go shopping. It was a terrible day, dark clouds and heavy rain, but there were things I needed to get, so I went out anyway."

She stares at me, hanging on every word.

"I was finishing up and had lots of packages to carry in the pouring rain, so many that I couldn't hold the umbrella too. I was running to the car, getting drenched, and all of a sudden my feet flew out from under me and I fell backward. My head hit the sidewalk really hard. It hurt so much that I started to cry."

"Was your head bleeding?" Valentina asked.

"A little bit, yes. But the worst thing was that when I got up, I didn't know who I was."

"You didn't know your name?"

"Sometimes when you hurt your head, Valentina, it makes your brain forget things. When I got up, I couldn't remember my name or where I lived. I was lost. But then Daddy found me and brought me home. And now we can all be together again." As I said those last words, I was trying to convince myself of them too.

What mattered, though, is that when I finished, Valentina's sweet face had a smile on it, and she wiggled closer to me. I put my arm around her, leaning forward until my face was just inches from hers, and gently tucked a lock of hair behind her ear. "I would never leave you on purpose." I hugged her close to me.

"I knew you didn't want to leave on purpose. I'm glad you're home, Mommy."

Suddenly I feel such love for this precious child that it actually hurts my heart. I know without a doubt that she is my daughter.

37
Blythe

Blythe reread the last page of Jim Fallow's report on Julian Hunter and closed the folder. There was nothing that raised alarm bells. Successful board-certified Boston doctor, married ten years, seven-year-old daughter. No criminal record, no medical malpractice lawsuits past or present, no liens or judgments, not even a traffic violation.

When she thought of all the possible pasts she had imagined Addison might have, the reality was a considerable surprise.

Addison, or Cassandra, had been married once before, for five years, she'd learned from Jim's report. Her first husband was a man named Zane Dryer. Days after her divorce was finalized, she'd married Julian. What kind of a person got remarried before the ink was dry on her divorce papers? It made Blythe jump to the natural conclusion that she must have been seeing Julian while she was still married. Now she was doubly glad that Addison was out of Gabriel's life. Cassandra had attended college for one year before dropping out to get married. She'd worked as an assistant buyer at Filene's, but she quit before her marriage to Julian. She'd apparently been a stay-at-home mother until her disappearance two years before. Jim hadn't been able to find records of any living family other than her child.

Blythe had kept her word to Gabriel; she hadn't up-dated Darcy. But it was only a matter of time before word of Addison's departure spread. Darcy was living in London now, and Blythe had received an email from her a few days before.

Hello, Blythe,

I am getting settled here and already loving London. Tomorrow will be my first day at the conservatory, and I am both excited and nervous. Gabriel may have told you that we saw each other before I left Philadelphia. I was sad to see how painful this whole thing is for him. I will always consider Gabriel a beloved friend, but I've accepted that there can never be anything more than that between us. You and I both hoped for something else, but that hope is firmly in the past. I would never want to be second best, and Gabriel does not deserve that either. I hope we will both find the happiness we seek. I trust all is well with you, Ted, and Hailey.

                                        Much love, Darcy

The note had surprised Blythe. She hadn't realized that Gabriel had seen Darcy, or that he'd told her what had happened. That fact gave her a sliver of hope; maybe there could be a future for the two of them. Gabriel had to get over Addison. The woman had come into their lives, turning everything upside down, and they were still reeling while she was back living her old life. Gabriel had told Blythe that he was still in touch with her. It infuriated Blythe that Addison was still holding on to him instead of making a clean break. But no matter what she said to her son, he refused to cut off communication with Addison.

When Blythe arrived at the gallery that day, Hailey was with a customer. Blythe gave her a little wave and went straight back to the office without stopping. Gabriel was sitting at one of the desks, his laptop open in front of him. Blythe had been going in every day now, ostensibly to prepare things for a new exhibit. The truth was that she needed to assure herself that Gabriel was all right, and for that she needed to see him, however briefly, every day. Her sunny, forward-looking son had become quiet and depressed. She understood that, but she was afraid that Gabriel would sink so low he might do something stupid. She couldn't let that happen.

"Good morning," she said, hanging up her coat.

"Hey, Mom," Gabriel said, not looking away from his computer screen.

Blythe sat at her desk. "How are you?"

He shrugged.

"What are you reading that's so fascinating?"

He finally looked up. "I've been doing some research on Julian Hunter. Not all his online reviews are great. I don't trust him."

"Really, Gabriel, there's no person, or business, that has all positive reviews. You know that as well as I do." She wasn't ready to tell him about hiring Jim Fallow, even though she wanted her son to know that he'd found nothing questionable about Julian Hunter.

"Why did she try to kill herself? What if she was trying to get away from him?"

Blythe sighed. "Who knows when that happened? It could have been years before she even met him."

Gabriel shut his laptop and shook his head. "I can hear the stress in her voice when I talk to her. What if she's not telling me everything, just pretending to be okay? Maybe I should go to Boston and see for myself."

"No," she said with such vehemence that Gabriel looked up startled. "You can't do that. She has a child. She needs time to figure things out, and it's not fair to her for you to complicate matters. Besides, she's still very much in touch with Gigi and Ed, and they would be on the first plane up there if they sensed anything was amiss."

"But—"

"No buts," she interrupted him. "You have to give her space. If you love her, you'll let her do what she has to do. They've been married a long time. They have a child together. If she's meant to be with you, things will work out, but as much as it hurts, you have to let her go for now."

"It's not that easy, Mom."

Her voice softened. "I hate that you're hurting, sweetheart, but try to be grateful for the love you felt. You will have that again in your life—if not with Addison, then with someone else. You must love her enough to let her decide what's best for her."

He took a deep breath. "Hailey said the same thing. Darcy too."

Since he'd opened the door, Blythe walked through it. "Darcy wrote to let me know she was settling in. I hadn't realized you'd seen her."

"Yeah, I wanted to see her before she left. I've always

felt bad about the way I ended things so quickly. She's a good friend."

Blythe was glad to hear it. "Maybe you should go visit her once she's settled. It might do you some good to get away for a while."

He shrugged. "Maybe."

Blythe said nothing else. *Maybe* was a start.

38
Cassandra

I remembered something! It was during my third therapy session, during hypnosis. It was my honeymoon. Now I know where the picture of the two of us on the beach was taken. On our way to Hawaii, we'd stopped in Los Angeles for two days and spent all day on the beach in Santa Monica. I remembered us holding hands as we walked along the shore, then going back to our room at Shutters and making love with the sound of crashing waves in the background and the scent of salt air permeating the room, filled with a sense of well-being and safety as Julian held me in his arms.

It's such a relief to finally have a piece of my past to call my own. I look at Julian differently now, and I'm so grateful that he waited and never gave up on me.

I'm finding solace in the solitude of my weekdays,

when Julian is at work and Valentina in school. After they leave in the morning, I sit in the sun-drenched conservatory, where I do a half hour of meditation. Today I feel the need to spend more time, as I try to recall more details of those glorious days in Santa Monica when I remember being so happy and in love. Nothing more comes to mind, though. The last month has shown me that trying to force a memory is an exercise in futility, so I decide to take a walk.

My phone rings. I look at the screen—Gabriel. I've been avoiding his calls for the past few days, texting him that I need some space. But it's time for me to have the conversation I've been dreading.

"Hey," I answer.

"Addy! I've been so worried about you. Why haven't you called me back?"

I sigh. Despite my rediscovered feelings for Julian, I still love Gabriel. Just the sound of his voice brings all my feelings back. "This is so hard. But we can't keep talking. I have to focus on my family. This is my life now."

"Please don't cut me off. You still don't know what made you leave. What if you were really unhappy? Or if Julian's not who he seems. I just need—"

"Stop. I'm remembering things." I don't want to hurt him, but he needs to hear the truth. "I was happy.

I think I was very much in love with him, and I want to find my way back to him."

There is a long silence. Finally he answers, his voice cracking. "Your memory's come back?"

"Not completely, just bits and pieces, but enough for me to know this is where I belong. If things were different . . . you have to move on. Please, don't call me anymore. You have to forget about me." I grip the phone tightly as grief envelops me. I feel as though I'm being ripped in two. Even though I still love Gabriel, I know that in time, when I'm able to fully remember my life with Julian, my feelings for him will recede. Now, it hurts so much to say goodbye. But I know it's the right thing to do.

"Addy, I can't promise you that. I'll leave you alone, but I'll never forget about you. And I'm only a phone call away."

The tears come now, and I can hardly speak. "Goodbye, Gabriel," I choke out, and end the call.

With a shaking hand, I swipe to Gabriel's contact information and block him. I grab my camera, throw on a parka, and go outside for that walk. Inhaling the fresh air and being surrounded by nature has a calming effect. I push thoughts of Gabriel from my mind and try to be in the moment. The ground is covered in snow now, the world quiet and peaceful. Two male cardinals are at the bird feeder. One of them drops to the ground, his bright red feathers brilliant against this early November snowfall. I raise the camera to my eyes, adjusting the lens as I focus on the bird. Once I begin, I can't stop snapping, from the colorful birds to the winter wonderland of pines, so majestic with their snow-covered branches. I've already taken hundreds of photographs since I've arrived. Lots of Valentina, of course, but for some reason I'm drawn to wildlife now. It's very different from photographing landscapes. The other day I was delighted to see a family of deer at the fringe of the woods, bordering the back of our property. The sight filled me with joy, the idea that even in nature, we're meant to be in a family unit.

When I return to the house, I'm feeling better. I take the antidepressant prescribed to me. It's supposed to make me think more clearly and open the pathways to remembering. Perhaps that's why I was able to regain some memories of our honeymoon. I'm supposed to take an antianxiety pill in the morning, but it makes me feel even more lethargic and confused then the afternoon pill sometimes does, so I've been skipping it. I haven't told Julian that I'm only taking one of the prescriptions, but I intend to, and I know he'll back me up. After all, I'm not feeling anxious, so that should prove that I don't need that extra pill.

I expect Valentina home from school at any moment. Della, another mom who lives a mile away, has been alternating carpool weeks with Julian, but he says soon I'll be able to take over from him. He wants me to give it a little more time, and I'm fine with that. I grab my coat again and go to the front porch to wait for my daughter. When I see the car pull in, I hurry down the front steps to open the car door for her.

"Thank you." I lean over, smiling at Della, and take Valentina's hand to lead her inside. Her cheeks are rosy, and she shrugs off her coat and removes her gloves the moment we're through the door. A few seconds after I've closed the door, Julian enters.

"You're home early," I say. I feel myself blushing and realize that I'm happy to see him.

He holds his arms out to Valentina, who runs to him, and he grins over her head at me. "I decided to cancel my afternoon appointments and spend some time with my two favorite people. What do you say we go out for an early dinner tonight?"

Valentina jumps up and down. "Yes, Daddy, yes."

He looks at me. "Not ruining any dinner plans you had, am I?"

"No, nothing that can't wait till tomorrow. That sounds wonderful."

Julian goes upstairs to change, and I follow Valentina into the kitchen, where I have a snack ready for her.

"Maybe you should only have the carrots and apple slices, since we'll be going out to dinner. Are you very hungry?" I ask Valentina.

"Hmmm. I guess not," she says, swinging her legs under the kitchen table and absently fingering a piece of apple.

Julian appears in the kitchen then, now wearing khakis and a button-down. This impromptu outing delights me, and as I look at both of them, my husband and my daughter, I think of all I would have missed if he hadn't found me. How fitting that it was my love of photography that brought me back to my family.

I feel a happy buzz as we go to the car, but then what I feared begins to descend—the wooziness and numb feeling from the afternoon pill. That's why I hate them, but I can tolerate the side effects better in the evenings. Besides, I don't dare skip all my medicine; for now, at least, they've put a stop to the disturbing images that have plagued me for the past two years.

39
Cassandra

I watch with amusement as Valentina holds her doll—
the one she's named Hannah—in her lap and reads
to her. After a few minutes she looks up from the book.
"I'm Hannah's mommy," she says. "Daddy's her grandfather, and you're her grandmother."

I laugh. "I know. I'm really happy to have a granddaughter."

Valentina's face turns serious. "How come I don't
have a grandmother?"

I feel my body tense. What do I tell her? It feels
wrong to tell a seven-year-old that both your parents
died in a fiery car crash, so you were raised by a series
of strangers in different houses. I don't want to frighten
her after what she and I have been through already.
When I think how close Valentina came to suffering

the same fate as I—losing a mother—it makes me sick. I decide on a partial truth. "Daddy's mommy is in heaven now. And my mommy is too. So you do have grandmothers, and they can see everything you do."

"How can they see me, if I can't see them?"

"Because we can't see things in heaven. But everyone in heaven can see us."

Valentina's expression becomes serious. "Will you be in heaven when you're a grandmother?"

I pull her onto my lap. "That's a long way away, but I plan to be right here."

"Good," she says, and leans her head against me. "But if you ever go to heaven, you can take the book I made with you."

I ruffle her hair and laugh as I look at the sweet little booklet she made in school today. There are four pages of red construction paper, and Valentina has drawn pictures of Julian, herself, and me on one of them. On the front cover she's glued a photograph of herself.

"I will always keep this book. And as I said, I'm staying right here with you."

That seems to satisfy her, and she begins reading aloud to her doll once again. She continues to occupy herself like this for a while, and I'm impressed at the expression and ease with which she reads books above her grade level. I still don't remember the little toddler that Julian tells me I taught to read, but I have come to feel a very strong bond with my daughter, and that makes the lost memory a little less guilt-inducing.

When I hear the front door close, and Julian calls that he is home, I look at my watch and see that it's five o'clock.

"Daddy's home," I tell Valentina as I get up from the chair. "Let's go see him." I take her hand, and we meet him halfway to the hall.

He scoops up Valentina with one arm and puts his other arm around me as we walk together to the living room. "How are my girls?"

"We're fine, Daddy," she says as Julian deposits her on the sofa and sits down next to her. "Guess what?"

"What?" he says.

"I have two grandmothers."

Julian raises his eyebrows and looks at me. "You do?"

"Yes. They're in heaven, but they can see me."

He nods. "I bet they think you're the coolest kid they've ever seen," he says, and starts tickling her.

Valentina squeals in delight, laughing until he stops.

"So tell me about your day, little one," Julian says, putting his arm around her, and I sit back and watch them as they talk. He is such a wonderful father.

When they've finished, Julian looks at me. "Our reservation is for seven. Shall I give Valentina her dinner while you go change?" It's our anniversary, and Julian's made plans for us to go out.

"Oh my, I didn't realize how late it was. That would be great. I'll go get ready." I pick up the book Valentina made and take it upstairs with me.

Yesterday I stood in the walk-in closet in the bedroom Julian and I used to share, and was astonished at all of the beautiful clothes. I slid the hangers over one at a time, wondering where I wore these dresses, and whether I bought all of them, or any were gifts from Julian. I chose a red silk dress for tonight, and it's waiting in my room now. I shower and dress, taking special care with my makeup and hair, and then slip on the dress. Immediately I can tell by the fit and the way it falls on my body that it is well-made and expensive. When I look at my reflection in the mirror, I see a stylish, impeccably put-together woman. It's a new look for me—or, I guess, an old one that I've forgotten.

The last thing I do is pick up Valentina's book. As I flip through it once again, my heart swells with love for her. In her sweet little hand she's written "You are the best mommy in the world. I love you to the moon and back." I open the top drawer of my nightstand and place the book there.

When I come downstairs, Valentina is in her pajamas, and Julian has changed into a dinner jacket. He looks . . . an old-fashioned word pops into my head. Dashing—he looks quite dashing.

"Wow, you look so beautiful," Valentina says, and reaches out to touch my dress.

"Yes," Julian says, smiling at me. "You are stunning."

I have no idea where we're having dinner. Julian said he wanted to surprise me, but even so, when we walk into Ricard's, I am momentarily speechless. I've never seen such an enchanting room. My shoes sink into the thick brown carpet as a waiter in black tie escorts us to a table. Soft music plays, and there is a muffled hum of conversation in the background. The walls are a deep burgundy, and in the dim light the crystal chandeliers make everything sparkle. We pass a dance floor, and when we are seated, our waiter lights the candle on our table.

"This place is wonderful," I say.

"This is where I proposed to you." He reaches across the table and puts his hand over mine. His blond hair looks golden in this light, and I notice again the curl that always seems to break away and brush his forehead.

"It makes me sad that I don't remember."

"I know. But one day you will. For now it's enough that we're together. You don't know how happy that makes me."

The waiter brings the bottle of pinot noir Julian ordered and pours us each a glass. Julian wraps his fingers around his glass. "To us. And to all the years I hope are ahead." He stops, and before raising the glass, he leans toward me slightly. "If you'll stay."

For a split second I think of Gabriel and all I've left behind, but then I push him from my mind. Lifting my glass, I say, "To tonight, Julian. Let's drink to tonight."

I see his eyes grow sad, but he lifts his glass to mine, and we each take a sip.

"I know it must feel to you like I'm rushing things. I'm sorry. It's hard to keep my feelings under wraps. I want so much for things to go back to the way they were that I forget how tough it is for you as well." He shakes his head and takes another sip of wine. "I'll try to be better. Take it slowly and give you all the time you need."

He's been so extraordinarily patient with me that it makes me feel guilty. What is wrong with my brain, that I could screw up so many lives? As I look across the table, however, I sense something happening. I realize that I feel comfortable with Julian. I trust him, and more than that, I like being with him. Maybe these are feelings of familiarity I'm experiencing, and soon more memories will follow.

"It's all right, Julian," I say. "You don't have to

apologize—I understand. You've been so patient, and you've given me all the space and time I need."

When the waiter brings our dinner, I see four musicians with their instruments seat themselves behind the dance floor. "Look, live music," I say, pointing to the stage. They begin to play, and suddenly I am swept back in time. My breathing grows rapid. The song. It means something. I close my eyes and try to see what it is, but like a puff of smoke it's gone.

"What is it?" Julian's voice brings me back.

"This song. I know it." My pulse has begun to slow a bit.

"'All of Me,'" Julian tells me. "Cassandra." He looks at me with tenderness. "This is the song we danced to the night we got engaged."

I am staggered. No matter how fleetingly, I've remembered something. I feel hope, and when I look across the table, Julian rises and extends his hand to me. "May I have this dance?"

I close my eyes as he wraps me in his arms, and we glide across the dance floor. I breathe in the familiar scent of his cologne. He holds me tightly to him, and through the thin material of my dress I feel the warmth of his hand on my back. I move my own hand from his shoulder to his neck, pulling him closer to me. He tilts his head so that his cheek is touching mine, and suddenly there is a tingling throughout my whole body. We move together as if we've done this a thousand times, and before our dance has ended, I feel like I'm finally home.

40
Cassandra

We are quiet on the drive home from the restaurant, as if to speak would break a spell. I feel dreamy and happy. This must be what it's like to be a teenager on the brink of something big. I look over at Julian, my eyes moving from his chiseled profile to his strong hands on the steering wheel and the gold wedding band on his finger. I look away and at my own naked finger, wondering what kind of ring I wore.

When we arrive home, he comes around to my side of the car and opens my door. I look up at him as he takes my hand, and I can see the same excitement in his eyes as we enter the house and climb the stairs together. Words feel unnecessary. We both know that I will not pass our old bedroom and continue to the guest room tonight. Julian stops and opens the door to the large room and waits for me to enter first. It looks different than it did yesterday when I went through my old closet and felt like an intruder. Tonight it's warm and welcoming, and I know I belong here.

I move nearer the bed and turn to Julian. I'm not sure what to do next, and he, seeming to sense my awkwardness, comes to me and takes me in his arms. I breathe him in again, my head on his shoulder. We stay like that for a while, wrapped in each other's arms, swaying gently. Then he pulls away and carefully guides me onto the bed. He lies next to me, and as we face each other he runs his hand along my cheek, letting it come to rest on my lips. And then he kisses me, a long, sensuous kiss that makes me shudder with desire. I watch as Julian gets up and removes his clothes. His body is toned and fit. He comes back to the bed and slowly undresses me, caressing my body until I am completely naked. He straddles me, taking my hands in his, and, lifting them to his mouth, kisses the scars on my wrists. I feel like I am drowning in him. When he lowers himself and our bodies meet, I am on fire.

Julian is asleep next to me when I awake in the morning. I realize that I have slept more soundly than I can remember and without any bad dreams. I lean on my elbow and rest my head against my open hand, watching him. His hair is tousled, and he's on his stomach, his face toward me. He's so handsome, I think, and shiver with delight as I remember last night's lovemaking. My shoulders start to feel cold, so I lie back and pull the covers up around me. The movement awakens Julian, and he moves over until our bodies are touching.

"Good morning, beautiful." He kisses my neck as he whispers the words.

"Hi," I say, feeling suddenly shy.

"I love you. Last night was incredible."

I smile and snuggle closer to him, feeling like I could go back to sleep again. After a few minutes, Julian turns away and gets out of bed. I immediately think I've done something wrong, disappointed him some-how. I sit up, holding the sheet over my breasts, and watch as he puts on a robe and walks to the bureau. He opens the top drawer, removes a small red velvet box, and comes back to sit next to me on my side of the bed.

"I've waited to give this back to you," he says, hand-ing the box to me. "Now seems like the right time."

I take it from him and close my eyes, holding it for a few seconds before opening it. I know it must be my engagement ring, and I try to visualize it, to bring the memory back before I look at it, but there is nothing. Sighing, I open my eyes and lift the lid, and there it sits, the ring I wondered about when I looked at the wed-ding band on Julian's finger last night. I'm struck by its beauty—a magnificently faceted emerald flanked on either side by brilliant diamonds in the shape of sparkling triangles. I look from the ring to Julian, stunned by its opulence.

"It's gorgeous," I say in wonder. "This was mine?"

Julian nods. "Your engagement ring," he says, taking it from the box and slipping it onto my finger. It fits perfectly, and I hold my hand out with fingers spread apart to admire it. Julian puts his hand under my chin, lifting my face to his, and kisses me on the lips. Then he puts his hand in the pocket of his robe and takes something out. "This is your wedding ring. You left them both on the dresser." He opens his hand, and resting in his palm is a thin gold band. I remove the emerald ring and hold my hand out so that he can place the wedding ring on my finger. I feel like the luckiest woman in the world.

"Julian," I say, "I'd like to move back into our bedroom."

His smile goes from ear to ear, and he hugs me. "I was hoping you'd say that."

We hear the sound of Valentina's voice, and Julian stands up. "She's up," he says. "I'll take care of her. You take your time. You have some robes in the armoire." He points to the tall piece near the window as he leaves the bedroom.

I throw the covers back and get up. The room is quiet, and as I walk to the armoire my footsteps make no sound on the thick Oriental rug that covers most of the wood floor. Taking a blue silk robe from its hanger, I slip it on and tie the belt around my waist. I see the room with different eyes this morning. The ceilings are tall, just as in all the rooms in the house, and in one corner are two deep-cushioned chairs in off-white linen. I wonder if Julian and I used to sit in them and talk before we went to bed.

Enough, I think, and head to the guest room I've been occupying. There's not very much to move, and I begin carrying to our shared bedroom the things I want to keep. I decide to leave some of the clothes I had in Philadelphia; they don't seem like they are me any longer. I'll ask Nancy if she knows anyone who could use them, and if not, I'll give them to charity.

After I've emptied the closet and drawers, I take the stack of books from the night table and turn to leave. But then I remember the book Valentina made for me. I drop the books in my arms and open the drawer to retrieve it. But as I open the drawer wider, I frown. It's empty. I scan the room. The book is nowhere to be seen. I know I put it there. Didn't I? Frantically I begin to search the room, opening every drawer, running my hands along their insides. I even check the bathroom, flinging open the vanity doors and drawers. Nothing. I sit on the bed and try to think. Did I put it somewhere else? No. I'm sure the last place I put it was in that drawer.

But I can't think about the book right now. I need to go downstairs for breakfast with Julian and Valentina.

Valentina is sitting at the table with a glass of orange juice in front of her, and Julian is at the stove, his back to me.

"Mommy! Daddy's making waffles," she says happily. "I want ice cream on top instead of syrup."

Julian and I laugh. Ever since she outgrew her milk allergy, she asks for ice cream at every opportunity. "I don't think so," I say. "We can have ice cream later. Promise."

"I know. I was kidding." Valentina laughs now.

"Need some help over there?" I ask.

Julian looks over his shoulder at me. "No, no. You sit. I'm serving this morning."

I sit next to Valentina, and before I can ask, Julian brings me a cup of coffee. "Thank you." I take a sip of the strong brew—too strong for my taste, but it's the way Julian likes it.

"Here we are," Julian says, setting down two plates of waffles, one for Valentina and one for me. He gets his own dish and takes a seat. Valentina chatters away about a movie she and the babysitter watched last night, talking nonstop. After I had been back a few weeks, we let the nanny go. "So," Julian says when Valentina takes a breath. "What's new with school?"

Valentina's face breaks into a wide grin, and her eyes are shining. "I made Mommy a book all by myself." She tugs on my sleeve. "Can I show it to Daddy?"

Julian looks at me expectantly. My stomach muscles tense.

"Yes, of course," I tell her. "I put it away in a special place so nothing happens to it. I'll get it later, and we'll show him, okay?"

"Okay." Valentina appears unbothered by the delay. She starts to tell us about a new girl in her class, but I'm only half listening. What will I do if I can't find the book?

41
Cassandra

Tonight we're going to the Huntington Theatre to see *A Midsummer Night's Dream*. Julian told me that we have season tickets and never used to miss a show. This will be the first night he's attended since I left. The sitter arrived half an hour ago and is giving Valentina dinner. I glance at my watch and see that I still have time before I need to start getting dressed. Christmas is just five weeks away, and looking at the silver watch that Gigi gave me for Christmas last year fills me with a sudden longing to talk to her. I tap her number into the phone, and she answers on the first ring.

"Addison! I was just thinking about you."

Hearing her call me by that name is jarring, now that I've begun to think of myself as Cassandra. I want to correct her, but I don't want to hurt her feelings. "I miss you," I say instead.

Her voice is warm. "Oh, sweetie, I miss you too. How are you? Everything okay?"

"More than okay, actually." I tell her about my breakthrough in therapy. "My feelings for him are coming back. I think I was happy here."

She doesn't say anything for a moment, and I almost wonder if the connection has been broken. "Gigi?"

"I'm here. Listen, that's wonderful." She clears her throat. "Have you spoken to Gabriel lately?"

So that's it, I think. I sigh. "I can't take his calls anymore, Gigi. I'm married. And a mother. There's no place for Gabriel in my life anymore."

She's quick to answer this time. "Of course, of course. I'm sorry. This is all just going to take some getting used to. But I'm thrilled that you're starting to remember."

This feels wrong all of a sudden. "Okay, well. I've got to go. We're going to the theater tonight. Give my love to Ed. I'll talk to you later."

I end the call, realizing that I need to put some space between Gigi and me. This is a time for me to concentrate on remembering, a time to recapture everything I've lost. Holding on too tightly to the life I had in Philadelphia will only make that more difficult. Gigi will understand.

I go to the bathroom and turn on the shower to warm up. Back in the bedroom, I take off my watch and rings and put them on the nightstand in the crystal box, then undress. After my shower, I take a minute to sit at the dressing table. I'm still thinking about my conversation with Gigi and how let down I feel. I know that as I become more and more established in my own life, the old one will have to recede. But I didn't expect to feel an awkwardness with Gigi, of all people. If I didn't know better, I'd almost believe she was hoping I'd be unhappy here, that I'd return to Philadelphia and take up where I left off. I shake the thoughts from my mind and concentrate instead on getting ready for the evening ahead.

After I've finished with my makeup, I open my closet and try to decide what to wear. I look through the garments hanging there and come across a turquoise silk tunic with gold piping. As my hand runs over the fabric, an image floods my mind. I'm looking at my reflection in a mirror in some kind of house. I'm screaming, my face red, filled with rage. *That's right. Run. Get the hell out of here before I kill you!* I let go of the hanger and back away from the closet, my breath coming in short gasps. Who was I yelling at? Was it my abusive ex-husband? I push the thought from my mind, trying to focus on the present. I still need to pick an outfit for tonight, so I slowly walk back to the closet. I hold my breath and scan everything, finally plucking a purple silk wrap from its hanger. I slip into it and choose a pair of nude heels.

As I turn around to leave, Julian comes into the room. "You look beautiful," he says. "I love that dress on you."

I'm tempted to ask him about the tunic, but I decide against it. I don't want to take a bad trip down memory lane right now. I want the evening to be beautiful and filled with promise. I smile back at him. "Thank you."

I walk over to the nightstand to get my jewelry and slip my rings on first. I reach for the watch, but then decide not to wear it. It's not really dressy enough. Taking a last look in the mirror, I'm pleased with what I see. The last touch is perfume. I move the perfume bottles around on my dresser, looking for the Creed Aventus for Her that Julian brought home to me yesterday. It's gone.

Turning to him, I ask, "By any chance did you see my new perfume? It was on the dresser this morning."

His forehead wrinkles, and in two strides he's next to me. "It's not here?" He examines the bottles himself but doesn't find it either. "Are you sure you left it here?"

"Absolutely," I say.

"Not again," he whispers.

"What are you talking about?"

His back is rigid. "Nothing. I'm sure it will turn up. Maybe you put it somewhere when you were moving your things. Shall we go see if it's on the dresser in the guest room?"

I follow him down the hall, but when we go into the room, there's nothing on it but the lamp and a book.

"We can look when we get home," he says. But his expression is still worried.

I nod mutely and follow him from the bedroom, replaying the words in my head. *Not again.* What does he mean? Did I put the perfume somewhere and forget? The way I did with the book Valentina made? I already know I can't trust my memory. Do I have to question my sanity now, too?

42

Cassandra

This morning when I went to put on the watch that Gigi gave me, it was gone. I'm hoping it's just the stress of adjusting back to my old life in addition to the work I'm doing in therapy. I've decided I need to start taking my antianxiety pill in the morning. I've read that anxiety can make you absentminded, and even though I don't think I'm anxious, maybe I'm more stressed than I realize. I hope it will help. I'm beginning to wonder if my brain is permanently damaged. I'm afraid to tell Julian; I don't want him to look at me differently, when we are just beginning to rediscover each other. Valentina is off to school in the morning, and then I have my therapy session.

Until I regain my memories, I'm having therapy daily, which is quite exhausting. But it's been a miracle of sorts. Many of the events of the year before I left have come back to me, Christmas especially. I remember the three of us choosing a live tree that we tied to the top of the car, and I remind myself to ask Julian if we will go out to get this year's tree soon. I can remember celebrating Valentina's birthday too, and other days and nights filled with activities both mundane and exciting. I can't yet recall what happened the day I left, or what caused me to have amnesia. And I still haven't been able to retrieve the dark days after Valentina's birth, when I tried to take my life. I've decided that I need to know the details leading up to the suicide attempt. Maybe if Julian tells me, it will trigger the memory, and then I can deal with it and move on.

I asked our housekeeper, Nancy, to take Valentina for the night so that we can discuss it in private. Then I texted Julian to let him know, and now he's on his way home. I pour myself a glass of wine. Julian has warned me that alcohol is not good in combination with my meds, but surely one glass can't hurt. I need it to relax. I leave a glass out on the counter for him, go into the living room, and turn on the gas fireplace. There's a chill in the air, so I grab an afghan to throw over my shoulders. Taking a seat on the sofa, I sip my wine and think about the questions I want to ask.

I hear the front door open and put down my glass.

When Julian comes into the room, he takes the chair across from me instead of sitting next to me. He doesn't say anything about the wine.

"I want to be able to see your face," he explains. "Make sure this isn't too much."

I shake my head. "I appreciate your wanting to shield me, but I won't break. I'm strong." My words are braver than I feel.

"I know you are," he answers.

I dive in. "I need to know why I did it. Both times."

Julian clasps his hands together and looks up, as if he is turning over in his mind what to say. I try to keep from tapping my foot or squirming in my seat as he thinks. His eyes retrace their path back to me, and he clears his throat. "This isn't an easy thing to tell you, but you have a right to know. You've suffered from depression for as long as I've known you, but the medication kept it in check. Then right after Valentina was born, things got bad again." He pauses, pressing his lips together. "You became very jealous of Sonia. Suspicious even. You worried that she was trying to take me away from you."

"I don't understand." I tilt my head. "Why did I think that? Was she flirting with you or something?"

"Not at all. She was nothing but professional. She'd done this for two other couples, and she had impeccable references. At first you were grateful to her, but sometimes your condition worsens with added stress. You can get . . . angry."

"My . . . condition?"

"I don't like labels. But you have suffered from paranoid delusions in the past. I'm not saying you're schizophrenic—"

I jump up as though someone has jolted me with electricity. "Schizophrenic! That's not possible. How could I have lived for two years off my medications and still had no delusions, if I was schizophrenic?"

He stands and gently places his hands on my shoulders. "Calm down, Cassandra. I said I *wasn't* saying you were."

"Why would you use that word, then?"

He guides me back to the sofa and sits with me. "I'm sorry. I didn't mean to upset you. It's just . . . well, you've been somewhat of an enigma. You can go along quite normally, and then you have an episode that renders you almost a different person."

I'm stunned. It sounds like I'm crazy. "What do you mean?"

"Well, like I said, at first you were grateful to Sonia for carrying Valentina for you, but then you started to hate her for it."

"Did she stay in touch after the birth?"

He clears his throat. "No. She was gone for good."

"So what happened next?"

"You were fine for a little while." His face darkens. "But then you started hearing voices."

I take a big gulp of wine now. I feel as though I'm going to be sick. "Voices?"

"Telling you that you should hurt Valentina. Very similar to postpartum psychosis."

This doesn't make any sense to me. "But if I wasn't pregnant, how could I have that?"

He shrugs. "Some women lactate even though they're not pregnant. The brain is a very powerful organ."

I take a deep breath and let it out slowly. "Go on."

He gets up and begins to pace. "We were worried for Valentina's safety, and yours too of course. We tried all kinds of medications, and they helped at first, but the voices always came back. The day you tried to kill yourself, though, you actually seemed better." He stands in front of the fireplace, his hand on the mantel, and shakes his head. "I know now that it was because you had made up your mind to do it, and that gave you peace. I left in the morning, and when I got halfway to the hospital, I realized I'd left my cell phone at home. I turned around and drove back. That's when I found you in the tub. You'd already lost so much blood. If I'd been five minutes later . . ."

I lean back and close my eyes, trying to absorb what he's told me. It's a terrifying story about a woman on the edge. I don't want it to be me, but a deep sense of dread makes me fear that the woman he's talking about *is* me.

"Where is Sonia?"

The pain in his eyes is immediate. "Don't ask me that, Cassandra. It's better if you don't remember."

"But—" I begin, and then stop. Is Sonia the woman I've been seeing in my nightmares? The one whose face is half gone? Suddenly I can't get a deep breath. I stand, trying to get the air into my lungs.

"What about the next time? When I drove into the wall?"

He sighs loudly. "You'd been doing much better, but then you stopped taking your medicine. That happens often with patients. You feel good, so you don't think you need it. It was the summertime, and Valentina was three. You started having delusions again, voices telling you to do bad things. You left Valentina alone in the house and drove your car into the brick wall of the fitness center." He swallows. "But then you got better. You took your medicine. I thought everything was going okay. Then you disappeared."

Julian rises and pulls me to my feet, encircling me in his arms. I begin to cry, and soon I'm racked with sobs.

He holds me tightly, murmuring that everything will be all right, until finally I am spent. The elation that I felt just a few days ago in finding him again is replaced with a feeling of desolation and dread so potent that I feel I will drown. Who is Cassandra, and what secrets is she keeping?

Whatever they are, something tells me that they have the power to destroy me.

43
Blythe

Blythe finished addressing the last of her Christmas cards, put her pen down, and took a sip of chamomile tea. Cold. She set the mug back on the kitchen table and spun it around as she looked at the depiction of the sculpture *Aeneas, Anchises, and Ascanius* that decorated it. Addison had given it to Blythe for her birthday last summer, knowing how much she loved the works of Bernini. It was a thoughtful gift. She sighed inwardly, thinking of Addison. Recently she'd said she needed to cut off contact with all of them. Hailey had been hurt, but understood. Gabriel, however, had been frantic with worry, convinced that Addison was in danger somehow, and there was nothing Blythe or Ted could say to convince him otherwise.

"Hey, Mom," Hailey said as she entered the kitchen, giving Blythe a hug.

"Hi, sweetheart. So glad you're here. Can I make you some lunch?"

"No. Can't stay long. I have to get back to work."

"How about a cup of tea then?"

"Yes, perfect."

Blythe put the kettle on, retrieved her own mug from the table, and grabbed another cup from the cabinet.

"Here you go," she said once the kettle boiled, and set the steaming mugs on the table before taking a seat herself.

"Did you have a good time in Miami?" Hailey asked.

"We did. It's always a wonderful event. I'm just sorry you two weren't there with us."

"Yeah, me too." Hailey made a face. "Gabriel probably would have been even more miserable there than he was here, though. All he talked about was how great his trip to Florida with Addy was, and how they'd planned to go back for Art Basel." She sighed. "I don't know. I guess it's not been that long, but he seems to be getting worse, not better."

Blythe sighed deeply. "I'm worried about him, too." She drummed her fingers on the table, shaking her head. "I knew something like this was going to happen from the very beginning. It was inevitable. There had to come a time when her other life was revealed and she'd have to make a choice. That choice was never going to be Gabriel."

They sat in silence for a while, sipping tea and thinking their own thoughts. Finally Blythe spoke. "I wonder if Gigi and Ed still hear from her. If she's in touch with them and telling them that her life is going well and she's happy, maybe Gabriel will stop believing she's in some sort of grave danger."

Hailey slid Blythe's cell phone over to her. "Why don't you call her now?"

"I will." Blythe picked up the phone, scrolled down her contact list, and tapped on the number.

"Gigi. It's Blythe. How are you?"

"Not too bad, just getting ready for the holidays over here. How are you doing?"

"I'm all right. I'm actually here with Hailey. We were wondering if you'd heard from Addison lately."

There was a sigh on the other end. "I haven't spoken to her in a few weeks," Gigi said. "She's stopped taking my calls, and her phone goes right to voice mail. I've tried texting her, and for a while she was answering, but a few weeks ago she wrote to say she was grateful to me and Ed for all we'd done for her and that she loved us, but she needed to give all her attention to her family for the time being. That maybe in the future we could be in touch again, but not right now."

Blythe was shocked. She understood that Addison needed to find her own way, but how could she just cut off Ed and Gigi, after they'd saved her life and helped her rebuild one?

"I'm so sorry, Gigi. I know how hard this must be for you and Ed. How did things seem to you when you *were* in contact? Did she sound okay, like things were going well?"

"They did. She seemed apprehensive at first, but as time went on, she sounded like she was beginning to remember things. It even sounded like she was happy to be back." She stopped again. "But then a few days ago Julian called me to tell me he's worried about her."

Blythe looked at Hailey and frowned. "Did he say why?"

"He didn't go into a lot of detail, but apparently she's back in therapy, and it's taking a lot out of her."

"I suppose that would be expected, given everything she's been through. And continuing to go through," Blythe said.

"Right. From what Julian says, she doesn't have any close friends, and he's been encouraging her to call me, but she won't. He even suggested to Addy that she should ask me to visit, but she refuses."

"Hmm. Strange," Blythe said. "You don't think he could be lying, do you?"

Gigi sighs again. "I don't know what to think anymore, to tell you the truth. But doesn't it seem like if things were bad, Addy would tell me and Ed? I know things are more complicated with Gabriel, but she'd have no reason to keep that from us, right? And Julian seems like he's on the up-and-up. If he didn't want to help her get better, why would he have bothered to find her and take her home?"

That was true, Blythe thought. "I haven't told anyone but Hailey this, Gigi, but I hired a detective to look into Julian. He's found nothing to indicate that he's a liar or dangerous or, I don't know, playing at some sort of crazy game. Maybe it's just taking Addison time to adjust."

"I hope you're right."

"Well," Blythe said, "if you hear anything that worries or alarms you, would you let us know?"

"Of course."

"Thank you. Take care, Gigi."

After she hung up, Blythe looked at Hailey and recounted the conversation to her. "What do you think?"

Before she could speak, the phone rang. Blythe's brows knit together when she saw Gigi's name. "Hello?"

"I thought of something after we hung up," Gigi said. "Did Gabriel ever tell you that when he and Addy were in Florida, some guy came up to her in a restaurant and insisted he knew her?"

"What? No. He never told me that."

"I guess that doesn't surprise me."

"Why?"

"Well, it probably wasn't something either he or Addy would want broadcasted. He told her he remembered her from the club in Fort Lauderdale where she used to work."

"What kind of club?" Blythe asked. She had a feeling Gigi wasn't talking about a country club.

"A strip club," Gigi said, almost in a whisper. "Addy was mortified. Naturally she didn't want anyone to know. Anyway," she continued, "Ed ended up going down to Florida to talk to this guy, see what he could find out, but it was basically a dead end."

"Do you have the man's name? Perhaps my detective can dig a little deeper, find some answers."

"I don't remember it offhand, but I still have his business card. I'll take a picture and text it to you as soon as we hang up."

Blythe sighed. "Thank you, Gigi."

"You'll let me know whatever you find out?"

"Of course."

"She's a wonderful girl, Blythe. I think she's been hurt by people who she should have been able to trust. I don't want that to happen again."

Blythe didn't want to say it to Gigi, but she was beginning to think that the untrustworthy one was Addison herself.

44
Cassandra

When I left this morning to go to the grocery store, I noticed a silver car parked on the side of the road outside the house. I didn't think too much of it at the time, but now as I approach the driveway, I see that the car is still there. It has Massachusetts tags, but I can't see if anyone is inside because the windows are heavily tinted. My heart quickens as I glance into the rearview mirror and watch as it pulls in behind me. We're not expecting anyone, and I'm starting to feel panicky. I don't know what to do. If I hit the remote and pull into the garage, whoever's in the car will have instant access to the house. I decide to park in front of the house and stay in the car, with the doors locked and the phone in my hand.

As I watch, the driver's-side door of the silver car

opens, and I'm shocked to see Gabriel step out. My heart begins beating faster. My first instinct is to run over and hug him, but just as quickly, my excitement turns to anger. He shouldn't be here. I told him I was trying to make my marriage work. To leave me alone. What if Julian were home? I think back to my phone conversation with Gigi a few weeks ago and wonder if she encouraged him to come and see me. Before I am out of my car, he's standing a few feet from it, waiting. Slowly I open my door and get out. He continues to stand there, looking at me but not speaking. He's lost weight. His face is hollow and gaunt-looking, and his eyes are haunted.

"Addison," he says finally, stepping closer.

My mouth feels suddenly dry. "What are you doing here, Gabriel?"

"I can't stand this, Addy. I had to see you. I can't reach you at all, and I was worried." He reaches out to try and hug me, but I shrink back. His eyes widen in surprise.

"You shouldn't have come. You don't belong here," I tell him, my voice hoarse with emotion.

"No." His eyes are on fire. "*You* don't belong here."

"How can you say that? Julian is my husband. We have a child together. This is my home."

Gabriel looks up at the house and makes a face. "Looks like a prison."

I feel myself growing impatient. "This isn't helping anything, Gabriel."

He looks down at the ground and runs a hand through his hair. "I'm sorry. I just—I miss you. I needed to see you, to make sure for myself that you were okay. You haven't been responding to any of my texts." Then, lifting his eyes to me, he says, "It's cold out here. I've come all this way; can we go inside and talk? Please?"

I hesitate, struggling to decide what to do. I'm torn. He looks so miserable that I can almost feel his pain. "Okay, just for a few minutes," I say.

He stands in the hallway as I hang my coat and shakes his head when I offer to take his. I'm relieved that he seems uncomfortable in Julian's house—he should be.

"We can go in the kitchen. I'll make some coffee." I deliberately choose the kitchen, where we can sit across from each other with a table between us.

Gabriel puts his coat over the back of the chair and sits while I make two cups of coffee. I pour cream into his and realize I don't even have to think about it, as if we're still together. Julian takes his black.

Setting both cups on the table, I take a seat, still feeling nervous about letting him come in. I know Julian wouldn't like it. "We said our goodbyes already. You shouldn't have come here. I don't know what you thought it would accomplish."

He looks at me for a long time. "I was worried. The last time we spoke, you sounded so different. You don't look happy, Addy."

I flinch, hearing his old nickname for me. I'm not Addy anymore.

"My name is Cassandra," I say defiantly.

"It's just . . . your being here. It feels all wrong to me."

I pinch the bridge of my nose between my thumb and index finger and close my eyes.

"Are you happy? Is this really where you want to be?" Gabriel pushes.

I drop my hand. "I'm happy to finally know who I am and to have found my family. You have to listen to me. My memory is coming back more and more. I married Julian because I was in love. I love my daughter. Yes, there are adjustments, and yes, some things are hard. But listen to me, Gabriel. This is my home and where I belong. I loved you, and I'm sorry I hurt you, but you have to accept that you are no longer part of my life, and I am no longer part of yours. It's time for you to move on."

Gabriel looks like I've just punched him in the stomach, but he has to see that it's futile to believe that I will come back to him.

He eyes travel around the room, then come to rest

on the row of medicine bottles lined up on the shelf next to the kitchen sink. He stands and walks over, picking up one and then the next, reading the labels. He shakes his head. "What are all these?"

I sigh. "Some things to help me with my anxiety and depression."

He frowns. "Since when are you depressed and anxious? This looks like some heavy-duty stuff. I knew you weren't happy here."

My face is hot, and anger surges through me. How dare he come here and judge me? I stand up. "You have no idea what I've been through. How hard it's been for me to be a blank slate. So now that I'm having to relive some painful things in my past, the meds are there to help me. I want you to leave. This discussion is over."

He puts the bottle down and looks at me. "I guess I made a mistake in coming here. I'm sorry." He takes his coat in his hands, and together we walk to the front hall.

With his hand on the door handle, he turns and looks at me one last time. "I'll always love you, Addy. You can reach out to me anytime if you need me."

Before I can say anything, he is out the door, striding quickly to his car, and a feeling of sadness rests heavy on me. "I love you too," I whisper when he is out of earshot, and realize that it's still true. I love him, *and* I love Julian. But my life is here, and I also know that in time I will remember more of my life with Julian, and Gabriel will be nothing more than a distant memory.

45
Cassandra

"**M**ommy, Mommy, did you hear me?"
I look down at Valentina, who's tugging on my shirt.

"Sorry, sweetie. What is it?"

"I'm hungry. You said you'd make me breakfast."

I've been even more distracted since Gabriel's visit yesterday, replaying our conversation over and over in my mind, hoping I've convinced him that it's really over. I don't want Julian to know that he came here. It would serve no purpose except to upset him, especially if he knew how hard it was for me to push Gabriel away. Julian is doing so much to help me and care for me; the last thing I want is to hurt him.

I cut some banana and apple for her cereal and sit down across the table from her.

"Sorry, sweetie. What did you say?"

I try to focus as she talks, but my mind continues to wander.

"What are you going to read to my class next week?" she asks.

I snap to attention. What is she talking about? "Next week?"

"It's your turn to read. Remember?"

"Yes, yes, of course." I have no recollection of this. "What time again?"

She shrugs.

"Don't worry. I'll figure it out," I tell her. I'll call one of the other moms and get the details. She finishes her breakfast and goes back to her bedroom to get dressed. I go upstairs and pull out my journal. Nothing about the class reading. I've been writing things down—everything I do, where I've put things, details or stories that Julian and Valentina have told me. I can't let Julian know how much I'm slipping, so I keep the journal in the guest-room closet, hidden beneath a pair of old boots in a shoebox from my Philadelphia days. I must have forgotten about going to Valentina's class next week. I feel sick. I still haven't found the watch Gigi gave me, but I did find the book Valentina made for me. When I took the recycling from the kitchen out to the garage, it was sitting in the large bin, folded in half. I grabbed it and took it to the kitchen, wrapped it in a tea towel, and hurried to the bedroom with it, putting it safely into a bottom dresser drawer under a pile of folded clothing. I don't know how it got into the bin, but I can't tell Julian. What would he think?

He is leaving this morning for a conference in New York and will be staying overnight, returning tomorrow afternoon. This will be the first time he's away since my return, and I hate the thought of sleeping in our bed without him next to me. But I've planned a fun Saturday with Valentina.

I've just turned the coffee on as he comes up behind me, puts his arms around me, and kisses the back of my neck. "I'm going to miss you," he says.

I turn around and put my hands on his shoulders. "Me too," I say, and stand on tiptoe to kiss him.

Over breakfast, Julian tells me about the paper he's just published and what he is going to talk about during his session. His acute intelligence never fails to impress me. It's no wonder he's so well regarded in his field. After a second cup of coffee, I walk to the entrance hall with him and take his overcoat from the hall closet, folding it over my arm while he kneels down to open his briefcase. He shakes his head and looks exasperated. "Damn. I left my phone upstairs. Stupid," he says, and bounds up the stairs.

In a few minutes he's back.

"All set?" I ask, and hand him his coat.

"I think so," Julian says as he puts it on. He fishes in his pocket, frowns, and then tries the other pocket, then feels around in his jacket pockets. "Hmmm," he says, and looks around.

"What is it?" I ask.

"My car keys. They were in my pocket."

"Are you sure?" I say, wondering if he's getting forgetful like me.

"Yes, I'm positive." He checks the pockets again. "Doesn't make sense." He shakes his head and takes the second set of Jaguar keys from the drawer in the console table. "I'll look for them when I get back. I'm already late."

We kiss again, and I stand in the doorway waving until his car is out of sight. As I shut the door, I feel a bit dejected at his departure. I try to shake it off, heading upstairs to dress, telling myself that today will be a good day with my daughter. It's only one night, and before I know it Julian will be home. Valentina and I are going to the Children's Museum this morning, then having lunch out. She asked if we could have pizza for dinner, and I told her I thought that was an excellent plan.

After I've showered and dressed, I go to Valentina's

room, opening her door a crack. When I see that she's dressed and sitting on her bed reading, I open it all the way and walk in. "You've been quiet as a mouse. How long have you been up?"

"Not long. I only read one book." She closes her book and jumps off the bed. "We're going to the museum now, right?"

"Yup. And Christmas shopping after that. I love what you've picked out to wear."

She's wearing a hot-pink turtleneck sweater, and a pair of brown-and-white cowboy boots. I watch as she brushes her hair and pulls it back with a purple-sequined headband.

"You look marvelous," I tell her, and we hold hands as we go down the stairs together.

"You do too, Mommy. But you should wear your cowboy boots too. Then we could match."

I look down at the comfortable wool-lined boots I'm wearing for all the walking we'll do today. I don't relish the idea of trading them for cowboy boots, but it's worth it for Valentina. "You're right," I say to her. "Let's go back upstairs right now, and I'll change."

Valentina claps her hands. "Yay."

Mission accomplished, we head downstairs, and I can see that she's anxious to start the day we have been planning for the last two weeks.

"Here you go," I say, handing her the down coat. "Do you need help with the zipper?"

She gives me a disdainful look. "I'm not a baby, Mom."

I swallow a laugh. "I know. Sometimes I forget what a big girl you are." That garners a kinder look from her.

I slip on my own down jacket and grab my handbag. "Off we go," I say, and open the kitchen door to the garage. When I take the car keys from my purse and hit the button that starts the car, nothing happens. I press on it again. Again nothing. I look at the keys in my hand and shrink back in horror. I am holding the keys to Julian's Jaguar. I'm hot all of a sudden, and Valentina is asking me what's wrong. I can't think. Why are these keys in my handbag? I always leave my purse on the console table in the hall, right next to the key holder. How could I have taken the keys from his pocket and dropped them in my bag without even realizing it? I fish around and find my own car keys and we leave, but I'm shaken and second-guessing myself.

I try my best to put it out of my mind and enjoy the day with Valentina, and mostly I am able to do that. We are both tired when we get home, and she gives me no argument when I suggest we change into cozy pajamas before dinner.

"I'm going to wear my Belle PJs and my Rapunzel slippers," she says as she prances up the steps singing "Be My Guest."

When she reaches the landing, I go and put the pizza in the oven before going upstairs to change. Still chilled from spending so much of the day outside, I put on a pair of flannel pajamas and a long fleece robe.

"Pizza's almost ready," I say when we walk into the kitchen.

"My favorite," Valentina says, clambering up onto one of the high stools at the island counter.

I take the round pan from the oven and slice it up, putting a piece on each of our plates. "Be careful," I tell her, "it's still hot."

She leans over so that her face is almost touching her dish and starts to blow on the pizza, short little huffs and puffs. I feel my mood lift as I watch her.

"Is it okay to eat it now?" she asks, poking it with her finger.

I laugh. "How does it feel? Is your finger hot?"

She looks at me, her eyes wide, then shakes her head and picks up the slice, taking a bite.

I can see her eyes begin to droop before I can offer her a second piece, and she rests her head on her hand. "I'm tired, Mommy."

"You had a big day. Why don't we read a story and get you tucked in?"

It's only a little after eight when she falls asleep, and I decide to get an early night myself. Taking my book from the night table and slipping into bed, I pull a second pillow on top of mine and begin to read. It's not long before my eyes grow heavy, and the next thing I know, the book falls on my chest, rousing me. I switch off the lamp, and as darkness fills the room, I pull the covers up and close my eyes. But sleep eludes me. I can't stop thinking about Julian's keys. I need to get some rest, though, so I begin the breathing exercises I learned in therapy. Inhale and count to eight, exhale and count to eight. I'm feeling more relaxed, listening to the silence, when suddenly all of my synapses start firing like it's the Fourth of July. Voices. Someone is talking, not in my head but out loud. Am I hallucinating? It's so loud! I lie perfectly still, my eyes wide open, holding my breath and listening. I hear it clearly now, a gravelly voice that sounds angry. *Evil. You are evil. Why do you want to hurt Valentina? What kind of mother wants to hurt her child?*

"Stop!" I scream, springing to a sitting position. "Who are you?"

All of a sudden, there isn't a sound. My heart pounding, I turn the light on and get out of bed. The room is empty, and when I peek into Valentina's room, she is sleeping soundly. In the hall I see that the alarm is armed, the front door securely locked. I tiptoe to the kitchen and take a long butcher knife from the block, clutching it in my hand while I check each room in the house. Every door and window is locked. There's no one here except Valentina and me. I drop the knife and sink to the floor in tears. I'm losing things, stealing things, and now I'm hearing voices. Is this what it's like to be going mad?

46
Cassandra

I wake up on the wood floor to see soft light streaming through the living room windows, telling me that it's almost dawn. My mouth feels like it's filled with cotton, and I'm still groggy after a night of agitation. Feeling something cold against my thigh, I lift my leg and see the knife. It all starts to come back to me. Now I remember taking the knife from the kitchen and searching the house, making sure all the doors and windows were locked. And I remember that voice. That horrible voice. Was it real? I heard it, not just in my head, I'm sure of it. But then I laugh bitterly through my tears. I've proved over and over that I can be sure of nothing. I must pull myself together, though, before Valentina wakes up. Valentina! Could I have done something to harm her? I sprint up the stairs, the rush of blood pounding in my ears, and run to her bedroom. The door is closed.

I stand there frozen, afraid of what I'll find. Then I press my ear against the door, hoping to hear her breathing. Hearing nothing, I turn the knob to find that the light is just beginning to seep through the pink shades. Valentina is sleeping soundly, her breathing deep and regular and her dark hair stark against the white pillowcase. I sigh with relief as I look down at my child and reach out to touch her cheek. I watch my hand move as if it belongs to someone else, and I see the steely glint of the knife, whose handle my fingers are wrapped around. Taking a step back, I blink several times, shaking my head as I continue to inch away from her. And then I turn and run from the room, the knife still in my hand. I forgot I had it, I keep telling myself. Yes, that's what it is. I forgot I was holding it. I wasn't going to hurt Valentina, was I?

I'm barely able to get to the bathroom and turn on the shower. I make the water so hot that it hurts as it beats against my body, punishing me for my horrible thoughts and for what the voices are telling me. I let the water continue to rain down on my back like stone pellets. When I finally turn it off and step out, I stand naked and dripping wet in front of the large mirror. My skin stings, and it's bright red and blotchy. My eyes are sunken and dark. I look as if I've aged ten years. I'm leaning in closer, running a hand through my wet hair, when suddenly something moves behind me in the mirror, making me jump.

"Mommy, what are you doing?"

I spin around to see Valentina standing there, a look of confusion on her face. "You're all wet." She takes a towel from the rack and hands it to me. "Here."

She smiles up at me, and I start to cry.

Her face clouds. "Why are you crying, Mommy? Are you sad?"

I wrap the towel around me and kneel, putting my arms on her shoulders. "No, I'm not sad. It just made me cry because you're so sweet, and I'm so glad you're my little girl. Sometimes when we cry it means we're happy."

This seems to appease her, and she's back to my sunny girl. "Now," I say. "Why don't you go get dressed while Mommy does, and we can go downstairs together for breakfast."

"Okay." She skips away, stopping in the doorway to look back at me. "Daddy is coming home today, right?"

My stomach sinks. "Yes. That's right," I say. What will Julian say if I tell him I'm hearing voices again? What if I ran away two years ago because I was afraid I'd hurt Valentina? I ponder this as I find clothes for the day. Maybe the voices are just in my head—my unconscious warning me—and that's why I only hear them when I'm here, near Valentina. I pull a red cashmere sweater over my head and slip my feet into a comfortable pair of house shoes. I'm not sure how much weight I've lost, but the waistband of my black wool pants is definitely looser.

I won't tell Julian about any of this when he gets home, I decide. Why ruin our evening? But I will have to tell him tomorrow. If I'm not honest with him, I'll never get better. I need to bring it up in therapy too. If it's even possible for me to get better, that is. Is that what I came to realize before, when I tried to take my life? That getting well was never going to happen?

It's too much. My head is spinning again, but I have to get breakfast for Valentina. I take one last look in the mirror and add a touch of blush to my pale face. As I head to the door, I see the knife. I must have put it on top of the bureau when I came into the bedroom. I don't know why, but I glance around the room as if someone might be watching me and then take the knife and shove it into the bottom drawer of my nightstand.

47

Cassandra

Valentina and I spend the rest of the day playing in the snow and tobogganing down the backyard hill. Afterward we bake chocolate chip cookies, which we take into the den to eat while we watch *The Incredibles* by the warmth of the fire. I made sure to take my pills as soon as we finished breakfast. Maybe if I'm more diligent about the meds, the voices will stop. I still hate how the pills make me feel groggy all the time, but anything is better than how I was last night.

By late afternoon, when Julian arrives home from his conference, I'm tired but feeling more together than I was in the morning. He hasn't even taken his coat off before he bounds into the den to greet us. "How are my girls? I missed you."

Valentina jumps off the sofa and runs to him, burying her head against him. "Daddy. I missed you too."

I get up and put one hand on Valentina's back and the other around Julian's shoulders in a three-way hug. His coat is cold from the frigid outdoor air, and I shiver.

Julian disengages from us and takes off his coat. "Did you have fun while I was away?" He sits down and pulls Valentina onto his lap. I sit next to them, happy that he's home.

"Look." Valentina points to the dish of cookies proudly. "We made your favorite. Chocolate chips."

"Yum," Julian says, covering my hand with his and squeezing. "I can't wait to have one."

"How about some dinner before we eat more cookies?" I say.

"Great idea. Let's see what we can throw together." Julian gives Valentina a little poke, and she slides from his lap.

"I made some lentil soup this morning, and I'll heat up a baguette to have with it," I say as we walk to the kitchen.

"Perfect," Julian says.

As we eat, Julian regales us with stories from the conference, making sure to throw in some silly stories he's concocted to make Valentina laugh.

Later, after we've put her to bed, Julian pours us

each a glass of chardonnay. "Why don't we take these upstairs to the bedroom and turn on the fireplace?"

I can't think of anything better. I take my glass, and we walk side by side up the wide staircase to our bedroom, where he clicks the gas fireplace remote and the flames spring to life, spreading a golden glow over the room. We sit in front of the fire, facing each other. Julian looks tired; he moves his head from side to side and massages the back of his neck. "How did everything go? It looks like you and Valentina had a good time together," he says, dropping his hand to the arm of the chair.

"Yes. We had a wonderful day. Just about finished all my Christmas shopping." I push the voices and the knife from my mind.

Julian looks at his glass and swirls the liquid around, then lifts his gaze back to me. "I see the Jaguar keys are back. Where did you find them?"

There's an uneasiness in my stomach. I try to think of a lie that makes sense, but my mind is blank, so I go with the truth. "They were in my bag." I move to the edge of my seat, keeping my feet on the floor to ground myself. "I don't remember putting them there, Julian. I mean, why would I? I never drive your car. I don't know how they got there." I can tell I'm talking way too fast, and all the words are running together.

"Hm. Yes." He sighs.

I wait, wondering if that's all he's going to say. His silence becomes unbearable, but then a thought strikes me. "Maybe Nancy put them in my purse by mistake."

"The thing is, Cassandra—how do I say this?" He looks away and sighs again. "The thing is that this has happened before. I was hoping it wouldn't start again." He's looking at me now, his eyes intense. "Stealing things and hiding them. Not because of any particular value given to or need for the item, though. Kleptomania is actually linked to a lack of impulse control."

The hysteria rising inside me makes me want to laugh. Kleptomania? How am I not in a padded cell by now?

Julian moves forward toward me. "But you really don't remember taking the keys?"

I shake my head furiously. "No."

He looks at me, and I see pity in his face. "I was wrong to mention kleptomania. I'm sorry. This is different because you don't remember taking the keys." He gets up and sits on the arm of my chair, patting my back. "We can work on this and help you understand why it's happening. Don't worry, darling." He kisses the top of my head. I lean back into him, but how can I feel reassured when there are holes all over my brain?

"We've both had a long day, so let's make it an early

night," Julian says, rising from the chair. "You'll be refreshed for your therapy session tomorrow, and we can talk more about this after that."

I soon hear the water running. While he's in the shower, I run to the guest room and take the shoebox from the closet, fumbling with the lid as I open it. My journal is in the box, underneath a folded necktie of Julian's and a child's heart-shaped locket studded with small stones that look like diamonds. I don't remember taking the tie or the locket. My throat feels like it's closing. I tear the journal from the box and open it, but the pages are blank. I'm sweating now, and my hands tremble as I shove everything back into the box and push it to the back of the closet as if it's a ticking time bomb.

Trying my best to steady myself, I return to our room. Julian is still in the bathroom, and I can hear the sound of his electric razor. After I glance up to make sure the bathroom door is firmly shut, I pull open the bottom dresser drawer and unwrap the towel to find Valentina's book. I feel a modicum of relief to see it's still there, but when I take a closer look at Valentina's photo on the front cover, I gasp. There is a big red X drawn over her face. I drop the book, swallowing hard, and shut the drawer just as the bathroom door opens and Julian comes into the bedroom.

"Care to join me?" he asks, pulling the covers back and settling himself in.

Nodding, I slide into bed next to him. While Julian reads, I hold my book, staring at the page without seeing the words while I try not to look at the dresser drawer. All I can see is the X over Valentina's picture. After a little while Julian closes his book and leans over to kiss me. "I missed sleeping next to you last night." He begins to caress me, but I am too full of pent-up anxiety to respond tonight.

"I'm awfully tired, Julian."

"Of course, sweetheart. You rest." He rolls over to turn out his light, and soon after I hear the steady sound of his breathing.

I am wide awake, though, my eyes open and all my senses on high alert. The minutes tick by with agonizing slowness. The house is quiet, the world is asleep, and I feel so alone. I close my eyes and try to relax every muscle, beginning with my toes and moving up my entire body. Concentrate, I tell myself.

Cassandra.

I freeze. The voice.

While you're in this world, Valentina is in danger. Evil. Evil mother.

"Stop, stop it!" I scream. "Go away. Stop."

"Cassandra." Julian's sitting upright, shaking me, and the light is on. "You're having a bad dream. Wake up."

I open my eyes as wide as I can. "Julian, did you hear them?"

"Hear what?"

"The voices. Could you hear them, too?"

He pulls me close and holds me, rocking me back and forth. "It's all right, my darling. I'm here, and everything is going to be all right. I promise."

48

Cassandra

When I come downstairs, Julian's in the kitchen. I inhale the smell of freshly brewed coffee. He has a few patient files in front of him, and he's writing something in one of them. When he sees me, he gets up and comes toward me, concern in his eyes. "How are you? Did you get a little more sleep?"

"I did," I say. "Thank you for—you know—for staying with me."

The mood is somber. The last thing I remember is falling asleep in Julian's arms last night, as he held my shaking body and whispered assurances to me. He let me sleep this morning while he took Valentina to school, but he came straight home after that. I heard him call his assistant and tell her to reschedule all of his patients, that he needed to be home today. I'm glad; I don't want to be alone.

"You don't have to thank me. Why don't you sit? What can I get you?"

"Maybe a cup of coffee."

"I'll make a quick decaf." He takes a pod from the stand and inserts it into the machine. "Caffeine is probably not the best thing for you right now."

I smile wryly at this and think he's right—what I could use is a stiff drink. "Thanks," I say, and take a sip from the mug he hands me.

"How about something to eat?" he asks.

"I don't think I could stomach anything." The coffee is making me feel nauseated, and I push it away. I rub the back of my neck, wanting to tell him what the voices have been saying, but I'm afraid he'll have me put away somewhere. But then again, maybe I should be put away. I can't put Valentina at risk. "Julian." My hand goes to my throat. "The voices I heard last night. I also heard them the night you were away."

He folds his hands on the table and leans toward me.

"I want to tell you what they said."

He straightens. "No, that's not a good idea. You first need to talk about it in your therapy session today where you're in a safe place."

"Julian, you don't understand. Nowhere is safe. Valentina isn't safe. They're telling me I'm going to hurt her." I can barely get the words out through my choking, and tears are running down my cheeks.

"You would never hurt Valentina."

I wipe the wetness from my face, shaking my head. "But what if I do? What is going to stop me?"

"Is this what the voices are telling you again, Cassandra? That you're going to hurt her?"

My head down, I whisper, "Yes."

He's quiet, and I'm afraid to meet his gaze. Now he knows. Maybe he's thinking he needs to lock me away somewhere so that I can't hurt her. But he takes my hand and leads me from the kitchen into the conservatory. He knows I love this sunny room, and I imagine he's thinking it will make me feel better to be in here. We sit together on the sofa that faces the window, and he puts his arm around me. Neither of us speaks for a while. Outside the sun is shining brightly, even though the temperature is freezing and there are four inches of snow on the ground. I'm already pining for spring. It feels like spring could bring new hope, but I am coming to believe that there *is* no hope for me.

With my head resting on Julian's shoulder, I continue to stare out the window. "The same thing is happening all over again, isn't it?"

He doesn't answer, and I sit up, facing him. "I'm right, aren't I?"

He nods sadly. "Yes."

"That's why I tried to kill myself." *And that must be why I ran away.*

He stands up and begins to pace back and forth, then stops suddenly. "Maybe it's time I told you the whole story."

I brace myself. "The whole story?"

He sits again and takes my hand. "About Sonia." He pauses. "Are you sure you can handle this?"

I nod silently.

"After Valentina was born, you were a nervous wreck. You kept going on and on about how Sonia was going to try and take your family from you. I've already told you how you were jealous of her. But you were also convinced that she was really Valentina's mother, and that we'd lied to you about using your egg. You concocted this elaborate fantasy where Sonia and I were in love and had tricked you."

I feel like I can't catch my breath. My pulse races as his words register. "Go on," I say. I want him to get it over with and tell me what I already know in my heart to be true.

"This went on for weeks, and even after I ordered a DNA test that proved you were Valentina's mother, you insisted that Sonia was going to try and steal her. You called her one day and asked her to come over and talk to you, pretended you had something important to tell her." He puts his head in his hands.

"What did I do, Julian?"

He looks at me sadly. "You found my rifle, the one my father gave me years ago. I never thought to lock it away. It hadn't been fired in years. I didn't even think you knew how to use it, but I guess there's a lot I don't know about your past." He sighs. "I came home to find her on the floor. You killed her, Cassandra. Put a bullet in her head. Her hand was still clutching the lamp that she'd used to try and fight you off."

I think of the gory image that's been running through my mind for the past two years. It *was* a memory. My stomach rises to my throat, and before I can get to the bathroom, I vomit all over the rug.

Julian is by my side in an instant, guiding me upstairs to our bedroom. He deposits me on the bed, then returns with a cool cloth and puts it on my forehead.

"Why aren't I in prison now? Didn't you call the police?"

"No, no. You weren't in your right mind. The voices made you do it. I wasn't going to let anyone put you away."

"What did you do with her—her body?"

"I took care of it. That's all you need to know. It's enough for now. No therapy today. You need to rest." He walks to the bathroom and comes back with a glass of water and two pills. "Take these. They'll help you sleep. We'll talk more later."

I swallow the pills and curl up into a fetal position, drawing the covers up to my chin. I want to go to sleep and never wake up. I killed some poor woman whose only crime was to help me bring Valentina into this world. Even in my worst nightmares I would never have guessed that my past was this dark, that I'm an actual murderer. I don't know how I can live with this. The tears start again, and I turn to Julian.

"You have to protect Valentina from me. I don't want to hurt her."

"Listen to me, Cassandra. We're going to find a way to make the voices stop."

But I know they'll never stop, and even if they do, I can't live a normal life. Now that I know what I've done, nothing will ever be the same. I start to tell him, but suddenly my eyelids are heavy and I feel the pull of slumber. Tomorrow is Christmas day and the last thing I think before I close my eyes is that I hope I never wake up.

49

Blythe

Blythe finished wrapping the last-minute gift and placed it under the tree with the other presents. When she learned that Darcy was coming home for Christmas, she'd picked out a lovely Escada scarf for her. Darcy and her father would be arriving for dinner soon, and Blythe had asked Hailey and Gabriel to come too. At first Blythe had thought about arranging a lunch with just the two of them, but the more she thought about it, the more strongly she felt that it should be a family affair. After all, the families had been friends all of their lives, so what was wrong with being together and helping them through a holiday season that was going to be difficult for them? When she'd casually mentioned it to Gabriel, he hadn't really reacted, and Blythe had taken that as tacit approval.

Blythe hadn't seen much of Gabriel since his return from Boston two weeks before. At the gallery he'd been his charming and friendly self with customers, but otherwise he kept to himself. Even lunches were spent alone in his office, and he made excuses any time Blythe invited him to dinner. She hadn't pressed him for the details of what had occurred in Boston, but he'd told her that things were truly over with Addison. She knew he must have shared more with Hailey, but Blythe wanted to respect the siblings' connection. It was enough to know that he was talking to his sister and not keeping everything inside.

Now she turned on the Christmas lights, and as she stood back to look at the tree and the gift-wrapped packages beneath it, she thought back to a few Decembers ago, when Darcy's mother was alive, Gabriel and Darcy were together, and no one had ever heard of Addison Hope. She sighed. How much had changed.

"It looks beautiful," Ted said as he walked over and put his arm around her. "We've had a lot of wonderful Christmases in this house."

Blythe leaned against his shoulder. "Yes." They stood quietly, and she said a silent prayer of thanks for this wonderful man and all that they'd shared together over the years.

The sound of voices made them turn. "I guess the party's starting," Ted said.

Blythe turned to see Hailey and Darcy come into the room. "Hello!" She spread out her arms, inviting each of them into a hug. Holding on to Darcy's hands, she stepped back to appraise her. "You look wonderful, Darcy. I'm so glad you were able to get home for Christmas."

"I am too. I couldn't bear the thought of Dad being all alone, even though he told me he'd be fine if I stayed in England."

"Speaking of your father, where is he?"

"He's not coming. I'm sorry. He's been sniffling and coughing all day. Feels like he might be coming down with something and didn't want to pass it on." She handed Blythe a wooden Di Bruno Bros. box tied with a large gold bow. "He sent his regrets and asked me to give you this."

"How nice of him. I'm sorry he's not well. We were looking forward to seeing him."

"I'll give him a ring tomorrow," Ted said. "See about getting together when he feels better."

"Why don't you all have a seat and I'll get some drinks. Any takers for a glass of eggnog?" Blythe asked.

"Your famous homemade eggnog? You bet," Darcy said.

"Come on, everyone," Blythe encouraged the group, but Hailey made no move to sit. "We'll give you a hand with dinner, Mom."

The kitchen was filled with a mouthwatering mixture of smells from the turkey and sweet potato casserole in the oven, and the glow of the fireplace lent a warmth and cheeriness to the room. On the mantel sat a simple nativity scene made from hammered tin that Blythe had made when the children were small. Ted uncorked a bottle of Cade Estate Cabernet to breathe, and Blythe ladled out cups of eggnog amid chatter and laughter. Darcy regaled them with stories of settling into London.

"I wonder where Gabriel is," Blythe said when they were on their second glass, and he still hadn't arrived. "Do you think I should call him?"

"Maybe he had a last-minute customer. I'll text him." Hailey picked her phone up from the counter.

"How is Gabriel doing?" Darcy looked from Ted to Blythe.

"Not well," Ted said. "He's been pretty down the last two months."

"He went to Boston two weeks ago," Blythe added. "Went to her house. It didn't go well."

Darcy sighed, shaking her head. "At first, when Gabriel broke things off with me, I hoped that he would come to his senses, and things would end as quickly as they began. I was angry and bitter, of course, but I never wanted to see him so hurt. It took me a while, but I finally reached a point where I felt sad instead of mad."

Blythe put her arms around Darcy, gently pulling her close. "I'm so sorry for what you've been through," she murmured.

"It's fine. I'm fine," Darcy said, stepping back. "Moving away was the best thing for me. New places, new people. I'm busy and enjoying myself. Really."

"Hey, everybody." Gabriel stood at the entrance to the kitchen. "Sorry I'm late. Got tied up at the gallery."

Blythe stood back as he greeted everyone, observing the very tentative brush against the cheek he gave Darcy before quickly moving to his mother for a kiss.

"Eggnog?" Hailey picked up a glass.

Gabriel shook his head. "Nah, I think I'll have a little vodka on ice."

Though Blythe had seen him recently, she was distressed by his appearance—he seemed to have lost more weight, and his eyes looked sunken. And where had the taste for straight vodka come from? Gabriel had always enjoyed a beer or a glass of wine, but he wasn't a drinker, and she wondered if this was a one-off. He put one ice cube in the glass and poured the vodka, swallowing it down in one gulp. Then he poured another round into the tumbler. There was an uncomfortable silence until Blythe spoke.

"Shall we take the appetizers into the living room, or would you rather sit in here?"

"In here," Hailey said. She picked up a tray of mini quiches and carried it to the low coffee table in front of the love seat facing the kitchen fireplace, flanked by two upholstered armchairs. The kitchen seemed to be the room that always drew them, a room whose walls had been privy to countless family conversations and tête-à-têtes.

"When did you get back, Darce?" Gabriel sat down in one of the armchairs, being careful, Blythe thought, not to sit too close to Darcy.

"Wednesday night," she said, her tone friendly.

"Nice. How's your dad?" It sounded perfunctory, and he looked down at the glass he held between his hands as he spoke. Couldn't he even give her the courtesy of looking at her?

"He's okay. Just a bit under the weather, or he would have been here, of course."

The conversation continued, everyone trying their best to keep it as superficial as possible. Addison was the elephant in the room that nobody wanted to acknowledge, Blythe realized. She'd begun to feel that it had been a mistake to invite Darcy. She and Hailey should have made a lunch date with her instead. Just as she was worrying that this was going to be an agonizingly long evening, Darcy changed the whole tone of the gathering.

"I don't know about the rest of you, but this feels really uncomfortable. You guys are like family to me. Gabriel," she said, looking directly at him, "we're not together anymore, but can't we be friends? I know you're still in love with Addison. That doesn't mean you have to treat me like a stranger, like if you talk about her, I'm going to shrivel up and die. We go back too far for things to be so awkward between us."

Blythe held her breath, watching Gabriel. He cocked his head and smiled at Darcy, really looking at her for the first time tonight.

"You're right. I'm sorry for acting like an ass. You're a good friend."

Darcy smiled. "Thank you."

Blythe felt like cheering Darcy's bravery in speaking up. She'd taken a big step, and Gabriel had responded. And isn't that how every journey began?

50
Cassandra

It took everything in my power to get through the holidays. All I can think about is what Julian told me about Sonia. No matter how hard I try, I can't remember anything about her or what I did. I'm sick with guilt over it; a constant state of nausea fills me. Julian is wrong. No matter how out of my mind I was, I have to pay for what I've done. I have so many questions and so few answers. Does her family know what happened to her? Has anyone ever come looking for her? When he says he took care of things, what does that mean?

The only thing I do know is that I can't live with this horrible secret. I start to plan, thinking about just going straight to the police and telling them the truth about what I did and how my husband hid it. But even if he was wrong to do so, Julian was only trying to protect his family. How can I betray him just to alleviate my guilt? And what about Valentina? If the police arrest Julian for covering for me, then our sweet girl will have no one, and be forced into the same system that ruined me. And a confession won't bring Sonia back, anyway. It's clear this can't be the solution. I sink down on the bed, putting my head in my hands, and try to take a deep breath.

I've slept all day. I need to get up and dressed, pull myself together and think this through. Maybe together, Julian and I can figure out a way to deal with this. I hear the garage doors open. I walk to the landing and call down, "Julian? Is that you?"

He appears, looking up at me, and as he climbs the stairs I can see from the look on his face that something is wrong. He is holding something in his hands, and when he is almost at the top I see that it is Valentina's stuffed elephant. When he reaches the landing where I stand, he holds the stuffed animal out to me without saying a word. I cry out when I see the mutilated elephant, its stuffing ripped partway out and the knife embedded in it. This is Valentina's favorite toy, the one she sleeps with every night. What have I done? Trembling, I run to the bathroom and vomit into the toilet. My stomach is empty but keeps heaving. Tears and snot run down my face as I gag and cough, and I rest my head on the toilet's edge. Julian sits behind me and lays his hand on my back, but I cannot be comforted. Finally it seems I am spent, and Julian hands me a towel to wipe my face.

"Where is Valentina? Is she all right?" I ask him, terrified of what he is going to tell me.

"She's at Nancy's house. I took her there after I picked her up from school."

Relief floods through me. "Where did you find the elephant?"

"It was in our bed this morning. You were holding it next to you." His voice is sad.

"I went to her room and took it? I don't remember. How can I not remember?"

He gets up from the floor and takes my hand to help me up. His voice is comforting. "You need to go back to bed and get some rest. I'll stay with you for a while."

Once I'm back in bed, Julian drags one of the easy chairs near to the bed and sits. I close my eyes and pray for sleep, but it doesn't come. I toss and turn, and all of a sudden, a light comes on and Julian is standing next to the bed. "Take this. It's a sleeping pill." He hands me a white capsule and a glass of water. I swallow the pill and lie back, waiting for it to take effect. Within a few minutes, my eyes close.

It starts softly and grows louder, a high-pitched

woman's voice with a thick southern accent, different from before. *She's crazy. She's gonna hurt that girl. We need to kill her. Kill her.* The deep raspy voice speaks again. *Evil lives inside you, Cassandra. You must kill the evil before it kills Valentina. As long as you live, Valentina is in danger. Death. The cure is death.*

"Julian, Julian, help me!" I scream. He is at my side immediately, his hands pressing on my shoulders, trying to restrain me as I twist and turn.

He turns the lamp on, and I cover my eyes with my hand to shield them from the light. "The voices again?" he says.

"You heard them, too, didn't you?" I plead, but I can see from his face that he has not.

"What did they tell you this time?"

"They said I'm going to hurt Valentina and that I have evil inside me." I look at him and try to hold back the tears. "They said I should kill myself."

Julian gives me a sad look and nods slowly. "I don't know how to help you anymore." He wipes a tear from his cheek. "We've tried everything. As much as I love you, I have to think of Valentina."

I rocket to a sitting position and look at him in horror. "You think I should do it?" I whisper.

He chokes back a sob. "I think it's the only way. There really is no hope that I can see. I'm not sure there's any way you can get well, and eventually you will hurt Valentina, the way you almost did before. I know you love her and want to protect her. The only way she will be safe is if you're gone."

Julian's voice is smooth, mesmerizing, and I nod as I wrap my arms around my body, rocking back and forth. It's like listening to a poem, and I want him to go on talking in that soothing, rhythmic way. This must be the answer. I can't endure this torture for another day, the guilt of having killed someone and the fear of hurting the one I love the most.

"Now, my darling. I'll support you in finding the peace that has eluded you all your life," he tells me. "No more pain, no more hurt, no more tears."

"What will you tell Valentina?" I ask.

"I'll tell her it was an accident. Valentina will remember you as the wonderful Cassandra I tell her about. How much better for her to grow up with the memory of a dead adoring mother than a living woman who wishes her harm. You want that for her, don't you?"

"I do, Julian. But I can't leave her without saying goodbye. Can I give you something you can show her when she's old enough?"

"Of course."

He leads me to the desk, pulls out a fresh page of

stationery, and hands me a pen. I look up at him. "Now I'm not sure what I want to say."

"Okay, I'll help you."

He dictates as he walks around the room, and I write:

My dearest Julian,

Please forgive me, but I can no longer live in this tortured state. I've tried everything to get better, but nothing helps. For a long time I was able to hide it. But now, the voices won't be silenced. They come to me almost constantly. They are relentless and they urge me to do bad things. All night they shout at me to kill my child, that she is evil and must be removed from the world. I can't endure it any longer. While I still retain a tenuous and fleeting hold on reality, I must do the only thing that will keep you and Valentina safe. Please tell her that I love her with all my heart and that all I do is for her. One day she will understand.

Your loving wife,
Cassandra

Then he takes the letter from me and scans it. "Very good," he says, and takes a brown vial from his jacket pocket, placing it on the desk next to me. "I promise this will be painless." Taking the empty glass from my night table, he fills it with water from the bathroom tap and then places it on the desk next to the vial. I look from the pills to Julian and back at the bottle again.

"Take them, my darling, and afterward you can lie down in bed. There will be no voices, no more nightmares." He smiles at me and picks up the bottle. "Open your hand, my sweet."

I hold my hand out, and he pours the pills into my palm. Placing one on my tongue, I wash it down with a sip of water.

PART III

4 Years Earlier

51
Julian

Cassandra is dead, but I've found a way to replace her. My new patient, Amelia, will take her place, like a gift sent from the heavens to make everything all right again. I'll make her believe that she is Cassandra. It's no coincidence that she has green eyes like my mother, and like Valentina. She can easily pass for Valentina's mother. I'm adept at using hypnosis with many of my psychiatric patients, and proficient in memory reconstruction, thanks to the work of my father. I refer all my other patients to colleagues, telling them that my wife has had a breakdown and requires my full-time attention. I'm already seeing a heavily medicated Amelia five times a week. She's completely withdrawn from anyone she knows; she's quit her job working at the museum and is living on her recent inheritance. She has been existing for our sessions; our work is the only thing tying her to reality. Even taking photographs has ceased giving her any pleasure. So when I suggest that she come and stay with me so that we can work more intensely together, it is an easy sell.

As much as I'm loath to part with her, I send Valentina to stay with my father. It's amazing to me, but he's proved himself to be a good grandfather since Valentina's birth. When I was growing up, he was too busy building his career and making a name for himself to play games or spend time with Mother and me at home. If he wasn't with patients, he was holed up in his lab doing research or in his office poring over patient files. Parkinson's slowed him down, though, and made him realize he's not immortal and that he needed to retire. He's managing the disease remarkably well, and spends his summers in New Hampshire, where he's eager to have Valentina visit so he can teach her how to fish and play cards.

I drive to Amelia's apartment building and text her, then wait for her outside. I don't want anyone to see me. Within minutes, she's downstairs, wearing tattered jeans and an old sweatshirt and carrying two suitcases, which she throws in the back seat.

"How are you doing today?" I ask as I pull away

from the curb. I notice her hair is unwashed, her face devoid of makeup.

She shrugs. "Nightmares again. Even the sleeping pills didn't help."

"It's going to get better now that we'll be able to spend more time on your therapy. I'm going to take those horrible memories away for you."

She stares straight ahead. "Can you bring my sister back? Or my mother? Please, I don't want the memories, the special times with them, erased."

I don't answer. We've been around and around this topic before. She's afraid she can't erase the memory of the tragedy they suffered without losing her memory of them entirely. But though I've respected her wish so far, thinking of them does nothing but bring her pain. If she's to become Cassandra, she will have to believe that her family died when she was twelve, as Cassandra's did. I won't burden her by adding false memories of foster care, but will re-create a past for her with a few good images of a nice early childhood, followed by a tragic accident that took her parents. The bulk of her memories I'll build for her, through stories I tell her, and the photographs I show will consist of our dating, our wedding, and our child.

I'd like to have her believe that she carried and gave

birth to Valentina, but in case she ever finds out that she's never been pregnant, I'll tell her we used a surrogate. If it ever comes into question, we can always blame the "doctor" who saw her, and who will turn out to be conveniently dead. I've had to work out every contingency; Valentina's happiness depends on my making this work. And this is why I'm doing it, all of it. It's for my beloved Valentina. But there's a silver lining. I'm giving Amelia a gift. This is going to save her, too. She'll have a new life, devoid of trauma and heartbreak.

We pull down the gravel road leading to the house. Amelia looks around. "It's so secluded here."

"I like my privacy," I tell her. I always feel a sense of relief coming home from the hospital. The moment fifteen years ago when I first saw the imposing home surrounded by tall hedges, I knew it was perfect for me. She will come to love it here.

I carry her suitcases for her, and she follows behind wordlessly.

"Are you hungry?" I ask once I've put her suitcases in the guest room and settled her in there. She's too thin, I think. We'll have to work on this.

She shakes her head. "No."

"We've talked about this, Amelia; you need to keep your strength up."

"I don't have an appetite."

For now I don't want to push her. The first time I was called in to be the psychiatrist on her team, she'd been enraged about her failure to end her life. The universe had other plans for her, I told her. If the apartment below hers hadn't flooded, the super of the building would have never found her in time. He'd gone in to check the leak and seen her in a bathtub full of blood, her arms sliced up to her elbows. It was a very serious suicide attempt. Fortunately, he'd been trained in first aid and was able to stanch the bleeding enough for the paramedics to get her to the hospital alive, where she was put on suicide watch. I saw her every day that first month on the psych unit, and when I was convinced that she was no longer a danger to herself, I signed for her release and she began to see me as an outpatient.

There's no time to lose, so I steer her into my private office. She looks around and smiles for the first time. "This is nice. Much better than your other office." I know my hospital office still feels institutional, despite my best efforts to make the space my own, and I hope this new environment will help advance the work we will do.

"I'm glad you like it. Sit wherever you like."

She chooses an oversize chair with a fleece blanket on it and snuggles underneath it.

"So Amelia, before we begin today, I want you to tell me again some of the things you have to live for."

She sighs. "My future. The future that I want to make. A good family, with a man nothing like my father. And my photos. I used to love losing myself behind the camera."

"Good. Good." A good family and kind husband are things I can provide her with. And she can always take photos of Valentina as a creative outlet. "Okay, let's work on the memories that have been giving you nightmares. Are you ready?"

She nods and pushes up the sleeve of her sweatshirt. The jagged scars are still red and angry. I prepare the injection, clean her arm, and push the fluid through. Within seconds, she visibly relaxes.

I sit and begin to speak in a quiet voice. "I want you to close your eyes, Amelia. Relax all of your muscles and let them become loose and limp. Now imagine yourself drifting on a calm river, with a gentle breeze wafting across your skin. Smell the air and allow yourself to relax more and more with each breath you take."

She is breathing deeply now. "It feels so good to relax and let it all go," I continue. "You are going deeper and deeper now, and you are open to my voice."

She is very still, in a deep trance. "I want you to picture that day. You're going to the door and ringing the bell. No one answers. You look inside, but no one is home. You're not related to anyone in this house. You're just going to visit your friend, whose name is Amelia. Your name is Cassandra, and your parents died in an automobile accident when you were only twelve. Amelia became your best friend, and you liked to pretend that her house was your house because you got moved around so much. But you're Cassandra, and you don't have to remember what happened to Amelia's family. Go back to the day and knock on the door again. No one answers. Do you see?"

She moans. "No one's there."

"That's right. You read about what happened in the paper. But it wasn't your family. And you, Cassandra, did nothing wrong. Remind me of your name?"

"Cassandra," she says.

We continue for another hour, building out her backstory and moments from the past we're creating for her, before I bring her back.

"How are you feeling?" I ask.

"Better," she says, looking surprised. "Calmer."

I walk over and take her hands in mine. "We still have a long way to go, but I'm optimistic." By the time Valentina returns at the end of the summer, she'll have a mother again.

52
Julian

"Tell me what you remember about our wedding," I prod.

"It was lovely. Here at the house. We had chocolate cake, and I drank too much champagne."

Amelia has been at home with me for three weeks now. I work with her for hours every day, much longer than is the norm, but in two months Valentina will be back home, and I need to fully convince Amelia that she's Cassandra before she returns. I've made good progress; she moved into my bedroom three nights ago, and already believes she's my wife. I'm working on implanting memories of Amelia with Valentina so that she accepts Valentina as her own when she is back. We're in the middle of another session now. I've inserted a port in her arm to avoid having to stick her every day, and attached the IV to it.

"Was it a happy day?"

She smiles. "One of the happiest of my life."

"Was your family there?"

A tear slides down her cheek as she shakes her head. "My parents died when I was young. I don't have any other family."

"But do you remember the necklace you wore? It was like having your mother with you. Visualize the pearls. A woman, your mother, giving them to you, and you've kept them safe, bringing them from house to house during all those years in foster care."

"Pearls?"

"Yes, can you see them? They are a long strand, lustrous and beautiful. And you were so happy to be wearing them on our wedding day."

She smiles. "Yes. My mother's pearls."

Now when she looks back at our wedding portrait, into which I've photoshopped her face, and sees the pearls around her neck, she'll believe it's her. It will evoke a memory of her mother's necklace.

"Now you have me and Valentina. Do you remember her birth?"

Her brows knit together. "I can't. Can you tell me about it?"

"You didn't carry her, remember? We used a surrogate. But she gave birth to her here in the house with a doula, and you were the very first one to hold her."

"I held her," she repeats. "Why couldn't I carry her?"

"Your uterus. You kept having miscarriages. But it's okay. We went to a specialist, remember?"

She shakes her head. "I can't remember."

"Take a deep breath," I instruct her. "We drove to the appointment in my Jaguar, and you were nervous and kept cracking your gum. When we met in the doctor's office and she told us the results, you cried, and I comforted you. Can you remember that room?"

She nods.

"I want you to see the desk she's sitting behind. It's a dark wood. There are pictures of babies on the wall. And you're sitting in a comfortable chair. It's beige with white piping. Can you see it?"

She nods again.

"What does the doctor tell you?"

Her voice shakes. "That I can't carry a baby successfully."

"Right. But you can still have your own child with your egg and my sperm."

"Valentina is my baby."

"Yes," I say in a soothing voice.

"She's with your father," Amelia says.

Good, she's making the associations on her own. "When was the last time you saw her?" I say gently.

"Before I went away to get better."

"Right. Why did you go away?"

"I was depressed. I tried to hurt myself. I was hearing voices. But I'm better now. I'm taking my medicine like I should. But when I stopped taking it, I crashed my car, and my face was messed up."

"Yes, so remember that Valentina might not recognize you at first. You have to let her get used to your new look."

"I'm her *mother*," she insists.

"Yes, you are."

I glance at my watch. We've been at this for five hours, and I need to stop for today. I bring her out slowly. When she opens her eyes, she looks exhausted.

"Are you okay?"

"Yeah." She sits up slowly. "I just feel tired. I think I'd like to go upstairs and rest for a while."

"Okay, darling."

I'm finding working with Amelia much more challenging than with Cassandra. Then, all I had to do was manipulate her existing memories. Now I'm creating a whole new set of memories for Amelia, in addition to erasing her old ones. Using drugs to aid the hypnosis is helping this along, though, and so far, it seems to be working.

She goes up to our bedroom and gets under the sheets. If I squint I can almost believe it *is* Cassandra; they look a lot alike, especially now, with Amelia wearing Cassandra's clothes and doing her hair the way Cassandra used to. Amelia's nose is smaller, and she's ten years younger, so her face is unlined. I've had to photoshop the new Cassandra into all my old photos. It pained me to have to replace my true love with this substitute, but it's the only way. Of course, I've kept our original wedding portrait, hidden along with other pictures and mementos I've held on to so that I can still feel her presence here.

I've taken Amelia for a new driver's license, pretending she lost hers. Even though she'll never truly replace Cassandra in my heart, I am growing to care for her. The more I shape her to become like my darling wife, the more I honor Cassandra's memory. I'm sure Cassandra would be pleased to know that she's not being supplanted as Valentina's mother by someone new. It's almost as though she were still here. And Amelia will be so much happier with the history I've created than the one that fate dealt her. She'll never have to remember what she saw that day in her family's house. She'll never have to mourn the sister, mother, and grandmother she lost. Instead, she's going to have a wonderful life with me and with her daughter. Things have a way of working out for the best, don't they?

One thing that I *am* worried about is Valentina's reaction to Amelia. I've never tried my protocol on someone as young as Valentina, but I have no choice. I'll have to try it when I pick her up from my father's. The fact that she's only three works in my favor. Memories from before that age are rarely accessible, as the hippocampus is not mature enough then to form and store them in a way that makes them retrievable later.

In the meantime, there is still plenty of work to do with the new Cassandra—I can't think of her as Amelia any longer, lest I slip and call her that. Henceforth, I will only think of her as Cassandra.

I draw the shades, unzip my pants, and shrug out of my shirt, folding my clothes and putting them neatly on the chair. I pull down the covers on my side of the bed and get in next to her. She's half asleep, but she responds to my caresses. Her arms encircle me, and she moves against me, moaning. She pushes me onto my back and sits astride me, her head forward, her long hair on my chest. The pleasure is so intense that I actually cry out, and as I do, I try to push away the disloyal thought that this Cassandra is much better in bed than the other one ever was.

As I lie there in a haze after we make love, I feel confident that I've made the right decision. In our sessions, I'll convince her that she loves being at home, that all she needs is Valentina and me. Perhaps I can convince her that she's come up with the idea of homeschooling. She won't get crazy ideas about working and being more independent, like the first Cassandra did. She won't need anybody but me. And I will never let her go.

53
Julian

Valentina is eagerly waiting on the porch for me when I arrive at my father's house in New Hampshire to pick her up. As she runs to me, I lift her up and hug her tight. I've missed her more than I could have ever imagined, and I promise myself this will be the last time we're separated for so long.

"My angel. Look at you. You've grown so much in just three months."

She plasters my face with kisses. "You too, Daddy!"

I laugh and put her down. She hands me a bouquet of pink and orange flowers made of tissue paper. "I made this for you and Mommy."

"I love it, and so will Mommy. She's waiting for you at home."

I was nervous leaving Cassandra behind; it's the first

time she's been alone since I brought her home. But I've arranged for Nancy, the housekeeper I hired two months ago, to stay with her. Though I feel her transformation is complete, one never knows what might trigger a regression.

Valentina scrunches her face up. "No. I want her."

Before I can answer, my father walks toward me. I notice that his gait is slower, his hair whiter, than just three months ago. For the first time I realize how much he's aged. He holds out a hand to shake mine.

"Come have something to eat before you head back," he says.

I'm anxious to be on my way, though; I have work to do. I've booked a hotel room on the way home, where Valentina and I can spend a little time preparing her to accept the mother she's about to see. "Just a quick cup of coffee," I say.

I follow him back into the cabin and take a seat at the kitchen table. "Why don't you do one last drawing for your mommy out on the deck," he says. "You won't see the lake again until next year." While he brews a cup for me, I marvel to see that the refrigerator is plastered with drawings and colored pages that Valentina has done. There are board games piled up on the coffee table, and toys stacked up in the corner. What he lacked as a father, he has more than made up for as a grandfather. He brings the cup over, and I notice that his hand shakes slightly.

"Thanks. I really appreciate your taking care of Valentina this summer."

"I loved having her here. But I wanted to talk to you alone before you leave. She was very upset at the way her mother just left without saying goodbye. You know that's not good for a child's self-esteem."

I'm momentarily stunned into silence, flashing back to the last time I saw my own mother before she executed her plan to end her life. I was only fourteen.

"Of course I know that."

His eyes grow sad. I'm surprised when he reaches out a hand to cover mine. "I'm sorry, son. Of course you do. That was a careless thing to say. I know what your mother's . . . absence did to you. I'm only worried about our sweet girl."

The truth is, I'm worried about Valentina as well. It's the reason I've taken such extreme measures. I won't allow Valentina to suffer the way I have, to grow up without the loving hand of a mother guiding her. But of course I can't say that to my father. I give him a weak smile.

"I know, Father. Cassandra hasn't been herself. You know how depression can be. But she's getting better now."

He shakes his head. "I still don't understand it. She never seemed suicidal to me. Of course, neither did . . ."

He doesn't finish the sentence. He doesn't have to. I blow out a breath. "She's taking her medication regularly, which Mother never did. Hopefully she'll stay on it, and this will never happen again."

He nods. "I hope so. You need to make sure."

"I will." I stand, signaling that the conversation is over. Unfortunately, we won't be able to see him for a long time. He'll never believe that she's Cassandra, even if he thinks she drove into a brick wall in an attempt to kill herself. He might believe that her injuries were substantial enough to constitute facial reconstruction, but her mannerisms are different too, and of course so is her voice. But he'll go back to Arizona next week, and it shouldn't be too hard to make excuses for why she won't see him if I paint a picture of a woman descending into agoraphobia. He's a psychiatrist too; he'll more than understand.

"I tried to keep some of it from you. I was embarrassed, but she's been struggling with anxiety and depression for a long time now. Before she tried to hurt herself, she'd started being afraid to go out. It's been very difficult, but I'm doing my best to shield Valentina."

"I'm glad that you're making sure Cassandra gets the help she needs. That child deserves two parents who love her."

If he only knew how much I agreed. "Yes, Father. I am. Speaking of which, we need to get on our way. Thanks again."

I call out to Valentina. "Time to go. Come say good-bye to Grandfather."

She runs into the room and wraps her arms around his legs. He laughs and picks her up, kissing her cheek.

"You will write to me and do the—what's it called, the Facecall?"

"Facetime. Yes, she will," I say.

I reach for her hand, grab her suitcase, and we get into the car.

As soon as we're on the main road, she turns to me. "Where's my mommy?"

"Sweetie, do you remember when I told you that Mommy got an operation?"

Her head bobs up and down. "Yes, a paration on her face?"

"Right. You see, Mommy had a car accident. Her face was hurt. But she's okay now. It's just that she's going to look a little different, but she's still your mommy."

"No! I don't want her to be different."

I glance at her quickly. She's pouting now. "Sweet-heart, it's okay. She misses you terribly and can't wait to see you. You'll get used to the way she looks, and she's still beautiful."

She doesn't answer, and I drop it for now; after I've spent some hours with her in hypnosis over the next two days, she'll be fine. Once she's back home and has spent enough time with the new Cassandra, she'll forget what her real mother looked like. She has to; otherwise this is all in vain, and I won't have it all be in vain. She needs a mother as much as I need a wife. I'm giving her the family that I never had, that her real mother never had, but that's the wonderful thing about life, and about psychiatry—it's always giving you the opportunity to reinvent yourself, to make things right. I'm filled with new resolve. Today is the start of our new family—one that nothing and no one will ever tear apart.

It took me years to finally meet the woman that destiny had in store for me. All through college and medical school, I had nothing but superficial relation-ships. Plenty of attention from women looking for a rich doctor-to-be, but there was never a true connec-tion. Until I met Cassandra. I knew, of course, that as her therapist, it wasn't appropriate for me to have a relationship with her. But sometimes rules are meant to be broken. It became apparent very quickly that she'd been sent to me for a reason. I was the one who held the key to her happiness, the key to unlock her from the cage of her unhappy marriage, to give her a new life with me. I couldn't have known how it would end up—that I'd lose her as swiftly as I'd found her. I won't mess up this time. This time is for keeps.

· · ·

After two days of sessions, Valentina and I are home. I've called ahead to alert Cassandra that our arrival is imminent, but despite all my preparations, I'm still nervous. I stop in front of the house instead of pulling into the garage, and before I've even turned the car off, Valentina is out of her car seat and trying to open the door, eager to see her mother. When I open it for her, she bounds out and reaches the front door just as Nancy, the new housekeeper, opens it. "Hello, Miss Valentina. Welcome home."

Valentina gives her a shy smile. "Mommy? Mommy?" she hollers, running from the hallway toward the kitchen.

"Where's Mrs. Hunter?" I ask.

Nancy points in the direction of the kitchen. "She baked sugar cookies for Valentina."

Sugar cookies are Valentina's favorite. I'm pleased that Cassandra is trying.

When I walk into the kitchen, Cassandra is kneeling, her arms opened wide, but Valentina is just standing there, staring at her.

"You're not my mommy. I want my mommy!"

Despite the hypnosis, I'm not surprised at her reaction. After all, aside from the dark hair and similar build, the new Cassandra looks very different from the mother she remembers. I've hypnotized Valentina to believe that her real mother had green eyes. It's a happy coincidence that this Cassandra has green eyes, like Valentina's; it should help to cement the belief in both of them that they are related. My mother's eyes were the same green.

I come up behind Valentina and put a hand on her shoulder. "Valentina, it's okay. Click in," I say, using her trigger words. She's quiet suddenly, and I whisper, "That's Mommy. You love Mommy. It's the Mommy you remember, she just looks different because of how her face was hurt in the car accident." I stand again. "You're with me," I say quietly, and she comes out of the trance.

She takes a tentative step toward Cassandra, whose expression is anxious. "Mommy?"

"Yes, sweetheart. It's me. I made your favorite. Sugar cookies."

Valentina allows Cassandra to hug her, but I can tell

that she's holding back. It's a start, though. They will have time to have new experiences together, and after a while Valentina will love her just as much as she loved her first mommy.

"Why don't you have a seat, and I'll get you some milk," Cassandra suggests.

Valentina puts her hands on her hips. "I'm lergic to milk." She turns toward me, her face red and angry. "I told you that's not my mommy."

How did I forget to tell Cassandra about Valentina's allergy? "Valentina, no. Mommy meant almond milk."

Valentina doesn't look quite convinced, but she sits down at her little table. Cassandra hands her a plate with two cookies on it. Cassandra's about to say something, I can tell, but I give her a look that says *I'll explain later.* When Valentina finishes, Nancy takes her upstairs to help her unpack.

Cassandra looks at me. "How could I forget that she has a milk allergy?"

"You didn't know, honey. She just recently developed an intolerance. You were in the hospital at the time, and then, of course, she was with my father. It's my fault for forgetting to tell you."

"Oh," she says. "I just feel so strange. Like I'm walking around in a cloud half the time."

I put my arms around her and pull her toward me.

"It's okay, my love. It's probably just the meds, which can make you feel a bit fuzzy at first. You'll get used to it."

I have her on a combination of Tofranil and Halcion. I can't depend on the hypnosis alone to ensure she doesn't remember who she really is. I have to keep a close eye on her and watch the interactions and side effects for any signs of tremors, but so far, the drugs are keeping her just confused enough to depend solely on me. It's my hope that over time I can wean her off them, once I'm confident that the rewiring in her brain is permanent. But as I know all too well, the brain is a most unpredictable organ.

She leans her head on my shoulder. "I just want to feel good again, to feel like myself."

I lift her chin and touch my lips to hers. "It will get better. And in the meantime, you can lean on me. I'll always take care of you."

"I don't know what I'd do without you," she whispers.

I smile. "Fortunately, you'll never have to find out."

54
Julian

"I don't want to wear a jacket. It will hide my Belle shirt," Valentina tells me, her arms crossed across her chest in defiance.

"Sweetie, it's cool today, and we'll be outside," I tell her. "You can take it off when we have lunch."

"No!" She stomps a foot.

Cassandra comes out of the kitchen and kneels down next to her. "That's your favorite princess shirt, isn't it?"

Valentina's eyes are large, and she nods solemnly, but her arms are still crossed.

"Hmm, let me think. What if we put a snuggly turtleneck under it, and that way everyone would still be able to see you're wearing Belle?"

Valentina smiles. "Okay, Mommy!"

I walk over and give Cassandra a kiss. "You're so good with her," I whisper, feeling vindicated. I made the right choice. It's been a little over four months since Cassandra was reborn, and things are going wonderfully. My concerns about her and Valentina bonding have been largely unfounded. With the exception of a few meltdowns on Valentina's part when Cassandra didn't remember a favorite story or foods she hates, the transition has been smooth. I've had to have a few more sessions with Valentina, but I'm confident that from here on out, things will develop naturally.

When we arrive at Belkin Farm to go apple picking, it's still early, and we get a parking space right up front. Valentina runs ahead of us to a stand selling apple cider and doughnuts.

"Can I have a doughnut?" she asks.

"You just had breakfast, sweetie."

"Please, Daddy."

I relent and buy one for each of us, since it's a special day. We walk down the field and look at the signs for the apples, discussing which area we want to start in.

Cassandra pulls out her cell phone and snaps a few pictures of Valentina. When she's finished, she starts typing something on her phone.

"What are you doing?" I ask.

She looks up. "Just posting this one to Facebook. She looks so cute."

I grab the phone from her hand, and she looks at me in shock. "Cassandra, are you crazy? Do you know how many pedophiles scan social media for pictures of children? I don't want any photographs of her anywhere on the internet."

Her eyes well up. "I didn't realize that. I'm sorry."

"What's a ped-phile?" Valentina asks.

"A bad man, sweetie. Forget the word," I say, so angry I'm struggling to keep my voice even. I hand the phone back. "I didn't know you had a Facebook account. Are you on any other social media?"

She shakes her head no. "Just Facebook."

"We'll talk more about it later." I need some time to figure out how to handle this. "Come on, let's go pick some apples," I say cheerily, trying to salvage the day. Cassandra smiles at me, but the smile doesn't quite reach her eyes.

After we finish, I put the apples in the car and slip an arm around her. "Where would you like to go for lunch? Your choice."

She shrugs. "I don't know." She's clearly still feeling hurt.

"Well, what are you in the mood for?"

"I guess some soup might be nice."

"How about the Chowder House, then?" I know it's one of her favorites.

She nods, a bit more warmly. "Okay."

"Let's go then. Nothing better than lunch with my favorite girls."

. . .

Cassandra's upstairs, putting Valentina to bed. I pour two glasses of cabernet and wait. Things are back on an even keel, but I'm still disturbed by the thought of her posting things on Facebook. Every time I think I've covered all my bases, something new crops up.

She comes into the room and takes a seat next to me on the sofa. "Finally asleep."

I hand her a glass and lift mine in a toast. "To the best mother in the world."

She blushes but taps her glass against mine and takes a sip.

"It was a nice day, don't you think?" I begin.

"Mmm-hmm. But we'll never eat all those apples." She laughs. "I guess I'll be baking some pies."

"That sounds delicious." Turning to her, I brush a stray hair from her forehead. "Cassandra, I wanted to apologize for what happened. I should never have grabbed your phone from you. I sort of lost it for a minute there."

She bites her lip. "Thanks. I was a bit surprised."

"You see, I had a patient whose daughter was kidnapped and murdered after a stalker saw her picture on social media."

She gasps. "What?"

I nod. "Yes, you can't imagine the ways in which things can be tracked these days. Apparently he got into her Facebook profile and saw the photos and began obsessing about the little girl. He found out their location because of the geo info on the images, and eventually took her from their house." It's not actually a specific case that I'm citing, but I know that these kinds of things happen all the time.

Her face is white. "That's horrible. I just downloaded the app last week. But all my privacy settings are on. I didn't think it was a risk."

"There are some very sophisticated hackers out there. Even when you think your privacy is protected, it's not. It's crazy how often big companies are hacked and all their customers' private data leaked. It's really not safe to put anything out there." I sigh. "And not just about Valentina, but you as well."

"You think?"

My mind is filled with thoughts of people from Amelia's old life coming across her image and tracking her down.

"I do. I'd die if anything happened to you. I think it's best if you stay off all social media."

"I guess you're right."

"Good, I'm glad that's settled. Relax and drink your wine."

She shouldn't actually be drinking with her medication, but one glass won't really hurt, and it tends to put her in a better mood, make her more compliant. We finish up, and I lean in to kiss her. "Do you feel like the medicine is helping the depression?" I ask.

She nods. "Yes, I think so."

"I love you so much, Cassandra."

"I love you too."

A feeling of contentment washes over me. Everything is as it should be.

55
Julian

"When are they going to throw the big ball, Daddy?" Valentina asks, for the tenth time already.

I give her an indulgent smile. I know that she'll be asleep on the couch by ten o'clock, but I don't want to dampen her enthusiasm. I've planned a lovely evening for our second New Year's Eve as a family. It's been over a year and a half since Amelia became Cassandra, and the transformation is complete. We are a family. Just the three of us, with balloons, streamers, and a smorgasbord of food—shrimp, filet mignon, lobster tail, and for dessert, all the fixings for ice cream sundaes. Valentina has been looking forward to it all day.

But Cassandra has been in a mood all day, complaining of climbing the walls and being sick of the dreary winter weather, and she went upstairs midafternoon to take a nap. We had another eight inches of snow last night, and the temperatures haven't been above freezing for weeks. I've tried to cheer her up, even promised that we'd take a trip somewhere warm in February, after the dregs have completed their postholiday travel. The last thing I want to do is be stuck inside a crowded plane with a bunch of tourists. But she remains sullen.

At five thirty, I go to check on her. When I enter the bedroom, she's awake, sitting on the edge of the bed, looking at her phone.

"Hi," I say, keeping my voice light.

She gives me a sour look. "I wanted to go out tonight."

"I've planned a wonderful evening. All your favorite foods." I list what's on the menu.

"I'm going stir-crazy. I know it's too late to get a sitter for Valentina, but can't we three at least go out for an early dinner?"

I take a deep breath and warn myself to answer carefully. "We've already been over this. New Year's Eve is amateur's night. The roads will be filled with drunks."

She rolls her eyes. "We haven't been out in ages. We don't have any friends. I'm going crazy. I need people!" She yells the last sentence, her eyes bulging in a way that's not particularly attractive.

I've never been one for large groups of friends, much preferring my own company, but before the first Cassandra died, we did socialize occasionally with some colleagues. I can't risk exposing the new Cassandra to them, though. Despite the cover story about her car accident, too many things could go wrong. And I don't have the energy to form new friendships. Why can't she be content with Valentina and me? We should be enough.

I walk over to the bed and take a seat next to her, then make my voice as calm as possible. "I understand that you want to go out. But you have to remember we have a young child, and it could be dangerous to be on the roads with her." She says nothing, just keeps looking down at the floor. "What if you and I go away next weekend? I'll see if Nancy can stay with Valentina, and we can fly out to Las Vegas. Sit by the pool, see some shows. Even play some slots. What do you think?"

She looks up, her eyes wide. "Really?"

I smile. "Yes. It will be good to get out of this dreary cold and just have some time to ourselves. I'll arrange it tomorrow."

"Thank you," she whispers, and leans in to kiss me.

Now that her good humor is restored, we can salvage the evening and make it a good New Year's Eve for Valentina. "Shall we go and celebrate?"

"Yes, I'm just going to grab a shower and change. I'll be downstairs in a few."

"Perfect. I'll get the apps ready."

Once in the kitchen, I open the refrigerator and transfer the food I picked up earlier to our china platters. The shrimp are plump and pink, the filet cooked to a perfect medium, and the fresh asparagus seasoned with oil and herbs. I pop the mac-and-cheese bites that Valentina loves into the microwave, humming as I go. I've already opened a bottle of wine, and I pour myself a generous glass and take a sip. I hear the sound of little footsteps and look up to see Valentina come in, precious in a dark-green velvet dress with a pretty red sash. Cassandra has fixed her hair into a French braid.

"Princess! You look beautiful."

"Thank you, Daddy. Is it almost next year?"

I pick her up and spin her around, then kiss her cheek loudly. "Not yet, my love. It's only six o'clock. Can you figure out how many more hours until midnight?"

She looks up at the ceiling, ticking off the numbers on her hands as she counts. "Seven, eight, nine, ten, eleven, twelve." She looks at me and shouts, "Six!"

"That's right, my smart girl. Do you want to help Daddy put these trays on the table in the living room? We're going to have some appetizers before dinner."

She nods. "What's a patizer?"

"Appetizer. Something to satisfy your appetite."

After we set everything down, she runs toward the stairs. "I'm going to go get Mommy. It's time for the party to start."

I find a jazz playlist on my phone and stream it to the speakers in the bookcase, then light the candles I've placed around the room. Just because we're spending the evening at home doesn't mean we can't have some atmosphere. Cassandra will see how much better it is to be safe and sound with the ones who love her.

Once everything is set, I bring the wine out and pour a small glass for her.

"Well, you've created quite a setting," she says as she comes into the room, holding Valentina's hand. She looks beautiful in a dress of her own, this one a deep-cranberry knit that hugs her body, and I feel a stirring of desire. When I came up with the plan to replace Valentina's mother, my only thought was for my child, and a part of me feels guilty that I'm enjoying the new Cassandra so much. Then again, if she and I are happy together, it *is* better for Valentina.

"Thank you. I wanted to make tonight special for my two special ladies."

Valentina giggles. "Look Mommy, appetite tizers." She points to the trays.

Cassandra laughs and takes a shrimp and pops it in her mouth. "Delicious!"

We chat and drink, and the evening goes as planned. We have our dinner around eight thirty, and I notice Valentina's eyes beginning to droop. After we settle her on the sofa under a soft blanket, she's asleep within minutes. Despite my warnings, Cassandra drinks two more glasses of wine, and then she's fast asleep on the couch too. I tuck her in and glance at my watch. Eleven thirty. Do I dare risk it? Deciding that they're both out cold, I grab two glasses, tiptoe from the room and open the door to the basement, then use my phone flashlight to descend the staircase to the wine cellar. I open its door and lock myself inside, then pull out the bottle of Opus One that I've placed dead center on the far wall. I push the button, and there is a whirring noise. Within seconds, the wall opens into my secret room.

I had this room created right after Cassandra died. I take a seat on the maroon velvet couch, the high-end Victorian look she loves, and set down the wine and the glasses on the marble-top table. The wall is filled with pictures of Cassandra and me from our life together. The real Cassandra. In the center of the room is a custom-made easel on which sits a life-size portrait of her from our wedding day. She looks magnificent, and I can almost believe it's really her, here and looking at me. Sighing, I turn around and pour two glasses of wine. Holding one in each hand, I lift mine in tribute.

A thrill of desire like molten lava courses through my veins. I haven't entered this room in months, not since I brought the new Cassandra home. "My precious. How I've missed you. You must forgive me for staying away so long. It wasn't safe to visit. But I'm here, darling, and I promise, I will come and see you every week." Now that I've experimented with the dosages, I can just give new Cassandra a little extra any night when I want to come and visit.

I pour myself a fresh glass of wine and add to hers, setting it on the table in front of me. "Cheers, darling. To a new year." Taking a long sip, I lean back and sigh. I hate that things turned out the way they did, and that instead of her being the one upstairs, alive and well, I have only her image to keep me company.

"You'll be happy to know that Valentina is doing very well," I tell her. "She believes that you're still caring for her. I hope you understand that's why I have to pretend to love your replacement. But please don't think for one minute that she's replaced you in my heart. No one ever will." I stare at her picture, thinking back to our wedding day and how much in love we were. "I'm sorry that I had to photoshop you out of the wedding pictures in the house. I did it for Valentina. But you will always be my one true love."

I stay with her for another half hour, until it's after midnight. I need to get upstairs, just in case anyone does wake up. But I'm happy, truly happy, for the first time in so long. Standing, I lift my glass one more time. "Happy New Year, darling Cassandra. It's going to be a good one."

56
Julian

Cassandra has been complaining that the medicine is making her tired all the time and giving her headaches. Another unpleasant side effect is that she's gained weight. I have to leave for the hospital in an hour, and I check to see if she's out of bed. I sigh. She's still sound asleep, her hair a mess, a slight snore escaping her lips. This slovenly, overweight, out-of-it version is testing my nerves. I wonder about adding Adderall to the mix as an appetite suppressant and make a mental note to look up the drug interactions.

I wrinkle my nose in distaste, then walk over to the bed and nudge her arm.

"It's time to get up."

"What time is it?" she mumbles, her eyes still closed.

"Seven thirty. You didn't see Valentina off to school.

Nancy had to get her breakfast." I stop myself before I say something I'll regret, but what I want to say is that she's not being a good mother. Over the twenty months she's been here, her moods have been up and down. Valentina is five years old. Even though she is thriving in her private school, I had hoped that Cassandra would be up to the task of homeschooling her, but she is incapable of it.

Her eyes open, and she brushes the hair from them. "Sorry. Just so tired."

I try to remind myself that it's not entirely her fault; the meds are making her this way. I take a gentler tone. "I know, we're all tired, but life goes on. I'm leaving soon for work, and I'd appreciate having my wife get out of bed to see me off."

She sits up and slowly lifts herself out of bed, the nightgown tighter on her body than it used to be.

"Once you're dressed, can you meet me in the kitchen? I'd like to go over your day before I leave."

She nods and heads to the bathroom, and I go downstairs to pour myself a cup of coffee and glance at the paper. It's time for me to give her a project. There was never any question about her going back to work, and in any case, her dependence and confusion have eliminated any desire she had to do so. I had planned on having her spend her days teaching Valentina, but since she can't do that, there's nothing to occupy her. I have to give her something to do. Otherwise she might *truly* become depressed, not just medicated.

She lumbers into the kitchen, pours herself a cup of coffee, and plops down in the chair across from me. "I had the nightmare again," she says.

I sigh. This is also getting wearisome.

She shivers. "It's the one where everyone's dead, and I'm screaming, but I don't know who they are or what happened."

I put my mug down and look at her. "I've told you before, it's all those horror books you read. You're very suggestible. You have to stop polluting your brain with such vile content."

"Maybe you're right. It's just I'm so bored. I need to get out of this house. Talk to some other people, make some friends. Why don't I have any friends?"

She's been asking this more and more. "We've talked about this, Cassandra. When you got so depressed, right before you tried to take your life, you cut off all your friends."

"I did?"

"Yes, you made quite a scene actually, remember? It was at your thirty-fifth birthday party. You drank too much wine, and when it was time to sing 'Happy Birthday,' you picked up the cake and threw it on the floor. Then you told everyone to screw themselves, but you used more vulgar language."

She puts her head in her hands and is quiet. I've told her this story enough times that she believes it now. "I was jealous. I thought you were sleeping with my best friend, and that everyone knew and was keeping it from me."

I nod. "Your delusions were at their height." I reach out my hand and rest it on hers. "I tried to tell you that I'd never look at another woman, but you wouldn't believe it. This is another reason you're on medicine now. Without it, you can get quite violent. And we can't have you hurting Valentina."

Her eyes go wide, and she shakes her head. "I would never hurt her."

I give her a solemn look. "You say that now, but you've done things. We won't speak of them now, since I promised you we wouldn't mention them again, but it's not a good idea for you to be around new people. Anything could happen."

She's crying now. "What am I supposed to do with myself all day while you and Valentina are gone? I'm stuck here all day. You won't even get me a car."

"You know it's not safe to drive on your medicine. The last time you did, you almost hit a child. Right before you crashed into the wall and ruined your face."

"What?" She looks horrified. Though she knows the story of the car crash, this is a new detail I am adding to the false narrative.

"Yes, we didn't tell you at the time because you were too vulnerable. But I can't withhold the information any longer if you're going to start talking about driving again. You were so intent on hurting yourself that you didn't notice a little girl on her bike and had to swerve into a fence to avoid hitting her. You didn't stop but kept going and then . . . you know . . . you ended up quite smashed up."

She swallows hard and looks at her mug.

I pull out a piece of paper. "You can do the things I've outlined here. I've left you recipes for soups, casseroles, breads. You can prepare healthy meals and start doing more for me and Valentina."

She takes the paper from me wordlessly and scans it. When she looks back at me, I see an emotion I haven't in a while. Anger. "You're joking, right? You expect me to just stay in this house and cook all day?"

I snatch it back and glare at her. "You're lucky I don't—" I stop myself and take a deep breath. "You need to think about everything I've put up with. Your depression, your moods, your crazy temper. Maybe you'd be better off back in the sanitarium."

The threat is enough to douse the rebellion in her

eyes. "Julian, please. I need more than this. I'm going crazy here."

I raise an eyebrow. "My thoughts exactly." But I realize that she does need something more. She's no good to me, and to Valentina, if she's this miserable. "I'm sorry, let me think about it. We can talk more tonight, okay?"

She nods. "Thank you."

A former patient of mine is the head librarian at the town library just down the road. I'll tell Cassandra to apply for a job there. I'll make sure she doesn't get it, of course, but the process of applying should keep her busy for a while. She'll appreciate the fact that I tried to help her, but won't blame me for the fact that she's not qualified enough. I'll get the credit for the effort and get to play the hero. A role I very much enjoy.

In the meantime, I've hired a trainer to come and work out with her in an effort to get her back into shape. Even my devotion has its limits. I need her to be as close to the original Cassandra I married as possible.

57

Julian

Even though Cassandra seems fully assimilated, I did have a scare last week. We were watching a television drama that takes place in Florida. I intentionally suggested it, wanting to see if I'd been as successful as I thought in eradicating her memories of growing up there. After the first episode, there was no reaction, but in the next episode there was a scene at the beach, and she began to get visibly agitated.

"Turn it off!" she shouted, standing up from the sofa.

"What's the matter?" I asked.

She began to tremble. "I don't know. The beach. It looks familiar. Something bad happened there." She was pacing then.

"But you grew up in Maryland," I reminded her,

sticking to the backstory that mirrored Cassandra's. "There are no palm trees in Maryland."

"Maybe I went to Florida with my parents, or one of my foster families," she suggested.

I needed to see how much she could remember. I went to her, took her hands in mine, and gently squeezed them. "Take a deep breath. Sit down and close your eyes. See if you can remember."

She did as I asked. After a few moments, I prodded again. "Picture that beach. What do you see?"

Her lip quivered, and a tear rolled down her cheek. "He's going to drown her." Her voice sounded young, childlike.

"Who?"

As if she hadn't heard me, she began to yell. "Let her up, let her up. Stop! You're killing her."

"Cassandra, listen to me. Who are you yelling at?"

Her breath was coming in ragged gasps. "My father, it's my father. He's holding her under. She didn't want to go in the ocean, and he made her. No no no no."

I needed to calm her down. "Imagine," I say, using our trigger word.

She became still.

"You are safe, and no one can hurt you. You're watching a movie. It's not happening in real time. Tell me what you see."

Her breathing became more even and her voice less frantic, though it still sounded young. "We're having a nice day on the beach. Building sandcastles. Mommy is reading a book. Shannon and I are running back and forth to the water to fill our buckets."

"Go on."

"He's drinking beer. Mommy tells him to take it easy, and he gets mad. Tells her to shut her mouth. She gets upset and leaves. He tells us it's time to go in the water, but Shannon's scared of the waves. He calls her a stupid baby." Then her voice changed, and she imitated a man. "Get your ass in that water now before I throw you in."

Wrapping her arms tightly around her torso, she shrank back into the sofa cushions. "Come on, Shannon. It's okay. I'm with you." Her voice changed again to imitate the man. "Come on, you piece of shit." And then it's her voice again. "He's dragging her by the arm, and she's crying. Then he's holding her under the water."

"Does he let her go eventually?"

Cassandra shuddered. "Finally. She grabs on to me, and he swims away and goes back to the umbrella."

"Hear me, Cassandra. This didn't happen to you. It was a movie you saw when you were little. It scared you so much, you felt like you lived it. But you grew up in Maryland. You've never been to Florida. Repeat after me."

"I've never been to Florida."

I made a note to reinforce this changed memory in our sessions later that week. I know firsthand how you can take someone's memory and manipulate it. Confabulation. The trick is to use truth laced with fabrication. A mother takes a trip to the park with her child. You talk to the mother about what happened on that day, based on the facts she has already told you. Now you insert a lie. You ask the mother if she remembers her child getting lost in the park. The mother looks puzzled. *No.* Ah, but don't you remember how afraid you were? you ask her. She thinks for a moment. *Oh, yes, now I remember.* And the most incredible thing happens next. She begins to build an elaborate scenario to describe in detail everything that happened while the child was lost, the panic she felt, the relief when she found the child. It's fascinating how the mind can so easily deceive itself. There is no such thing as ethics when it comes to the mind and its manipulation.

I suppose it's a little like being God, this power to influence the mind. The more time passes, the more convinced I am that I can mold anyone into anything as long as they trust me enough to work with me. I've thought about writing my own book, trumpeting my victories, but as much as I'd like to share my discoveries, I can't risk unscrupulous people using my techniques to their own advantage. I use it to make my patients' lives better, to rid others of pain, and to make a happy family for myself. What higher purpose is there than that?

· · ·

I made some more adjustments during subsequent hypnosis sessions, and Cassandra is behaving much better. After the Las Vegas memory I embedded last New Year's worked so well, I've been planting "memory outings" more frequently, and she has stopped complaining about not going out.

One good thing is that she's lost that extra weight and isn't walking around like a zombie anymore. I've been able to wean her off most of her medicine and give her only an occasional benzo. Benzodiazepines have been known to impair long-term memory, which reduces the chance she will remember her actual past, but I have to be careful because they can cause permanent brain damage. The fact that she's been on them for six months is already dangerous. So now I give her an Ativan a few times a week to relax when I feel she's beginning to become agitated, and that is helping to keep things on an even keel.

Valentina is still happy, and she and Cassandra have

completely bonded. Two years after Cassandra's return, there is no question in my daughter's mind that she has her mother back, and that makes all of this worthwhile. Naturally, I still miss the true Cassandra, and must admit that this version is not as interesting to me, or as good a match. But at least I can visit with her on Sunday evenings, the night I give the new Cassandra a tranquilizer.

School will be out in a couple of weeks, and we plan to spend a month at the cabin in New Hampshire that my father left to me after his sudden death last month. I always thought it would be the Parkinson's that got him, but he had a heart attack in the middle of the night and died all alone in his Arizona home. His death hit me harder than I anticipated. Since his retirement, our weekly phone calls have been something I've looked forward to and enjoyed. I couldn't have him come to the house and meet Cassandra, of course. But I managed to take Valentina to see him for a long weekend a few months ago. Cassandra wanted to come, but I convinced her that she had a fear of flying, so she stayed home. He was a good grandfather to Valentina. I'm sorry that she has to lose another close family member. But the silver lining is that I don't have to worry that he will discover that I've replaced the real Cassandra with another woman.

58
Julian

It's a beautiful summer day, and we're strolling around Faneuil Hall. Valentina and I are in line for ice cream, and Cassandra waits for us on a nearby bench. Just after we've paid and start to walk toward her, I notice a woman approaching my wife from the other direction. Frowning, I take Valentina's hand and hurry over to see what's going on.

The woman calls, "Amelia!" and I freeze.

But Cassandra just gives her a quizzical look. "Excuse me?"

"Amelia, it's me, Rena. From work."

I watch Cassandra closely to see if there is any spark of recognition, but she shakes her head. "I'm sorry, but you must have me confused with someone else. My name's Cassandra."

The woman starts to speak again, then puts a hand up. "My mistake. I thought you were a woman I worked with at the museum." Her eyes narrow as they travel over Cassandra's face. "Are you sure . . . Oh, never mind. Sorry to bother you." She walks away, clearly embarrassed.

I'm relieved that Cassandra didn't recognize the woman, but this worries me. Cassandra is still staring after her. She turns to me with a puzzled expression. "That was so strange. She must have confused me with someone else."

Before I can answer, Valentina comes running up.

"Mommy, Mommy, here's your ice cream cone." Valentina hands her a chocolate cone while taking a lick from her own strawberry one. Cassandra takes it, but I can see she's still thinking about Rena.

"Valentina, go over to the stand and grab some napkins, please." I turn to Cassandra. "I'm sure she was just mistaken," I say. "*Imagine.* She was just confused."

Cassandra nods, a faraway look in her eyes.

"You've never seen that woman before."

"I've never seen her before."

"*Come back,*" I say.

Cassandra blinks.

Valentina comes running back with a hand full of napkins.

"Shall we walk around a bit and window-shop while we eat our ice cream?" I ask.

She nods, and we begin to walk.

"I love it here," Cassandra says.

I smile. This is the last time she'll be out of the house for a long time.

. . .

Why can't new Cassandra just be contented to be a stay-at-home wife? I've given her everything she could ask for. A sweet and loving child, a doting husband, a housekeeper to attend to her every need, and a beautiful home in which to live. But she continues to be unhappy as fall approaches. Despite my modifications to her weekly hypnosis sessions, now aimed at convincing her that she's afraid to leave the house, she's begun to complain more and more about being "stuck at home." Her bad moods are even starting to affect Valentina, who begins kindergarten in two weeks, and that I cannot have.

She's still hounding me about getting a job, but I can't have her out in the world; it's too risky. And I can't hire her to work at my office at the hospital, because my colleagues have met the real Cassandra. It's a dilemma I've been struggling with since we got back from the lake. The only conclusion that I've been able to come to is that we have to move far away, somewhere

where the chances of anyone from her past life seeing her are minuscule, where no one knows me or my first wife. The inconvenience, of course, is that I'd have to give up my practice and start again. Fortunately my father's estate was sizable, and I've accumulated a good amount of savings over the years. We have plenty of money, and I could get another position at a new hospital so that I can continue my work.

"Julian, can I talk to you?"

She's standing at the door to my home office, looking disheveled again.

"Of course."

She comes in and takes a chair across from my desk, but doesn't say anything for a moment. Instead she looks down at her lap, her hand twisting the cord of the pullover she's wearing. When she lifts her gaze to meet mine, I see that her eyes are red-rimmed from crying. "I wanted to wait until Valentina was asleep. I appreciate your patience with my recovery." She looks at her wrists. "Now that I'm off most of the medicine, I do feel well enough to go back to work. I know you keep saying it could stress me out and send me back into a depression, but being trapped in this house is not good for me. I know it didn't work out with the library job, but there's got to be something I can do."

I smile at her. "You're absolutely right."

She gives me a surprised look. "Really?"

I nod. "Yes, I was thinking about it too. You are much better, and I have been a bit overprotective. What kind of work do you think you'd like to do?"

She shrugs. "That's just it. I don't know."

I'm not surprised. She has no idea that she has a bachelor's degree or that she used to restore photos at a museum. The story she knows of herself is one of a woman constantly on the brink of a breakdown. She thinks she's never had a job since we've been married, and that I've stood by her through depression, delusions, and her attempted suicide.

"Well, before we were married you were working at a department store, trying to get on your feet after being released from foster care," I tell her. "You liked it enough, but I think we need to figure out what your interests are and then go from there."

She gives me a helpless look. "I do love children. Maybe I could get a job at Valentina's school."

I think. The old Cassandra doesn't have a bachelor's degree and I'm not sure what position she'd be able to obtain with only a high school diploma. Maybe the answer is not getting her a job, but having her go back to school. In fact, she could do online courses from home, solving both our problems at once.

"Do you mean a teaching job?"

"Maybe."

Annoyance fills me. "You need a degree for that. And besides, you weren't interested in homeschooling your own child. Why would you want to teach other children?"

"It's not the same thing, Julian."

I sigh. "Why don't we look into some of the local universities and see if you could work toward your bachelor's degree?"

She seems appeased. "I like that idea."

"It's settled, then. We'll look into it first thing on Monday. It'll be a lot of work, but I'll help to pick up the slack at home."

"Thank you, Julian," she says, throwing her arms around me. "I'm excited."

I return her embrace. "Great, let's go celebrate."

We go to the bedroom, and I shut and lock the door. As we slide under the covers, she presses her body against mine, kissing me deeply. "I love you," she whispers.

"I love you too," I answer, and lose myself in her while we make love. Afterward, I gaze at her while she dozes. Maybe we won't have to move after all. We'll get her enrolled in some online courses, and I'll ramp up the hypnosis to make her believe she's an agoraphobic. The wonderful thing about today's technology is that her world can be confined to the four walls of this house.

59
Julian

I have the house to myself overnight for the first time that I can remember, and have decided to open the Odette Estate Reserve in honor of the special occasion. Valentina and her mother are at a group sleepover for kindergarten children and their parents at the New England Aquarium. Cassandra insisted upon going, but our hypnosis will begin again tomorrow, and soon she'll be too afraid to leave the house at all. I'm confident I'll be able to make her believe that the only safe place for her is within these walls. Why not let her have one last outing with Valentina?

"Hello, my darling," I tell the real Cassandra as soon as I enter the secret room, wine bottle and glasses in hand. "We have the whole night to ourselves." I pour my wine and take a sip, and then put hers down on the table. I tell her all about Valentina's latest exploits. How well she is doing in kindergarten, and how much she reminds me of her mother. "I miss you so much. The last two years without you have felt like an eternity." I lean back and take another sip, thinking of all the nights the two of us would sit together and talk about our day. "You won't believe it," I tell her, "but Valentina has asked for horseback riding lessons. Her best friend rides, and she's now insistent that she try it. At first I said no, after all, it's dangerous, but then I thought of how much you used to talk about wanting to ride. You never had the chance, so I think I will make sure our daughter does." I don't mention that the new Cassandra has reservations about it. I don't think she'd appreciate hearing about her replacement. Suddenly I feel gloomy. It shouldn't be this way. She should still be with me, watching our daughter grow up together. Despite having told her a hundred times, I find myself apologizing once again. "You don't know how much I regret losing my temper. If only you'd been willing to listen to me, to calm down. We could have worked this all out. I would never have had to replace you." As I pour myself another glass of wine, I close my eyes, remembering the last time I saw her.

It had been a long day, and I'd been looking forward to a quiet evening at home. When I turned the key in the lock, I heard the sound of the television blaring from the den.

Valentina was by herself, watching a children's show, and Cassandra was nowhere in sight. What the hell had possessed her to leave our daughter in the room alone?

"Hello," I called out.

Valentina was sitting on the sofa, mesmerized, and didn't even hear me come in. I walked over and stood in front of the television. She looked up, and a wide grin lit up her face.

"Daddy!" She jumped from the sofa and ran to me.

"Hello, princess. How's my girl?"

"Did you bring me something?"

I pretended to think. "Hmmm, I don't know. Let me see." I opened my briefcase. "What's this?" I pulled out a Moana doll.

"Yay," she said as she reached for it.

"Uh, where's my kiss?" I leaned down, and she gave me a peck on my cheek, then grabbed the doll and started playing with it.

Something was wrong. Valentina was only three years old. Cassandra would never leave her by herself for longer than a few minutes. "Where's Mommy?" I asked Valentina, hoping she couldn't hear the trepidation in my voice.

She pointed a finger toward the stairs.

"Come with me," I said, and taking her by the hand, I led her upstairs and to her room. "Play with your toys, sweetheart. Daddy will be right back." My unease built as I headed to our bedroom and saw that the door was closed. What was Cassandra doing in there with the door shut, making it hard for her to hear Valentina, and why had she left our young daughter alone? It wasn't like her. I wondered if she was getting depressed again. It might be time to have her start another round of therapy.

"Cassandra? Where are you?"

There was no answer. I turned the door handle and entered to find Cassandra sitting at the dressing table, a book in her hands.

"Cassandra?"

She spun around and glared at me. Her face was puffy and her eyes red from crying. "I can't believe this. You beast!"

I flinched. "What are you talking about?"

"Shut the door. I don't want Valentina to hear."

I obeyed, and started to go to her, but she put up a hand. "Don't come any closer."

She was completely unhinged.

"What is the matter with you?"

She stuck her chin out defiantly. "You lied to me. All that time, I believed my husband hurt me, and you tricked me into believing it. I left him because of you, my *therapist!* What kind of man does what you did?"

It was then that I noticed she was holding my personal logbook from her file. How had she gotten it? Everything important had been locked in my safe. The room began to spin. I sat down on the bed, taking deep breaths.

"How did you get that?" I said finally.

She laughed, a bitter sound. "That's your first question? How did I get it?"

"I can explain."

"Oh really?" She looked down at the book in her hand and began to read aloud:

August 17: Cassandra Dryer, 27-year-old female, married, presenting with acute depression brought on by 3 miscarriages over a period of 2 years. Family history: Orphaned at age twelve, foster care until age eighteen, six different homes.
September 9: Husband emotionally absent and unsupportive. Intuition tells me he is not only emotionally but physically abusive as well, perhaps the cause of Cassandra's miscarriages, although she does not admit this. A careful step-by-step program will give her the strength to leave the marriage. It will take meticulous guidance and support. Swiftness is critical,

so I will need to see her several times a week, perhaps even daily. If she stays with this man, she will die, just as all of her unborn children have died.

September 30: Disclosure of sexual abuse at age fourteen, first foster home. Hypnosis has revealed more than one abuser over four years. Working on memory erasure to eradicate trauma. Explained the potential pitfalls of this treatment, but she's insistent. She has not shared any of this past abuse with her husband. Becoming clear to me it's because he is also abusive. She feels ashamed and, on some level, has chosen a man who mirrors her earlier abusers. Despite her insistence that he has never physically harmed her, it is clear she's adept at repression. I'm convinced that he has abused her, that he is in fact the reason she keeps having miscarriages. Her depression will never go away if she stays with him.

She glares at me, turning to another page, and continues reading.

October 20: Implantation of false memory of Zane pushing her down the stairs, causing miscarriage. In a few more sessions I'll implant enough false memories of his abuse to make sure she never wants to see him again. We will work together to modify in her memory *the horrible things that happened to her growing up but leave the planted memories of her abusive husband intact. She will need to remember those in order to leave him and live with me. Only I can save her, I see that now. And this way, she'll always be grateful that I saved her.*

She looks up from the book to me, and her eyes narrow with contempt.

"You're taking that out of context," I tell her, pleading. "Your husband did hurt you. I love you, Cassandra, we have a family."

"Don't! *I* have a family. You have nothing after today. I'm going to report you to the medical board. You'll never be able to do this to anyone again."

"You have to understand, I didn't do anything except love you."

She threw something at me. A book. I picked it up, and dread filled me. My father's book: *False Memories: The Unreliability of the Brain.*

She had started talking fast. "I stopped by my office to see about going back part-time. They'd been holding a box Zane dropped off. There was a note from him inside. They hadn't known how to get in touch with me, so they'd kept it for me all this time. Your father's book was in the box, along with my diary. I called Zane, and he told me how you made sure he couldn't get in touch with me." She gave me a venomous look, and her fists were convulsed with suppressed rage. "That horrible day you had me 'remember'?" She puts the word in air quotes. "The day Zane threw me down the stairs? That was over the Fourth of July weekend. Zane was out of town that whole time." She walked over to me with her diary and pointed. "It's all here. He wasn't even around on that other weekend when you made me believe that he'd raped and beat me. You made me believe my husband was abusive, when he never did anything wrong! I ruined his life and my marriage because of your lies. I can't believe I came to you for help, and you brainwashed me and then seduced me."

I felt like I was stuck in mud. Her words were flying at me too fast for me to process them, much less defend myself. The only way for me to get out of this was to hypnotize her again, then administer more sodium amytal, but there was no way I could start the hypnosis session when she was in that state. I had to try and calm her down, prevent her from taking any rash actions, and then maybe I could do it when she was sleeping.

So I said the only thing I could think of. "I know it looks bad. But I can explain. He did abuse you. Maybe not physically, but emotionally. The same way my father withheld emotion from my mother. She killed herself because of that. You were depressed. It was your husband's fault. I was saving you."

"*Saving* me? By implanting false memories? Making me believe things that weren't true?"

"I was trying to help you."

"After I read my diary and realized that Zane couldn't have done what you said, I knew I had to find my files. I went to your office at the hospital earlier today. I knew you had your appointment for your physical this morning and wouldn't be there."

"What? How did you get inside my office? It's locked."

"It's amazing the things people will do for you when you ask nicely. I convinced the custodian that I was going to surprise you by redecorating your office. He let me in." Her voice is tinged with menace. "I found all of your notes. It's all spelled out in black and white, how you implanted those memories of him hurting me." She was raging, her voice rising hysterically. "Why, Julian? Why?"

How could I make her understand that I did it because I knew instinctively that her husband wasn't right for her, and she needed a push to leave him? It wouldn't have been enough to convince her based on his indifference or his cruelty about the miscarriages. He *was* abusive, maybe not physically, or maybe she blocked it out, but I knew that if she believed he'd hurt her physically, she'd feel justified in leaving. Abuse is abuse, but she couldn't see that emotional abuse is as potent as physical. I couldn't save my mother, but I could save her. All I did was alleviate her misguided sense of right and help her to do the best thing for her.

Instead, I just said, "I love you. More than he ever did. You needed to be with me."

"You're sick. I'm leaving, and I'm taking Valentina. And I'm filing charges tomorrow." She grabbed the papers and books from the table and held them to her chest. I reached out to stop her, and she snatched her arm away. "If you touch me, I'll tell them you've been abusing me as well. As it is, I hope you go to prison for what you did."

She started to leave the room, but I was behind her. I pulled her back.

"You can't do this. What about Valentina? I'm her father!"

She gave me a look that sent shivers down my spine. "She won't even remember you. I'm going to make sure you never see her again. I'll find another man to be her father, and she'll love him, think of him as her father. You'll be nothing to her . . ."

All I saw was red. I reached out and put my hands around her throat and squeezed. I couldn't listen anymore. "Shut up, shut up, shut up!" I screamed, over and over, at full volume. Suddenly she went limp, and her knees buckled. I let go, and she fell to the floor. It was then I heard a cry.

"What's wrong with Mommy?"

Valentina! Had she been standing there the whole time? I ran over to her and scooped her up. "Mommy's sleeping."

She tried to get out of my arms, crying and kicking. "Mommy, Mommy."

I let her go, and as she ran to Cassandra, I bounded down the stairs for my doctor's bag. I was careful with the dosage, but I quickly filled the syringe and took the steps back up two at a time.

I grabbed Valentina by the arm. "I'm sorry, sweetie. This will just hurt for a minute." I plunged the needle into her skin, and she was out within seconds.

I feel a tear slide down my cheek as I come back to the present, in Cassandra's cellar room. How many times have I replayed that scene over and over in my mind, changing the ending, making things turn out right? But the past can't be changed. The only thing to do is to look ahead. And everything I've done since that dark day has been in service of protecting our precious child.

I swallow the rest of the wine in my glass, staring

at her portrait. "I know it must bother you to think that she's using all your things, wearing your clothes, taking on your identity. I'm sorry that I had to let her take your name. It hurts me every time I have to call her that, but I do it for Valentina. And for you. I can't have anyone figuring out that you're gone, my love. They'd come for me, and then Valentina would be all alone."

I continue, wanting to explain everything to her. I wish I could go and visit her out in the open, put flowers on her grave, but it's not possible. "My darling, I'm so sorry that I couldn't give you a proper burial. But I can't risk anyone finding out the truth and taking Valentina. And in some ways, by turning Amelia into you, I've reincarnated you."

Suddenly I hear a scream. As I spin around, I realize it came from the new Cassandra. Before I can say anything, she bolts from the room and flies up the stairs. I run after her, panting, yelling, "Wait! You don't understand." I have to stop her before she tells someone. She slams the basement door behind her, and I bang into it, slipping back down a couple of steps. Jumping up, I scale them again, push the door open, and run into the foyer. The front door of the house is wide open.

She's running down the driveway now. I try to catch up, but it's dark. "Cassandra!" I yell, but she doesn't stop. I've almost caught up to her—I can almost touch the back of her shirt. She sprints across the street, and I follow. I hear the scream of a horn, and then everything goes black.

. . .

I open my eyes. Everything is blurry. I realize I'm in a bed, but where? There is buzzing and beeping all around me, and it hits me that I'm in a hospital emergency room. I try to sit up, but a wave of dizziness makes me fall back onto the pillow. My hand feels around, and my fingers close on something hard. I see the button for the nurse and press it. The effort exhausts me, and I close my eyes.

"Dr. Hunter?"

My eyes open again. A woman is standing by the bed.

"What happened?" I ask.

"You were hit by a car. You've been unconscious for several hours."

"What?" Then it starts to come back to me. Cassandra. Amelia found out that she is not really Cassandra. Where is she?

"Do I have a concussion?"

"I've paged the doctor. He'll be here shortly."

As I wait for the doctor to arrive, I try to piece together the events that have landed me here. I can remember now being interrupted while I talked to the old Cassandra. Why did the new Cassandra come home? She was supposed to be at a sleepover with Valentina at the aquarium. Has something happened to Valentina? Why did Cassandra come home without her? What time is it? My eyes scan the room and fix on a clock high up on the wall opposite my bed. Three a.m. Suddenly, I'm panicked. Where is Valentina, and what has happened to the new Cassandra? If I've been out for hours, she'll have had plenty of time to go to the police and tell them everything. They could be at the house now. If she heard everything I said, they could be searching for Cassandra's body in the backyard. I have to get there before they do. I sit up, despite my vertigo, and swing my legs over the side of the bed.

"Whoa, whoa." A man in blue scrubs walks in. "Where do you think you're going?"

"Home. I have to get home. My daughter—"

He interrupts me before I can finish. "I understand, but you're in no condition to drive right now." He pulls the chart from the side of my bed. "I'm Dr. Brown. Do you remember what happened?"

I shake my head.

"You were hit by a car. The driver said you ran out into the middle of the road. He called 911. You're lucky you didn't break anything. But you do have a nasty bump on your head. Luckily, the CAT scan was clear. No concussion, but since you were out for several hours, I'd like to keep you for a while more."

I have to get out of here. "Absolutely not. I'm a doctor too. If my scan was clear, there's no reason for me to stay."

He starts to argue, but I put a hand up. "I won't drive, I'll call an Uber. But I really need to go."

"I can't keep you here, but I strongly advise you stay. If you leave, you'll have to sign that you're leaving against medical advice."

"Fine."

It still takes almost an hour for me to get out of there, but I'm feeling more steady now, and my Uber, a gray Volvo SUV, is waiting out front. My mind races throughout the twenty-minute drive to my house, hoping against hope that Valentina is there and the police aren't.

When we pull up the driveway, the house is dark, and all is quiet. Once I'm inside, I sit at the kitchen table to catch my breath. I notice Cassandra's handbag on the counter and jump up to grab it, dumping the contents onto the kitchen table. Her cell phone, wallet, keys. All of them are there. She took nothing with her. I unfold a piece of paper and see the name Lindsay and a phone number. I dial it.

A sleepy-sounding voice comes over the line.

"This is Julian Hunter, Cassandra's husband. There's been an accident. I found this number in my wife's handbag."

"Oh my gosh. Is Cassandra all right? She asked me to watch Valentina at the aquarium sleepover and bring her home with my daughter in the morning. The girls are still sleeping. Cassandra wanted to surprise you with a night alone."

My daughter is safe, thank God.

"She's fine," I lie. "Can you give me your address, and I'll come get Valentina?"

We make arrangements, and I end the call.

But where is Cassandra? She must have left on foot. Maybe she tried to flag someone down. She was either hurt or . . . could the trauma of what she saw have sent her into shock? I think of all the manipulation my therapy has done to her mind, her memory. One thing's for sure: I can't call the police. They might discover who she really is.

I stand up and pace. The new Cassandra must be out there somewhere. I've got to find her before she remembers—before she turns me in, and everything I've done over the past two years to mold her into Cassandra is for nothing. And when I do, I'll make her believe that she's crazy, that the best thing for everyone is for her to end her life. It will be sad for Valentina, but better for her to grow up with a loving father than for her new mother to remember the truth and put me in prison. Then Valentina would be utterly alone, thrust into foster care. There is no way I will let that happen.

PART IV

Present Day

60
Blythe

As the car sped along, Blythe opened the folder on her lap and reread the email Jim Fallow had sent to her in the morning. He'd looked into the past of Connor Gibbs, the dead owner of the nightclub, questioning those who'd worked for him, finally discovering the identity of the mysterious Blue Mirror stripper—a woman named Shannon Foster from Orlando. He'd attached a four-year-old article from the *Orlando Sentinel*. Blythe scanned the headline once again—"Police Investigating Murder/Suicide in Orlando Home"—and moved to the body of the article:

Orlando, December 26—Ernest Foster, a commercial airline pilot, killed his wife, their daughter, and his wife's mother on Christmas Day, before taking his own life, investigators said Tuesday.

The authorities found the bodies on Monday afternoon after a call from another daughter, Amelia Foster, a photographer living in Boston who had arrived Christmas morning and found the bodies of her parents, grandmother and twin sister. She is the only surviving relative.

Investigators searching the house found Jean Foster, 49, in the living room with gunshot wounds to the head and chest, said the Orange County district attorney. Daughter Shannon Foster, 23, and her grandmother, Jeannette Everly, 70, were both dead of gunshot wounds to the head.

Deputies found Mr. Foster in an upstairs bedroom with a fatal and self-inflicted gunshot wound. Investigators said no note was left at the scene.

The authorities would not speculate on a motive but said Mrs. Foster had applied for a restraining order against her husband in 2003, saying Mr. Foster had beaten her and had broken furniture in their home.

She later dropped the complaint.

From the back seat Blythe stared out the window as the four of them—herself, Gabriel, Ed, and Gigi—

drove to White Plains, New York, to question Zane Dryer, Cassandra's ex-husband. Zane, an investment broker, had agreed to meet them at his office that afternoon. They hadn't told him much on the phone, only that they were friends of Cassandra's and that they were concerned about her well-being.

Blythe looked down at the page once again and brought it closer to her face, squinting as she once more examined the family photograph the newspaper had published. There was no question in her mind that Amelia was Addison. She and Shannon were obviously identical twins, and if Addison and Amelia were one and the same, Addison would be only twenty-seven now. Blythe closed the folder and leaned back in her seat, closing her eyes. She hoped they would get the answers they were seeking when they met with Cassandra's ex-husband, Zane. He might hold the key to the truth.

"When did the detective say they were divorced?" Gigi asked, shifting in her seat on the passenger side to look back at Blythe.

Blythe opened her eyes. "Almost ten years ago."

Ed scoffed, looking from the driver's seat into the rearview mirror at Blythe. "Impossible. I don't care what Julian said, I knew there was no way Addison was close to forty."

"Of course she's not. This must be her. Julian is hiding something. I think he's tricked her . . . and all of us . . . somehow," Gabriel said.

"Well, we'll know soon enough," Blythe said.

They pulled into the parking lot of Soundview Investments at three. The receptionist in Zane's office took their names and picked up her phone to announce them.

Moments later a trim man with sandy hair and wire-rimmed glasses approached them, holding out a hand. "Zane Dryer."

Blythe estimated that he was in his early forties, a friendly-seeming guy. He led the group down the hall to his spacious office.

"Thank you for agreeing to see us," Blythe said, getting right to the point. "As I told you on the phone, we live in Philadelphia, where we knew your ex-wife as Addison, though she was forthright that it wasn't really her name. She'd had amnesia for the previous two years and was unable to remember her real name."

"Very strange. The last time I spoke with her was around four years ago," Zane told her. "We hadn't exactly stayed in touch." He shook his head. "I didn't want to get divorced. I thought we were happy enough, even though we'd struggled to have children. But she accused me of some horrible things, then essentially ghosted me and had me served."

Gabriel leaned forward. "What kind of things?"

Zane threaded his hand through his hair. "Look, I don't want you to get the wrong idea, so let me back up. She was in therapy to deal with depression. She'd had three miscarriages and was grieving deeply over them. Instead of helping her, her therapist convinced her that I'd caused the miscarriages by hurting her."

Watching her son, Blythe saw the color rise to his face. "Hurting her how?" he asked, his tone aggressive.

Zane threw his hands up. "Hold on. He was lying. He's a specialist in post-traumatic stress disorders. He started her doing hypnosis, some sort of treatment thing to get rid of traumatic memories." He sighed. "Cassandra grew up in foster care, and she'd had some very bad experiences there. At first he seemed to be helping her, but then she started to change."

"In what way?" Blythe asked.

"Pushing me away, spending a lot more time in therapy sessions. She was going every day—it seemed like overkill. The next thing I knew, she told me that she'd moved in with him, and she had her attorney send me divorce papers."

"She moved in with her *therapist*? Doesn't that

violate every professional standard?" Blythe asked, indignation in her voice.

Zane looked straight at Blythe, and before the words left his lips, she knew what he was going to say. "Her therapist was Julian Hunter."

Gabriel sprang up from his seat. "I knew that guy was full of shit. Didn't you have any recourse? Couldn't she be deprogrammed?"

"I tried, but he made sure I couldn't get in touch with her at all. Finally I gave up, and the divorce went through."

Blythe was outraged. "You're telling me that this man used his position as her therapist to turn her against you and marry her?"

"That's exactly what I'm telling you."

"Why didn't you report him?" Ed asked. "He'd lose his license, maybe even go to jail."

"I wanted to, but they'd made me out to be an abuser. It was her word against mine, and she threatened to tell my boss I'd beaten her. He'd convinced her that I threw her down the steps and caused her to miscarry. A few years later I moved down here from Boston for this job, and when I was packing up, I found her journal. There was an entry about the time she 'remembered' me throwing her down the stairs. I knew that I'd been away for work then, away that whole week—

and I could prove it. I took the diary to her job and left it there for her. She called me a few months later. I told her that Dr. Hunter—her *husband*—must have tricked her somehow."

"What did she have to say to that?" Gabriel asked, his tone softening.

"She was upset, rambling about him being controlling, possessive. She was going to take their little girl and leave him." He sighed. "I just wanted to prove to her that I wasn't a bad guy. That was the last time I heard from her."

"With good reason," Gigi said. "She must have confronted Julian, and he probably did something to hurt her. That's probably why she was on the road that night."

Zane looked dejected. "Maybe I shouldn't have reached out to her."

Gabriel shook his head. "You're not responsible for what happened." He held out his phone to Zane. "But can you confirm that this is your ex-wife?"

He took the phone and studied the picture for a brief moment. "No, that's not Cassandra." He glanced down at the screen again. "It looks a little like her, but it's definitely not her."

Blythe and Gigi exchanged glances.

"Julian Hunter claims that she had a bad car accident, and her face needed to be reconstructed," Ed said. "Is it at all possible that this could be her, after a round of plastic surgery?"

Zane's brows knit together. "Let me look again." He enlarged the picture and shook his head more vehemently. "Unless the car accident changed her cheekbones, and made her eyes go from brown to green, it couldn't be her." His face went white. "If Julian is pretending that the woman you know is Cassandra, what happened to my ex-wife?"

"I don't know, but we need to get to Boston. Now," Ed said. "Something is very wrong."

Blythe's stomach was in knots as they all gathered their things to leave. She hoped they weren't too late.

61

Cassandra

I close my eyes for a moment, squeezing them shut so hard that it hurts, and ready myself to take the pills. As I breathe deeply and slowly, building my courage, I feel Julian's hand on my shoulder and shudder. He's telling me it's time. I open my eyes and look at the mound of white pills resting in the palm of my hand, and then raise my eyes to the ceiling, hoping that a feeling of peace will descend.

Instead of feeling a calming sensation, I spot something in the upper corner, where the walls meet. I blink, squinting to make sure it's what I think it is. An understanding begins to dawn on me.

Julian's hand tightens on my shoulder. He moves in front of me and thrusts the water glass into my other hand. But I don't swallow the pills. The infinitesimally small camera mounted in the corner tells me that I'm not crazy or paranoid. He's been spying on me. Out of the corner of my eye, I look at the camera again. There's a speaker too. The voices were real, but they were Julian's. I am not crazy. Julian is the crazy one.

"Come on. You're going to feel really sick if you don't take the rest soon," he prods, his voice tinged with impatience.

My mind races. I have to do something, buy some time, think.

"There's one more thing I want to write in my letter," I blurt out, spilling the pills from my hand onto the desk and pulling open the drawer where I saw him place the letter. Instead of the letter, though, the drawer contains the watch that Gigi gave me, as well as the bottle of perfume I thought I'd misplaced. Julian laughs. "Well, what do you know? Here's the watch you were so careless with."

"You took my things and hid them. You wanted to make me think I was going insane," I say, searching my brain. "Valentina's book? Your car keys?"

"You're finally catching on," he sneers, gathering the pills in his hand. With one hand gripping my chin and pulling down my lower jaw, he shoves the pills into my mouth and orders me to swallow.

Raising my head to meet his eyes, I spit the pills at him with as much force as I can and hurl the glass of water across the room, where it crashes against the wall. He wipes his face, glowering at me. A vein in his neck is throbbing dangerously.

"You bitch," he says, grabbing a hunk of my hair and hauling me out of the chair.

I try to pull away, but his grasp is too tight, and he drags me across the floor. My scalp is hot, seared with pain. I manage to grab the leg of the bed, and Julian finally lets go. He looks down at me, his eyes narrowed in contempt, as I scramble up to stand.

"You." He puts his hand on my chest and shoves me backward. "I should have gotten rid of you long ago. You were nothing but a cut-rate replacement for Cassandra." He shoves me again until my back is against the wall. "You never deserved her name. She was everything to me. And she gave me Valentina. You could never measure up, Amelia."

I frown at him.

"Yes. Amelia. That's your real name. The dreams you had of people's faces getting blown off? That was your family, Amelia. Your sick family, all of whom are dead now." He spits out the words with malicious glee.

I'm dumbstruck. I search my mind for those memories, but to no avail. "What do you mean, she gave you

Valentina? I thought Valentina was mine. What about Sonia?"

He laughs. "There was never any Sonia. And you're not Valentina's mother."

"I don't understand. I know she's my child—I love her."

Before I can think, Julian slams his fist into the wall, inches from my head. "I tried to help you forget, but did you appreciate it? No. You ran away from me. From Valentina. That's how you repaid me for all I've done to help you. You ungrateful bitch."

Julian's eyes are crazed. If I don't somehow temper his rage, he will try to kill me. "I'm sorry, Julian," I say, bowing my head. "You're right. I never should have left. I don't know why I did it." I raise my eyes to him. "I was so glad when you found me, Julian, and brought me back. Remember how happy we were when we danced together, the night of our anniversary?"

He looks confused for a moment, and I rush on. "You put the ring on my finger, and later, when we got home, I came to our room and we made love." I want to shudder at the recollection of his hands on my body, but I try to keep my body language neutral.

He laughs and takes another step, his face just inches from mine now. "Very good, Amelia. I see you've learned something from all your years of therapy, but you should know better than to try and out analyze the analyst." He lifts his hand to my chin and squeezes. "Face it, Amelia. You're better off dead. Your brain has been damaged with trauma, drugs, and hypnosis." He laughs again, his lips curling in disgust. "But you've been a great test subject, one that's been enormously enlightening to me." His hands move to my throat.

"Julian, please, let me go," I beg as he tightens his grip. Then I ram my knee into his groin with all I've got.

He cries out in pain, doubling over. I run to the door, but before I can open it, he grabs the back of my nightgown and spins me around to face him. He's grinning like a madman, spittle running down the sides of his chin. I beat against his chest with my fists, and when he grabs my wrists to stop me, I start kicking, but he's too strong for me. I'm panting. The next thing I see is his giant fist coming at me. It hits my face with such force that I drop to the floor, banging my head on the night table as I fall. Every inch of my body is throbbing in pain, and I am losing hope. I scramble into a half-sitting position.

Julian stands over me, his legs on either side. "I tried to make this easy for you, but you had to make it difficult, didn't you? Just like she did."

Suddenly I remember the knife I hid in the nightstand. I need to stall him. "I'll take the pills, Julian. Give them to me."

He squints at me. "It's too late, Amelia. No second chances for you." He takes my arm and wrenches me to my feet. As I rise, I close my other hand around the drawer handle, pulling it open and grabbing the knife. Before he realizes what is happening, I've plunged the blade into his thigh. He lets go of me and falls to the floor, screaming and cursing as he rolls around. There is blood on the floor, lots of it, and I think I am going to vomit. Forcing myself to turn away, I run to the door, out of the bedroom, and to the stairs. When I look behind me, Julian is dragging himself along the floor, leaving a swath of blood in his wake. His face is engorged with rage, and his mouth is moving, but the thundering in my ears is so loud that I can't hear the words he's screaming. I spring down the steps, grabbing the banister for help when I lose my footing near the bottom. Looking back, I can see Julian on the landing, one hand clasped around his leg, the other gripping a spindle. My breath coming in ragged bursts, I run to the kitchen and seize the cordless phone, dialing 911 as I rush into the bathroom and lock the door. And then I wait.

62
Blythe

Blythe's heartbeat quickened as she spotted the flashing lights down the road. As they approached the gates, she took in the two police cars and an ambulance parked in front of the house.

"What the hell is going on?" Ed said, pulling over to one side of the circular driveway.

"I'll kill him if he's hurt her!" Gabriel flung his door open before the SUV had come to a full stop.

"Gabriel, wait!" Blythe jumped out of the car to follow him, Ed and Gigi close behind.

They caught up with Gabriel, who'd been stopped by a police officer. "Sorry, sir. I can't allow you access. This is a crime scene. Only authorized persons are allowed."

The EMTs shut the ambulance doors and started

down the driveway. "Please move back, folks, and let this official vehicle pass," the officer said.

The four of them stood there waiting in an eerie silence—Gabriel, his head down, walking back and forth; Gigi teary-eyed and leaning into her husband's broad chest; Blythe doing her best to quell the increasing dread she felt.

The ringing of a phone ripped through the silence, startling all of them. Ed took the mobile from his pocket and put it to his ear. "Hello?" He was quiet a moment. "It happens that I'm in her driveway," he said finally. Another nod and then, "There are a few friends of hers with me." He listened another few seconds, then said thank you and hung up.

"What is it?" Gigi said.

"Addy's okay. She's in the house," he said, and Blythe could tell that he was doing his best to hold back tears.

"Thank God." Blythe let her breath out, realizing she'd been holding it.

"They're taking her in for questioning," Ed said. "When they asked if there was someone she needed to call, she told them the only people she knew were in Philadelphia and gave them my name and number—"

"Why didn't she give them *my* number?" Gabriel

cut in before Ed could tell them more. "She should have given them *mine*. Is she in trouble?"

Blythe put a restraining hand on Gabriel's arm. "Gabriel, this isn't helping. Let Ed finish."

Gabriel scowled, but he was quiet.

"She's not being taken into custody," Ed said. "They just want to ask her some questions. When they told her we were outside, she asked if I could accompany her." Ed put his hand on Gabriel's shoulder. "So we'll follow them to the police department and go from there, okay?"

Gabriel nodded just as Addison appeared in the doorway, an officer next to her. With her head down, she got into the police car. Ed pulled out right behind them.

"I knew that Julian Hunter was a lying shit from the very beginning, but nobody would listen to me," Gabriel said. He stared out his window as Ed drove, his fists clenched and resting on his knees.

No one had much to say to that, and they rode the rest of the way in silence. They got out of the car outside the station just as Addison was being escorted inside.

"Addy!" Gabriel yelled to her.

She turned at the sound of her name but appeared not to see them in the darkness, and then she was through the door, out of sight.

At the station, Ed was permitted to accompany Addison while she was being questioned, and the other three sat in the waiting room. Blythe was struck by the overwhelming dreariness of the place, with its green-and-black tile floor and rows of gunmetal-gray seats attached to the wall. It was cold and impersonal, intentionally so, she assumed.

When after forty-five minutes Ed finally emerged with Addison, Gabriel jumped up from his seat and rushed to her. "Are you okay? What did he do to you?" He tried to take her hands in his, but she shrank from him, holding her arms rigidly at her sides.

"Why don't we all sit for a minute, and I'll fill you in," Ed said, guiding an exhausted-looking Addison to a chair. He recounted the whole story to them—all that he'd heard Addison reveal to the officer who'd questioned her. How Julian had tricked and manipulated her into believing she was someone else. How he'd searched for her these last two years, trying to get her back so he could murder her and keep his secret safe.

"He can't hurt you anymore," Gabriel said. "Come back to Philadelphia with me, Addy. There's nothing for you here."

Addison shook her head firmly. "My daughter is here."

"You're not her mother, Addy." Gabriel's voice was

soft. "We'll have our own children. Ones that belong to you."

Addison's nostrils flared. "I love her, and she needs me. She's all alone, just like I am. I'm sorry, Gabriel, but you need to go home without me."

Gabriel knelt before her. "But Addy, I love you. I want you with me."

She held up her palms. "No, Gabriel. You're a good man. You'll find someone who loves you the way you deserve to be loved." She closed her eyes, rubbing her forehead as if in pain. "Things are so complicated. I have a lot of work to do to find my way back to myself. I can't ask you to wait while I do that."

"You're not asking me to wait. I want to."

When she opened her eyes, they were full of resolve. "That's not fair to you. You should go back to Philadelphia and forget about me. All I've done is bring you pain."

"You brought me joy, too, Addy. So much joy. I'll leave now, but when you're ready, I'll be here." Gabriel touched her lightly on the arm and kissed her cheek before he stood and turned to go.

Blythe felt an immense flood of relief. She'd done all she could to find the truth about Addison. She'd fought for her, but she believed now more than ever that their marriage would have been a troubled and difficult one.

She rose from her chair and turned to Ed. "I know you and Gigi will want to stay. Gabriel and I can take a car to the airport and fly home."

"I'm happy to drive you to the airport, Blythe," Ed said.

She waved her hand. "No, no. You need to find a hotel and get settled. I know Addison will be happy to have you here." She looked at Addison. "Goodbye, Addison. And good luck."

Addison stood and embraced her. "Thank you, Blythe. You were always kind and generous to me. I'll never forget that. You taught me a lot about what a mother should be—loving and protective but knowing when to let go and support your child's dreams. I hope I'll do as good a job with Valentina."

Blythe looked at the young woman standing in front of her and wished that things had turned out differently. She was glad that the truth had finally come out, though. She took Gabriel's arm in hers, and they walked out the door together. It was time for a fresh start for all of them.

63
Amelia

"It's time, Amelia. I believe you're ready." I've been seeing Dr. Anita Pearlson for six months, and she looks at me now in encouragement.

"I . . . I'm not sure I am," I tell her. "It feels like I'm standing on the edge of a mountain, and if I take a step I'll fall off. And keep falling."

Her face relaxes, and I see understanding in her eyes now. "I promise you that this step will only take you to firmer ground. The more you remember, the less you will fear."

I close my eyes. Dr. Pearlson takes me back to that day a little over two years ago, and we begin.

I remember leaving the aquarium alone. I was going to surprise Julian by coming home early and leaving Valentina with a friend for the night. I see it so vividly—

the quiet and empty rooms when I entered the house and the basement door ajar, which was unusual. I descended the stairs to the wine cellar to find another opening into a small room, one I'd never seen before. Julian was sitting there, his back to me, facing the wall, talking in a quiet voice. He didn't know I was standing behind him, listening, but I heard everything he said, every shocking word.

My darling Cassandra, I miss you every minute of every day. I will never love her the way I love you. But she's good to Valentina, and she tries her best. You will always be my truest love, but she needs me. Was sent to me, I believe, to fill in the huge hole you left. She suffered trauma just like you did, only it was at the hands of her own father. Oh, Cassandra, we would still be together if only you hadn't gone looking at something you shouldn't have. We could be sitting together right now, drinking wine, listening to music, talking, flirting, laughing. But you left me no choice.

I couldn't stop looking at the enormous wedding portrait of Julian with a different woman. It didn't make sense. Who was she, and why was he calling her Cassandra? And then I heard him say he'd never meant to hurt her, that it was an accident. He begged her forgiveness and said he was sorry that he'd had to bury her in the backyard. I stood rooted to the ground, trying to stifle the scream that was surging to a crescendo inside me. And Julian kept talking, as if the woman in the picture was going to respond. When he turned to me with a sudden jerk, his eyes blazing, I realized that the scream had burst forth from me. I was wailing and sobbing, my body shaking, as he came toward me. I backed up, gasping for breath, and all I could think was *Run, run for your life.*

I turned to the door and felt his hand trying to grab my arm. Something said *Don't look back, don't stop. Keep running.* When I reached the top of the stairs, I slammed the door behind me and heard him curse as he crashed into it. I ran blindly through the house, feeling like my legs were made of lead, wondering if I'd ever reach the front door. And then finally my hand closed around the handle. I flung the door open and flew down the stone steps to the driveway.

"Stop running!" Julian shouted. "You don't understand!"

I stumbled at the sound of his voice, scraping my palms on the gravel as I righted myself and continued running along the driveway. All I had to do was cross the road and get to the thick woods on the other side, and I'd be safe. It would be impossible for Julian to find me in the woods. My sides ached, and my lungs were on fire. I didn't know how much longer I could keep running.

Then I heard a car horn, screeching brakes, and a loud thud. I stopped and turned to see a car stopped in the middle of the road. The driver opened his door and ran to the body lying in the road. *Julian.* For an instant I debated whether to go back and see how badly he was hurt, but I knew I had to get to the police and tell them what he had done.

The adrenaline pumping through my body began to ebb as I slowed to a walk. My hands stung where the gravel had bitten into them, and my face was caked with tears and dirt. I'm not sure how long I walked through the woods before I finally came to a hill that led down to a dark empty street. I turned my feet sideways, moving slowly and carefully down the steep slope until I reached the side of the single-lane road. No cars passed for what felt like an eternity. When finally I saw headlights coming toward me, I got a little closer to the road and stuck out my thumb. To my relief, a red pickup truck slowed down and stopped. The driver slid over and rolled down the passenger window. "Need a lift?"

"Yes. Thank you." He opened the door for me, and I stepped onto the running board and pulled myself up onto the seat.

"Where you headed?" he asked, glancing briefly at me and then putting the truck in gear.

He looked to be in his late twenties or early thirties, stocky, with the start of a beer gut, his hair pulled back in a short ponytail. He reached his hand into a can on the console, scooping out a dollop of brown glop and putting it in his mouth. I realized with disgust that it was chewing tobacco, but he'd been kind enough to pick me up, so I couldn't complain.

"Would you drive me to the nearest police station? I have to report a murder."

He whipped his head around to look at me. "What? You some kind of crazy person?"

"Please," I begged. "I'm not crazy. My husband murdered someone, his first wife. I have to get to a police station."

His mouth moved in slow motion as he rolled the tobacco around and then spit a ball of brown juice into an empty water bottle. "No way. I'm not taking you to the police."

He looked like someone who had probably had his share of run-ins with the law, so I tried another tack. "Just drop me off a few blocks from one. Or in any town center, really."

"Nah, I don't think so. I have a better idea."

Little fingers of fear crept up my neck. "Please. Stop

the truck. I'll get out here." I could hear the shakiness in my voice as I pulled on the door handle. Nothing. I kept pulling on it, but it wouldn't budge.

He just laughed.

"Stop. Let me out. Please."

He stared straight at the road ahead, ignoring me.

I knew I was in trouble now. I had to get out. "Look," I said, trying to keep my voice steady, "I really appreciate the ride. You were very kind to stop and pick me up. I don't want to get you in any trouble, so I can just get out here, and you can pretend you never saw me. Okay?"

"Shut up!" He reached over and backhanded me. My head exploded in pain, and the force knocked me into the passenger door. I must have passed out, because when I looked at the dashboard clock I saw that it was two in the morning. We'd been driving for over four hours. We suddenly jerked to a stop, and I lurched forward. He turned off the engine and spit again into the water bottle. There was nothing around us except trees. No streetlights, no houses, no stores. Desolate. No help that I could see.

"Get out," he said in a guttural voice. I heard a click as he unlocked the doors.

Shaking my head, I pushed my back harder against the seat.

"I said get out," he snarled. He grabbed my arm and dragged me to the driver's side and out onto the hard ground. "Get up, bitch. We gonna have some fun." He laughed, taking hold of my arms and yanking me up to a standing position before pulling me into the woods behind him.

I heard the sound of an animal whimpering; it wasn't until he slapped me across the face that I realized it was coming from me. "Shut up," he hissed, his face almost touching mine. My stomach turned as I smelled his foul breath. And then his mouth was on mine, his tongue pushing my lips apart. The rank taste of tobacco burned. I pushed my hands against his chest in a vain effort to shove him away. He took a step back and pushed me to the ground. "No," I cried, my voice rising hysterically. "Please let me up."

As I frantically felt around in the dirt with my free hand, it hit upon a rock. Mustering all my strength, I swung my arm and smashed it against his face. He howled in pain and rolled off me, grabbing at his cheek. I jumped up and ran blindly, not daring to look back, hearing the thud of his footsteps behind me, briars and branches tearing at my skin and clothes. Finally I heard him yell, "You ain't worth it, bitch!" The sound of his footsteps receded.

I knew he wasn't close, but I couldn't stop running.

The last thing I remembered was a low-hanging branch bashing into my forehead. I have no idea how long it was before I came to, but when I did, he was gone. Now I understand why I was wandering on the highway, clothes torn and dirty, with no identification on me. The doctors tell me that the shock caused me to go into a fugue state. That and the combination of drugs, hypnosis, and psychological abuse I suffered at the hands of Julian Hunter have kept my past elusive to me. I know my name now, thanks to Blythe's detective, but I can't connect Amelia Foster, the woman in the newspaper article, with myself.

I'm thankful every day that I'm working with a therapist I can trust now, a woman who's helping me to put the jigsaw-puzzle pieces of my past back together. Dr. Pearlson is hopeful that over time I'll recover most, if not all, of my memories. Knowing that the horrific discovery of my murdered family resides somewhere in my mind terrifies me to the core. But I'm through running. No matter what, I have to connect with the past so that I can make a new future.

64
Amelia

"Are you ready?" Dr. Pearlson asks.

"Yes," I say, nodding vigorously.

I feel stronger than I have in a long time. I finally know who I am. My name is Amelia Foster, and I grew up in Orlando, Florida. I had a twin sister, Shannon, a mother I loved, and a father I feared. I left Florida after high school for college in Boston, where I earned a bachelor of fine arts in photography from the Massachusetts College of Art and Design.

My world came crashing to an end on Christmas Day, the year I was twenty-three. Today I am going to relive that event, and I take a deep breath as I prepare to be hypnotized.

"All right, Amelia, close your eyes and relax. Breathe in slowly and deeply. And now exhale. I am going to count backward from ten. On each count you will go deeper."

I feel my muscles relax as I listen to her voice and begin going into a hypnotic state.

"It's December 23. You are alone in your apartment. What are you doing?"

"I just hung up with my mother. I told her I'm not coming home until the morning of the twenty-fifth. I don't want to be there any longer than I have to. I lied and told her I have a work obligation."

"Look around your apartment. What do you see?"

"Presents I still have to wrap. A pair of size-six Lucky Brand jeans for my twin sister, Shannon. Pearl earrings for my mom, a scarf for my grandmother, and a pair of Ray-Ban sunglasses for my father that I saved up for six months to buy. He doesn't deserve them, but maybe he'll be nicer to everyone if he gets the best present."

"What do you do next?"

"I call Shannon. She's disappointed that I won't be there early, but she understands. I'm worried about her, though. She tried college but fell in with a partying crowd and flunked out her first semester. She lives in Fort Lauderdale now, and tells us she's a waitress, but I heard from a friend that she's really an exotic dancer at some bar. I tell her I want her to come back to Boston with me after Christmas, and she tells me she'll think about it."

"Christmas morning, you fly to Florida. What happens when you get there?"

"I take a cab from the airport to my parents' house. I'm standing outside, steeling myself before ringing the bell. My father says that since my sister and I no longer live at home, we've lost the privilege of entering without knocking. There's no answer, and I ring again. I'm starting to sweat, and I take off the heavy coat I wore on the plane. Still no answer. I rap loudly on the door, and finally I punch in the key code, hoping he hasn't updated it since the last time I was there. I hear the familiar turning sound, and the blue access light comes on. I turn the knob and slowly open the door. Something's wrong. It smells terrible, like rotting meat and shit. I bend over, gagging, my hand over my nose. I step over the threshold and enter the house."

"Stop for a minute, Amelia. Take another deep breath. This is going to be difficult. Are you ready to continue?"

"Yes."

"What do you see now?"

"It's too quiet. I'm walking into the living room. I see the Christmas tree in its usual spot in front of the window, with the lights twinkling and piles of wrapped presents beneath it. There's someone sitting on the couch. No! No! Mom! Shannon. They're not moving." I squeeze my eyes shut more tightly and cover my face. I can't breathe, my heart is going crazy, and I can't make sense of what I'm seeing in my head.

"Take a deep breath, Amelia, and stop for a moment. This is a memory, it's in the past. You're safe. You're in my office."

Her voice grounds me, and I go back to that day again. "No! Oh please God, no! My mother is on the sofa, her eyes open and staring like she's surprised. There's a round hole in her forehead, and her face is caked in blood. It's run down her nose and cheeks and all over her white blouse. My sister is slumped face-down against my mother's shoulder. There is a huge hole in the side of her head, and splintered bones and gristle and tendons are oozing out of it. I vomit on the rug and stumble backward, away from my mother and sister, and when I look down, I see my grandmother sprawled on the floor. Half of her face is gone, but her one remaining eye is open. She is still clutching a lamp in her hand. And blood. I can smell it, like wet copper, sickly sweet. It's everywhere, on the wood floor, smeared on the furniture and walls, a bloody handprint on the mantel."

"Amelia, I want you to come back slowly, count to ten, come back to this room, to me."

I begin to count, listening to her voice.

"Open your eyes."

Dr. Pearlson is looking at me with a somber expression. "You're safe. I know that was extremely difficult."

I wipe away my tears with the back of my hand. I'm shaking. I reach out for the blanket thrown over the side of the sofa and clutch it to my chest. "I remember it all now. So horrible. So horrible."

"Do you remember what you did next?" she asks.

"I called 911." I'm speaking fast now. "I was rushed out of the house as soon as they arrived. They found my father's body in the bedroom. He slaughtered all of them, and then he killed himself." I clench my fists, wanting to punch something. "My grandmother must have tried to stop him by hitting him with the lamp, but he shot her." I'm sobbing uncontrollably by this point.

"Let it out, Amelia. Just let it all out. I will sit with you for as long as you need."

I wail as I let all the images bombard me, and Dr. Pearlson just sits, a quiet and comforting presence across from me, the picture of compassion. I think about all the years of silence in my family about my father's abuse. All the secrets we kept. He was a respected and intelligent airline pilot with a spotless reputation and an arsenal of guns. No one knew that behind closed doors he carried out a reign of terror. There were so many guns that he never missed the one I took and hid under my pillow for all those years. How many times had he pointed a gun at my mother's head in front of us and threatened to kill her? And the beatings, always making sure the bruises were in places no one could see. And then afterward he would send my mother flowers. Roses. Dozens of them, filling the house with their nauseating smell.

I escaped his murderous Christmas Eve rampage, in a physical sense. But he took everything from me that day. My beloved mother, sister, and grandmother. I'll never know what happened to set him off that day, I only know I should have been there. What if I had gone home sooner? Maybe I could have saved them. My sister's words echoed in my ears, what she sobbed when I told her I was staying on in Boston after college and had gotten a job at the museum. "Please don't leave me. I'll die here without you." Her words had been tragically prophetic.

After a long while, I can speak again.

"How can I ever forgive myself for not being there?"

Her eyes are filled with kindness. "You have nothing to forgive yourself for. I think you know deep down that there's nothing you could have done. You survived, Amelia. You're healing and building a life. Take this life and live it for yourself, and for your mother and your grandmother and your sister. This is how you will honor their memory and keep them alive in your heart."

I look away, blinking back tears. "Healing seems a long way off."

"You're strong, Amelia. It won't be easy, but you'll find your way again. And I will be here to help you at every step."

"I know," I say resolutely. "I have to. Not just for me, but for that little girl who still believes I'm her mother."

65

Amelia

Dr. Pearlson is big on forgiveness. At first I thought she was crazy. I had no desire to forgive my father or Julian for the atrocities they'd wrought. But I'm beginning to realize she's right—holding on to all my rage and anger only hurts me, keeps me in chains. I won't lie and say I'm there yet, but I am working on it, open to the possibility that one day I can come to terms with all they've both taken from me.

Julian is paying for what he did. They found Cassandra's body buried in the backyard, and he confessed to killing her, although he claimed it was an accident. He's been charged with her murder and unlawful burial of a body. He's awaiting trial and has already been stripped of his medical license.

Valentina is the only reason I agreed to visit Julian

in prison after his arrest. I was nervous, my stomach in knots, as I waited in that dreary visitors' room next to Ed, who'd insisted on being by my side. When Julian entered, I was shocked at his appearance. His face had become a pallid gray, his eyes dull, his posture hunched. Adrenaline shot through my body nonetheless as I remembered his attempt to kill me before. Ed seemed to sense my discomfort and squeezed my hand under the table.

"Thank you for coming, Amelia," he said.

"Speak your piece," Ed said. "We don't want to be here any longer than necessary."

Julian didn't look at him but took a seat across from me, his eyes downcast. "I know you hate me, and I don't blame you. I never meant to hurt you. I thought we could be happy. I was only doing what I thought was best."

I put a hand up. Even now he was justifying his actions. "I won't get into this with you. I'm only here to talk about Valentina."

"I'm willing to give you custody," he said, and my heart soared. "But I need to know if you can love her like she's your own."

I didn't hesitate to answer. "I do love her. Absolutely. I'm her mother." The truth was that even though therapy was helping me to recover my past as Amelia, I still had memories of being Valentina's mother during the two years I lived with her before I ran away, and then in the months after I came back. Even before then, there were early false memories Julian had programmed into me. I couldn't separate the true ones from the false, but regardless, I loved her, and I knew I always would. Even though she hadn't been born to me, she belonged with me. Together we would heal and become strong, despite the tragedies we'd both endured.

"She loves you and she needs you," Julian said. "I don't want her in the system. It may take a while for the courts to allow you to adopt her, especially given your suicide attempt after your family was murdered."

"Not to mention your crazy-making," I couldn't help adding.

"Yes." He looked down at his hands, clasped on the table in front of him. When he looked back up at me, his face was serious. "My lawyer advised me to plead insanity, but I've refused. You see, I must be considered legally competent in order to petition the courts to grant you legal guardianship of Valentina." He frowned. "Besides, I'm not crazy. I was only doing what I had to do to protect my daughter."

Of course, he *was* a man filled with madness, but the one pure thing about him was his love for his daughter. I took a deep breath. "My therapist will testify that I'm stable. I'll work with the courts for as long as I have to until she's legally mine."

"I've instructed my attorney to transfer most of my assets to you."

"No—" I began. I didn't want his money, like some kind of payoff to alleviate his guilt for all he'd done.

"I want you to have it for Valentina's education and care. I'm never getting out of here—what do I need it for?"

We left then, Ed's arm around me as we walked from the building, and this fine man held me close to his side as I wept. For the first time in my life, I felt that someone might be watching over me, as if the universe was in some small way making up for the kind of father I never had and the daughter Ed lost.

Epilogue
One Year Later

Julian was convicted of murder in the second degree and is now serving a twenty-five-year sentence. I've put all of his money in a trust and use it only for Valentina's benefit. I sold the house and rented a small Cape Cod in a neighborhood in Lexington where there are lots of other children for her to play with. I'm technically her foster mother, as we work with the family courts to prove I'm a fit mother. I love her even more fiercely than I did before, and I can't wait for the day when I can legally call her my own.

I haven't told her the truth about her father yet, or about her birth mother, and her therapist agrees it's best to wait. She thinks that her dad had to leave the country for work, and we're still figuring out how and when to tell her he's not coming back. When she is old enough to know more, perhaps she will want to visit him, but I'll leave it up to her. In the meantime, Gigi and Ed have become surrogate grandparents to her, and their presence in her life has somewhat mitigated the loss of her family. I'd love to move back to Philadelphia with her so I can be closer to them, but I can't leave the state until I'm able to adopt her. I hope that day will arrive before too long.

There are other reasons I'd like to go back. Hailey and I have remained close, and we talk a few times a week. Gabriel took some time away from the gallery to get his head together, she tells me, and he spent some time working for an organization in India that helps street children. I haven't seen or heard from him since that terrible night we said goodbye in the police station, but Hailey's told me that he's coming home next month, and she's invited me to his welcome-back party.

I told her I'd think about it. In truth, I've thought about it quite a bit. Imagined it really, seeing him again after all this time, embracing, maybe starting anew. But a lot can change in a year, and reality has eluded me for so long that I'm not going to indulge in fantasies. It's enough to know that I'm no longer filled with missing pieces, to know myself and be rid of the doubts that used to plague me. Whatever happens or doesn't happen with Gabriel, I will continue moving forward with hope and purpose.

I am coming to terms with all I've lost, but I'm learning to be grateful for what I do have. I now look in the mirror and recognize the reflection looking back at me. I like her. A lot. I am even beginning to appreciate all I've been through, the good and the bad. Those experiences have all contributed to making me the woman I see in the mirror today. A woman who is learning to become just as comfortable in front of the camera as behind it. A woman who is no longer a stranger.

Acknowledgments

We give grateful thanks to our readers and hope we will continue to entertain and surprise you. Our gratitude also to the wonderful librarians and booksellers everywhere—your support means everything to us.

It's a rare privilege to love the work you do and to be fortunate enough to also love those with whom you work. Our heartfelt thanks to our amazing team at HarperCollins. Thank you, Jonathan Burnham and Doug Jones, for your continued support. Huge thanks to Emily Griffin, our wise and talented editor—you are the one who perfects the work and brings out our best. Heather Drucker, our brilliant and tireless publicist: we are so lucky to be in your capable hands. Immense thanks to Katie O'Callaghan, our superb marketing guru, and the wonderful Sales, Marketing, and Production teams. Thanks also to Virginia Stanley and the fabulous Library Marketing team for your steadfast support and enthusiasm. Deep appreciation to Miranda Ottewell for your eagle eye in refining context/chronology and helping to keep track of details. Our heartfelt thanks to Julia Wisdom, Kathryn Cheshire, Fliss Denham, and the team at HarperCollins UK, for your creativity and all you do an ocean away.

To Bernadette Baker-Baughman, our extraordinary literary agent, everything began with you. We are forever indebted to you for your faith in us and your steady and judicious navigation of our careers. You are the perfect partner. To Victoria Sanders and the VSA team, thank you for all you do for us. We love working with you.

To our exceptional film agent, Dana Spector, deepest gratitude for your unwavering efforts to bring our characters to life on film. We so appreciate your dedication to us and your belief in our stories.

To Travis Seal, huge thanks for sharing your immense knowledge and love of Philadelphia, which was invaluable. And thank you, Sharon Seal, for connecting us.

To Lieutenant Steven B. Tabeling III, retired from the Baltimore Police Department, our thanks for always being at the end of the phone whenever we have a police procedural question. Your helpfulness knows no bounds.

Thanks to Special Agent Chris Munger for your help with our law enforcement questions, your generosity in sharing your time and knowledge, and your friendship.

Many thanks to our first readers, Dee Campbell, Honey Constantine, Lynn Constantine, and Cindy Graham, for your time and much-valued feedback.

And finally to our families. Your love and encouragement really do make it possible. To Rick and Colin, you are our rocks and safe landing places—and the best decisions these *sisters* ever made.

About the Author

LIV CONSTANTINE is the pen name of sisters Lynne Constantine and Valerie Constantine. Together, they are the internationally bestselling author of the Reese Witherspoon Book Club pick *The Last Mrs. Parrish*, *The Last Time I Saw You*, and *The Wife Stalker*. Their critically acclaimed books have been praised by *USA Today*, the *Sunday Times*, *People* magazine, and *Good Morning America*, among many others. Their books have been translated into 27 languages, are available in 32 countries, and are in development for both television and film. You can find more about them at: livconstantine.com.

HARPER
LARGE PRINT

We hope you enjoyed reading
our new, comfortable print size and found it
an experience you would like to repeat.

Well – you're in luck!

Harper Large Print offers the finest in
fiction and nonfiction books in this same larger
print size and paperback format. Light and easy to read,
Harper Large Print paperbacks are for the book lovers
who want to see what they are reading without strain.

For a full listing of titles and
new releases to come, please visit our website:
www.hc.com

HARPER LARGE PRINT